Sigil Online: Hellions

Jeff Sproul

ISBN-10: 1982084928

ISBN-13: 978-1982084929

CONTENTS

ACKNOWLEDGMENTS

I want to thank everyone that had a hand in making Hellions possible. And to everyone that read Paragons, your support has been amazing and makes being an author all the more worthwhile and enjoyable.

PROLOGUE

A hooded figure ran through the dark streets of Gargantuan City. Night had fallen within the virtual game world of Sigil Online. Lamp posts shone, but light had difficulty reaching the many alleyways between the large and numerous structures that stretched into the sky.

The figure's footfalls splashed as they dashed down an alley. The rain was still falling, pattering against the figure's shoulders and covering everything with a glistening sheen.

A flash filled the night sky as a bolt of lightning streaked miles away. Thunder boomed seconds later, followed by another flash of lightning and another rumble.

Fingers made of pale white bone curled around the edge of a nearby roof. An avian skull lifted and a pair of dark purple glimmers of light peered out from hollow eye sockets.

The skull turned slowly, those purple specks following the hooded figure's movements. Another boney hand lifted to brush along the balcony it was peering over.

Its movements were fluid as it was spurred into motion, moving swiftly along the roof. Long bone-tendrils clicked quietly and propelled the creature along. The tendrils looked almost like a human spine, ending with a sharp clawed tip. The monster's appendages hovered inches away from a humanoid central rib cage.

As the hooded figure slipped down another alley, the bone-creature pulled itself from over the ledge of the roof. The taps of its tendril tips were drowned out by the sounds of rain and thunder. Each bolt of lightning illuminated and shined off the monster's form, but the figure below didn't appear to be aware of its presence.

After another lightning strike, the creature leapt from the side of the brick wall. Silently, it plummeted. Then, with a multitude of loud cracks, its clawed tendrils pierced and broke the concrete ground as it swung a lengthy arm out. Its fist closed and smacked the running figure toward a wall.

The runner didn't have any time to react as the monster assailed him. His body thudded against the bricks. He grunted with the impact and fell to the wet ground. His hood fell back, and his head lifted to see his assailant.

The monster's bone-tendrils clicked against the concrete as it stood before the fallen young man. The tendrils extended out, closing him in.

"Nowhere to run," a screeching voice said. "When I was a player killer, I would've at least tried holding you up to see what loot you'd give me for not killing you. But as a monster, killing you is just so much more rewarding for my progress." The monster cackled as it brought one of its many tendrils back into the air, prepared to strike the rising player.

The young man slowly rose from the ground. Another lightning strike lit the alleyway and illuminated his face, showing off his longer black hair and his soft androgynous features.

Just behind his hip, his fingers moved rapidly in a predetermined pattern.

"You think you're a monster?" his voice rose, in defiance to the creature surrounding him.

With one final movement of his fingers, a small white sphere materialized in his palm, outside of the monster's line of sight.

The young man stood upright and stared into those purple pins of light in the avian skull.

"You have no idea what it means to be a monster." With that, his hand clenched and shattered the translucent white sphere. The ensuing sound of breaking glass was hidden behind another roar of thunder.

The young man's body changed rapidly. His clothes and skin seemed to meld together and transform into a chitinous hide, almost like the bleached bone of the monster before him.

The bone-creature let out another horrendous screech and drove that readied tendril into his chest.

But the transformation only needed a matter of seconds to complete. The clawed bone tip clattered back and rang off the impossibly hard exoskeleton of the being that now stood before it.

Instead of a young man wearing a hoodie, something else entirely was standing before the bone-creature.

A pair of dark eyes like black holes stared back at those pinpoints of purple light. It was still humanoid in appearance, but with its chitinous exoskeleton, it resembled something between a man and an insect. Its appendages were elongated and the pale white matched that of the bone-monster.

There was no mouth. But he didn't need to speak.

"You're a monster too!" came the screeching voice of the bone-monster. "But why were you—" Its voice cut off as its form noticeably shifted back and away from the humanoid insect before it. "No!" it screamed. "I thought the White Weevil was—"

A clenched fist smashed into the avian skull, cutting the sentence short. The bone-monster's body crashed into the nearby wall. Dust and bricks fell as its large body broke into the structure, but it wasn't finished yet. Not by a single attack.

The White Weevil, who had come to light as 'Arbiter,' dropped to the ground after leaping and smashing the monster in the face. As soon as his feet hit the ground, he darted for the bone-creature.

The monster pulled itself out of the wall with its many tendrils. It swung at the fast-moving insect-like player. Its large fist—easily the size of the other player's torso—was deflected by Arbiter's arm. Arbiter's fists clenched and one after another, they pummeled the bone-creature's ribcage as its tentacles thrashed around in an attempt to deflect and pull away from the insect.

Arbiter didn't relent. He landed blow after blow upon the monster while also managing to deflect the oncoming tendrils.

As Arbiter's arm pulled back for another swing, the bone-monster managed to pull away, digging its clawed tendrils into the brick wall. It propelled itself upwards, its purple eyes brighter than they'd been before. Those sharp bones crunched into the wall, but it suddenly came to a halt and was pulled back to the wet ground below, as long white fingers clutched one of its spiney tendrils and yanked it back.

"No!" the monster screeched as it came crashing down.

Arbiter leapt upon the fallen monster and drove his fists into that avian skull.

Crack crack, crack crack, crack!

As the last blow landed, the beak broke off. A second later, every bone that comprised the monster's body broke apart into thousands of glimmering white particles.

Arbiter dropped through the defeated monster's body. His feet smacked against the wet stone ground. Another lightning strike lit up the alley, followed by a thunderous boom a second later.

In front of Arbiter's feet rested an item left by the dead monster-player.

He bent over and picked it up with those long thin fingers. He held it up to his eyes, turning it over and side to side. It looked as though it could've been one of the avian hellion's glowing purple eyes, but it was hard like a rock.

Above the item, a readout appeared for the Arbiter's eyes only. It read:

-

Gem of The Pale Impaler

?

?

?

-

Arbiter's shoulder's slumped. He shook his head and gestured with his fingers to bring up an inventory screen. After a couple taps to various buttons on the overlay, the claw dematerialized and a new icon appeared within his inventory.

He turned his head and looked around

his surroundings. There didn't appear to be anyone else around. He turned and continued running the way he'd been going, before the monster had jumped him.

The rain pattered against his exoskeleton as he darted through the alleyways. Eventually he reached a larger street, but he remained in the shadows out of sight. He lifted his hand and brought up a status-screen for his character. He tapped several times at miscellaneous icons. When he was finished, the screen disappeared. A moment later, his chitinous body began to fragment. The pieces broke and fell away like the shell of a hatching animal. The white bits of exoskeleton dissolved on the ground, leaving no trace of what he'd just looked like. He was now an unassuming young man with a hoodie. He pulled the hood back over his head and went into the street. The closest pedestrians were dozens of feet away. He was confident that no one had been watching him.

He was surrounded by tall buildings, but ahead of him was a pair of doors with blue neon lighting. Above the doors, a neon orange sign read 'Neon Nest.'

He reached the door and pulled the metal handle.

Inside the Neon Nest were various

pieces of comfortable furniture, anything you'd find in a social bar and lounge. There was a long counter with a bartender standing behind it. He was a bald man with bright pink eyes, and was chatting with two people sitting at the counter. There were at least a dozen other people conversing quietly amongst themselves.

No one paid Arbiter any mind as he went to a doorway that led to a stairwell that descended. He went down about two floors before he reached a door. He opened it and went down a short hallway. At the end of the hall was a simple blue door surrounded with blue neon lights. He opened it up, seemingly not needing a key of any sort.

Once inside, he pulled his hood back. There was a bookshelf with only a dozen or so books upon it. There was also a simple bed across the room, along with a desk and other bits of furniture. He went right for the bed and laid down. He lifted his hand and gestured to bring up another holographic display screen, then tapped a button that said 'menu.' Then, he tapped the one that said 'logout.'

The screen disappeared. In its place was the number ten.

It changed to nine, then eight.

He closed his eyes and waited.

"Now I'm going to be late," he murmured in a soft voice.

The countdown reached zero and the game world faded away.

CHAPTER 1: ADJUSTMENT

A young man with dark hair and fair skin sat alone in a booth in Paragon Cafe. The cafe was located at the end of a street with a one-way street passing by it. There was plenty of foot traffic, as it was local to many apartment complexes and a larger shopping plaza.

Paragon Cafe was the young man’s usual real-world meetup spot for him and his best friend, but the time of day had changed recently to evenings and nights, instead of their morning meetups.

Riley sat on his usual side of the booth. His elbow rested on the table while he held his head up with his palm. He glanced through an open menu and read over the descriptions for the various items.

He flipped another page on the menu. The offerings at Paragon Cafe seldom ever changed. Sometimes there was a special item for the day or week, but the owners didn’t do much to change away from the norm.

Riley yawned and flipped another page. He stared at the imagery for blueberry and strawberry glazed pancakes with bits of chocolate strewn throughout. He turned the page and was greeted by a selection of sandwiches. One was on multigrain bread with crisp lettuce and a succulent slice of tomato. The description said that it was a turkey sandwich, but the amber slices of bacon made him think it was a bit better than your regular turkey club.

He wasn't sure why he was even looking through the menu for the fifth time.

Movement in the corner of his eye caught his attention. He looked up just as another young man entered his view.

"Sorry, got held up," said the boy with soft androgynous features and shoulder-length black hair. He sat down across from Riley and sighed. His chest rose and fell beneath his hoodie, which wasn't too dissimilar from the one his virtual character had been wearing earlier in Sigil Online.

"No worries," said Riley. "I'm just sitting here decompressing. Was a really weird day in-game."

"Tell me about it," said Aaron, who reached over and grabbed the other menu that was laying on the right side of the table. "It was a rough day, even with the regular monsters. But once you throw in all the player-monsters, it just… ugh, makes me tired thinking about it," he grumbled. "I didn't even think about what I wanted to order," he said as his gaze ran over the selections. "Everything looks delicious right now."

A dark-haired waiter in uniform walked up to the table, carrying a large plastic tray with two plates and drinks. He stopped beside the table and set a plate in front of Riley.

"Chili cheese fries," said Paul, the waiter.

The savory aroma of the fried food wafted up to their noses. Riley took in a slow, deep breath.

Paul set two glasses of water down before placing a plate in front of Aaron.

"And here's your double chocolate blueberry pancakes with bananas." Paul then looked between the two of them. "Anything else I can get you?"

"This is good, thanks Paul," said Riley.

Aaron just sat there, staring at the pancakes before him.

A thin slice of banana—covered in blueberry syrup—slowly slid down the edge of the dark, fluffy hotcakes.

"Paul said they're short staffed today, so the food would take longer to prepare. So I went ahead and ordered for you," said Riley. "Was that a good choice?"

Aaron's jaw had lowered, still staring

at the plate. He closed his mouth and swallowed. "This is perfect!" he said as he grabbed his fork and began cutting into the pancakes.

Riley took a sip of water and began pulling out french fries covered in meaty chili sauce and nacho cheese.

No words were exchanged as the two of them dug into their respective plates.

"Mmm," Aaron murmured, chewing a bite.

Riley crunched on one of the crispy fries and swallowed it before finally speaking. "So it was a rough day?"

Aaron took several long seconds to finish his bite before speaking.

"Yeah," he murmured, then swallowed. "The monsters in the enchanted asylum are really mobile. I kept getting patrolling monsters that wandered into where I was fighting. So I'd be controlling one and having it fight something a little smaller, only to have something even bigger wander over. I had to reposition and waste stamina to deal with it all. It was just… I dunno, it felt really unproductive. Then, on my way back to logout, I got jumped by this crazy looking bone monster."

"A player?" asked Riley, before

crunching on another fry.

"Yeah," Aaron confirmed. "I had to use my bug form to get rid of him, and he dropped one of those usual monster-player items."

"That's a pain," said Riley. "Did you already identify it?"

Aaron shook his head. "No, I was too concerned with getting here. I'll see what it is tomorrow. Hopefully it's something with elements I can use."

"Was the player strong?" asked Riley. "Is that why you were so late?"

Aaron took a moment to get another bite of pancake. He took his time and chewed it before swallowing. "Kinda," he said. "I was already late, because my last encounter with the monsters in the asylum was taking way longer than I expected. I couldn't queue a cheap taxi near the portal location, so I decided to run back. That's when I got jumped. It didn't take long to get rid of him. I don't think he was even a tier-two hellion yet. But he sure had that 'air of superiority' about him that most of the monster-players seem to have."

"I know what you mean," said Riley. "But there weren't any cheap taxis? Has there been a lot of monster-player activity in your area? I heard that over in Tall City, a bunch of the districts have had issues with taxi services due to the amount of monsters there. They keep targeting the local vehicles and NPCs to increase their progress. It was on the news a few minutes ago," he said, gesturing over to one of the televisions that was always on a channel that had Sigil Online news.

Aaron shrugged. "It's been the same as most of the other cities, I guess," he said. "We've been keeping their nests to a minimum. Well, I guess I should say, the players in my city have. I've been delving into that enchanted asylum to see if there's any sweet loot from all those new regular monsters. If I can find awesome things to sell to the players in my area, then I'm helping keep the city safe from the monster-players."

Riley nodded. He knew that Aaron couldn't always trigger his powerful bug-form, known to many players as the White Weevil. Apparently there was some 'cooldown' or 'time limit' effect that Aaron had loosely mentioned. His friend also made it seem as though triggering the transformation was a bit of a burden on him.

"I guess the hellions expansion hasn't been the best for you then, huh?" prompted Riley.

"Oh no, it's great, I love it!" said Aaron. "It's just… well, the monster-players are proving really problematic. There's more conflict going on within the city. Everyone has to keep on their toes, you know? It's tough. But there's a lot of awesome features that I've been enjoying. Like all the new crafting stuff has been really cool. And when I do kill a monster-player, I usually get something that I can use in crafting."

"I guess being a crafter is really paying off then. Even though you live a double life," Riley said a bit accusingly, but smirked afterwards.

"For the hundredth time, I said I'm sorry!" said Aaron. "And I wasn't lying about being a crafter. I do a lot of crafting! I kinda had to, when I kept getting loot I couldn't sell. It's just… you know, I didn't really tell you about how I acquired all my materials."

"I always thought you were some sorta business mogul, with your shop and your crafting" said Riley.

"Well, I'm kinda that too," Aaron quipped. "But I've made a bunch of in-game friends who are also crafters. I've got this nice little tight-knit community of crafting friends. We have some pretty rare recipes."

"I still have yet to find a cool recipe for an item," said Riley. "I found a couple when I was playing as Radiance, but it feels like there's just less recipe drops lately."

"Yeah, I've been hearing that as well," said Aaron. "Maybe they lowered the drop rates a little?" He then paused for a moment. "Which reminds me," he shifted gears and even lowered the hand he held his fork with. "There's something I wanna tell you. Or I guess I should say, show you. In-game, that is."

Riley lifted his eyebrows. "What do you mean? Why can't you tell me about it now?"

"I… well," Aaron murmured at first. "It'll just be a lot easier to show you. It's kind of a secret, a crafting secret. I honestly shouldn't even be talking about it, but I really hate that I kept the Weevil thing a secret from you. And I want to help you out, you know? Something more than meeting up with you and your friends to control bosses for you."

"Everyone loves you," said Riley. "I think they love you more than me, in fact. They really like my power stealing buffs, but I'm pretty sure that getting to watch two bosses fight it out, while they damage the weaker one, is a bit cooler."

Aaron smiled. "Well, I wish I could pop over more, but you're really far away and I have my shop… and I know the economy better in my city and I already have my crafting friends I do things with occasionally, and—"

"It's alright!" said Riley. "It's not a problem." He smiled. "I'm glad that we can at least hang out a little bit in-game now, is all. Even if it's only once a week or so."

Aaron nodded, his lips still curled. He looked down to the messy pancakes. "Me too," he said, as he slowly cut into them again.

"So tomorrow's the big day for you and your friends, isn't it?" asked Aaron.

Riley groaned. "That's one of the reasons this week has been a pain. Rushing to get things together by tomorrow."

"I thought you'd be happier?" asked Aaron. "You're all forming a guild! That's something to be happy about."

"I *am* happy," said Riley as he prodded the pile of fries with the one in his hand. "It's just been a lot of work to get it going. Items, mini quests, all sorts of stuff. You know how guild-forming goes," he prompted.

"Actually I don't," said Aaron.

Riley looked up with raised eyebrows. "Really?"

Aaron nodded. "Never been in a guild, and I've never bothered looking up what it takes to make one."

"Damn, I thought with your boundless knowledge of Sigil Online, that you'd have that info ready and waiting."

Aaron shook his head. "Nope."

Riley chuckled and sighed, as if remembering a painful memory. "Guild creation is a series of quests. You can't do them by yourself. Or, well, most people can't. Maybe you could, but some of them have been beyond what I think you're capable of when you're solo. But anyway, we get choices on what quests we want to do. It's so that different players with various powers can tackle things that are more suited to their group composition. So that's what we've been doing. Knocking out quests, killing monsters, acquiring special items, and some of our newer members to the group are taking over some of the crafting stuff."

"Didn't you say Constructor was a crafter?" asked Aaron.

"Yep, He's our main crafter currently. He has the most skills in it. So he's been sitting on the sidelines back at his place in Gargantuan City. Which he doesn't seem to mind, apparently. Even though his pylon things are pretty cool. We've been knocking monsters out really quickly, most of the time. But finding the correct ones and getting the drops we need have been the hardest parts. Also, getting to the correct zones where the creatures are. Then, factor in all the monster-players that think they can jump us… it's… just been a really rough week," he grumbled finally.

"So you're all done the quests?" asked Aaron.

Riley nodded. "We're all done. We finished earlier today and I've just been looking through my items and taking account of everything. We're going to do some votes tomorrow, once the guild contract is signed by all of us. That'll decide if we stick to Bunker 7 as our main base of operations. At least temporarily. We'll then start looking for a small place to buy for ourselves."

Aaron chewed another piece of hotcake, then murmured through the bite. "You have the money to buy a place?"

Riley shrugged. "If we all pitch in an equal amount, there's a couple places we could consider buying. But I think we're going to settle for Bunker 7, for the time being. I can only imagine how expensive the

Rook Den was when Warcry bought it. They must've really earned some serious money, for a bunch of mostly tier-zeroes."

"You going to buy Bunker 7?" Aaron questioned.

Riley laughed. "No way, that place is way out of our price range. The owners of the bunker know what they're doing. There's a lot of players who operate out of it. It was one of the earliest group spots. I'm sure they're making enough money to cover their rent in the real world, if not more. I'm not sure what costs are associated with running a spot like that, but they do put some money back into it to help us out. And they pay people to work there. But based on my rent and the fact that so many people use it as a hub, I imagine the owners are doing well for themselves."

"Yeah, that must be nice," said Aaron. "Wish I could've taken out a small loan when the game first came out. Then I could've bought some property and rented it out to players."

"I'm sure some people had the same thoughts at the time," said Riley. "I bet plenty of people lost money on that very risk." He munched on a fry and then swallowed it. "So how's your mom?"

Aaron was cutting into the last portion of his pancakes, having almost finished them. "She's doing really well. The doctors say that there's no complications and that the cancer's all gone. She had a rough couple of months there, with the therapy and everything. But she's doing a lot better and I think she's applying to a new job. Or a couple new jobs… not too sure. But I'm sure she'll get something and then want to get her own place again."

"I'm glad everything worked out," said Riley. "I'm sure it was tough."

"Yeah, me too," Aaron murmured as he poked at his pancake.

"Maybe you won't have to take so many risks nowadays," said Riley. "You've still got money from that interview, and don't think I haven't seen the ads on TV for Weevil-strength bleach. So I'm sure you're not doing too bad financially. So if that's the case, maybe you could keep your head down for a bit. You seem to be having trouble with the monster-players, since you can only deal with them in your bug form. Your infamy has waned with all the new monsters running around. So maybe take it easy for a bit? Or even come join us more often, so we can watch your back."

"There's also the 'Strong enough to

kill the White Weevil' bug spray," Aaron sighed, but smiled. He looked back to his friend. "I'm doing what I enjoy. I love exploring new content. I've gotten used to playing alone."

"You know," said Riley. "You might've killed Paladin, but he could've destroyed some monsters, I bet. He was really powerful in one-vs-one fights. As you saw. But you're only strong in solo fights when you're in Weevil form. He was powerful all the time."

"Are you criticizing me for killing Paladin, now that we have all these monster-player troubles?" asked Aaron, with a slight frown.

"No, that's not what I'm saying," Riley sighed. "What I'm saying is that Sigil Online has all sorts of players with different powers. Paladin was really powerful when he could directly fight someone, you're powerful when you can directly fight someone as the Weevil, but both of you have a hard-counter."

Aaron nodded. "Yeah, I've noticed," he murmured. "When I fought your friends back in Death's Chasm, the ones that could pin me down and use their powers to grapple me were really problematic. Todd, Snow, Erica. If they had more damage behind their abilities, I'd have had some real trouble. If Erica and

Todd had been paragon, I might've been crushed even faster."

"Yeah, that's what I'm saying," said Riley. "For every player out there, there's several power-types that are good against them. It's like one giant game of rock-paper-scissors. Which you're well aware of. All I'm saying is that maybe you should be more careful. You have money, you don't need to risk yourself to make even more money."

"I like being ahead of the curve, though," said Aaron. "I really enjoy delving into places others can't."

"I know," said Riley. "Just… be aware of your surroundings. There's tons of monster-players out there that would love to beat you, if they knew where you were. For right now, most of the player-killers are having a great time fighting monster-players, instead of regular players. So that's given you some reprieve from being hunted."

"Also, that monster that attacked me earlier seemed extra surprised when he realized who I was," said Aaron. "Lots of people seem to think I died, since I haven't been making my presence known."

"Which is good!" said Riley, leaning forward slightly. "Let that protect you.

Come hang out with us more. Keep your shop, sell your items, whatever you want to do. Just… be careful, alright?”

Aaron looked up to his best friend and offered a smile. He nodded. His plate was empty, save for lines of fruit-flavored syrup. “I’ll be careful,” he said. “It might be annoying to fight these new monsters one on one, but they’re going to need to try a lot harder to bring me down.”

Riley leaned back in his seat. “I guess if a few of them get lucky and manage to kill you, you’ll have no reason *not* to come join us, huh?”

Aaron narrowed his eyes. “Don’t you go planning my demise just to have me come party with you.”

“There’s a lot of cool pact powers out there,” said Riley. “That’s what Seth ended up doing. He got tired of being tier-zero and got himself a pact.”

“Ehh,” Aaron shook his head. “The pact system is cool and all, but it’s way too ‘double-edged-sword’ for my taste.”

“Seth seems pretty happy with it,” said Riley.

“After weeks without powers, I’m sure he was happy with anything.”

The two friends continued to chat. There was never much silence between them when they met up at Paragon Cafe. With the arrival of Sigil Online's newest expansion just a month prior, the two had even more to talk about with each passing day.

CHAPTER 2: BUSINESS AS USUAL

Riley's eyes opened. His room was dimly lit, as he always had his heavy brown curtains pulled tight to block the sun’s rays from ebbing into his room. Sleep came easy when he spent so much of his day hooked into Sigil Online. Now that he wasn't in such a dire situation financially, he was able to stay asleep as well. The stress and nightmares had abated. He was enjoying life again. Even if that life involved removing himself from the real world and inserting his mind into a virtual one.

He slid out of bed and went about his normal routine. Bathroom, breakfast, news articles. He went through his usual schedule in about an hour. Breakfast consisted of a meager bowl of oatmeal. He'd started to cut back on coffee, bit by bit. It wasn't *really* needed when he spent most of his time in-game. But he always enjoyed the taste of it as part of his morning routine.

After going through the usual motions of preparing for a day in Sigil Online, he laid back in bed and pulled his headset on.

He grabbed his crescent-shaped visor from the nightstand and pulled the strap on the back and situated it around the base of his skull. He flipped a switch on the side and a familiar mechanical whir sounded from inside the headset.

He closed his eyes and rested in bed, as the countdown began to initiate his connection to the online world. He exhaled slowly. The login countdown was almost a part of him, like brushing his teeth or unlocking a door. He subconsciously counted down in his head, and the moment he reached zero, his senses faded.

-

The world of Sigil Online embraced him. When his eyes opened, he found himself within his in-game apartment, a meagerly furnished room within a concrete bunker.

He was lying on a bed that was nicer than the one he had in the real world. But in the game, his bed counted towards his 'apartment furnishings' and helped his character by giving him a 'rested buff,' which helped his stats throughout the day.

His attire hadn't changed much since he took on this virtual persona. He wore a pair of dark brown denim pants and a brown leather jacket. He had on a light gray T-shirt beneath.

When he made this character months ago, he'd gone by his real name, 'Riley,' up until he'd acquired his sigil and became a paragon. Now, he was called Relinquisher. Some people called him 'Reli' for short. But the friends he'd made before he became a paragon still called him Riley. It made things somewhat confusing, but luckily the names were similar, so people tended to figure out what was going on. He wasn't sure why no one ever called him by his full paragon name. Perhaps it was too much to say?

He pulled himself out of bed and immediately went for the door. He hadn't put much money in increasing his apartment's furnishings. His money was better spent on gear and items. Furnishing your apartment was something that crafters or rich players usually did.

He left his room and went into the hall. He stepped quickly, but was in no particular hurry. He was by no means 'late' to the meeting, but he doubted he'd be the first one there.

He got to the stairwell and ascended it swiftly. When he got to the top, he opened a door and entered the main room of Bunker 7. There was a bar counter, plenty of drinks, couches, a lounge area, tables, booths, and a number of televisions. Most of the TVs were set to some news station or web-channel, talking about Sigil Online in some fashion or another. With the release of the latest expansion, there was even more buzz on the many stations and streamers that spoke about the game.

Riley stopped several feet into the room. He slowly scanned the area. The televisions were on, the music was playing. But for the first time in the history of playing Sigil Online, he didn't see anyone around. Not Marcella, or any of the other workers that staffed the bunker. It was dead, lifeless.

He looked over to the table that he and his soon-to-be guildmates were usually seated around. There were a few glasses and mugs set on the wooden tabletop, but that was it.

Riley directed his attention on the televisions as he headed over to the set of heavy double doors. None of the televisions were showing anything particularly interesting. Nothing that would warrant the bunker being empty. Maybe something was going on outside?

Riley reached the doors and pushed the right side open.

The moment he did, a cacophony of sounds assaulted him.

"There's more coming from the left!" someone shouted.

"I didn't know so many NPCs were in the entire city!" came another.

"Where are they all coming from? This is crazy!" came another voice, but this one Riley recognized. It was Seth. He was one of the first friends he'd made after he'd lost his last character.

Riley looked around as the telltale sound of shotgun bursts assaulted his ears, coming from the far right.

The scene before him was utter chaos. There were several dozen people clustered around the street near the entrance to Bunker 7. But coming from both sides of the street, and pouring out of alleyways, were hundreds of figures. They looked like ordinary people, just like those around him, but with less flashy and eccentric clothing and features.

Upon further inspection of his surroundings, Riley watched as his friends from Bunker 7 fought off the mass of bodies scrambling towards them.

Riley's eyes widened further as he noticed that the bodies were sickly and pale. They weren't moving naturally. They were frantic and clawing. Some of them were missing limbs or chunks of skin.

They looked like zombies.

Riley wasn't sure how it had happened, but he found himself dead-center in what looked to be some sort of outbreak event. Hundreds of non-player-characters (or NPCs for short) were rushing towards the actual players nearby.

He spotted Red Shotgun, pumping her fists and releasing torrents of red energy bullets, which smashed and obliterated small groupings of zombies.

Nearby, he spotted Seth. His friend was easy to pick out of a crowd, with that pure white hair and silvery outfit he wore.

Seth was moving his hands in a circle, creating a net of white glowing energy. When the net had grown to sufficient size, he threw it out and propelled it towards the mass of oncoming zombies that were scrambling to overtake his position.

The net caught five of the zombified NPCs, and caused them to stumble and slow down the zombies behind them. Seth still had a single white thread connecting his hand to the net. With a squeeze of his fist, a bolt of white lightning shot through the webbing and shocked the trapped monsters, causing them to shock others around them. Some of the zombies burst into colorful particles of light as they were destroyed.

Half of the people fighting the zombies were actually just a single player. There were roughly twenty copies of a young Asian woman with blue denim pants and a purple long-sleeved shirt. Each of them wielded a melee weapon of some sort, and were engaged with the zombies at all sides. This was Laura's power. She could create duplicates of herself, and split her stats amongst each of them.

Everything he saw took place in the span of seconds. Red Shotgun, Seth, Laura, and many of the others he often grouped with were all fighting around him, using their unique powers to deal with this horde of enemies.

A hand seized his shoulder.

He flinched and turned, thinking that one of the zombies had broken through and reached him.

But instead of a monster, he saw one of the many Lauras. This one had a revolver in her right hand.

"Good of you to join us!" she said, in a collected and even-tempered voice. "Everyone's good on health. How ‘bout you do some of the hard work this time around?"

"You sure? This doesn't look like we have things under control!" said Riley.

She slapped his shoulder and stepped away from him. "Get to killing!" she said, as she turned and lifted her revolver, firing off shots at oncoming zombies. Her weapon made a loud crack with each round she fired.

Large slabs of concrete had been pulled out of the street, creating barricades and walls to protect the group of players at certain angles. It was definitely Todd's handiwork, since he was the only earth-mover that Riley knew.

Riley brought a hand up and made a quick gesture. A holographic screen appeared before him. He tapped at it swiftly, selecting an item in his virtual inventory. With one last tap of his finger, the screen dissipated and a six-foot-long black metal staff appeared in his left hand. He gripped it tightly, but turned his attention to the scene around him. More specifically, to the other players fighting nearby.

Laura, who could make copies of herself.

Seth, who could create electrified webbing.

Erika, who could pull vines and plants from the ground.

Brenda, who could utilize a magical

crossbow.

Todd, who could move the earth at his whim.

Carla, who could deploy seemingly harmless lotuses, which could explode, freeze, or poison.

There were several others in the area, but his sights set on Red Shotgun. She had intense red hair and a red jacket to match. The woman could fire searing red energy pellets from her fists when she punched.

Riley flicked his wrist in Red's direction. As he did, a dark spike shot out of his palm. It stuck Red in the back, which caused her to look over her shoulder. "The hell?" she said, then caught sight of Riley. "There you are!" she said, before diverting her attention back on the battle. She pumped her fists and decimated the zombies around her as if nothing had happened.

With a moment's concentration, Riley focused on the spike that he'd stuck Red Shotgun with. A glob of red glowing liquid rushed from the back of the spike and towards his palm, from roughly twenty feet away.

Riley absorbed the red essence as it smacked into his palm. He left the spike where it was for now—it wouldn't bother Red

Shotgun too much.

A moment later, Riley's eyes took on a red glow to match the essence he'd absorbed. Without hesitation, he ran to the right side, where there were fewer players fighting the zombies. He made sure to keep out of Red's line of fire as he closed in on the NPC monsters.

Several of the scrambling creatures spotted him, and directed their attention on him as he raced towards them.

Riley smirked. He'd been wanting to try this.

With an iota of will and a squeeze of his left hand, he expelled the red glowing essence. The red glow around his eyes faded as quickly as it had appeared.

This time, Riley wasn't sending the essence to another player. He was sending it into a specialized weapon. A weapon capable of accepting the essence he'd absorbed.

A deep red energy blade extended from the top of the staff. But with the blade at the end, it was no longer a staff, but a scythe.

Riley reached the first several zombies and swung the essence empowered scythe. The energy blade cut through three of the zombies before him, severing the head of the first, then cutting through the torso of the next, and then one of the legs of the third.

The brainless creatures groaned as he dismembered them. Their blood was like oil, as it leaked and poured from their fallen bodies. A second later, their bodies dissipated in a flare of colored particles, their forms dying.

"Don't let ‘em touch you!" Red Shotgun called. "There's something really wrong with them, they're not just some regular zombies!"

"Got it!" Riley replied as he brought his scythe up and swung in the opposite direction. The reach of the weapon was invaluable to him in this situation. A sword might've allowed the zombies to get too close.

He hadn't had a good opportunity to use this weapon yet, at least not in a combat scenario. Despite the fact that they were being surrounded by an overwhelming force, his lips curled. He slashed and cut with his new weapon, rending deep gashes and tearing off limbs. This was the most fun he'd had in weeks!

Minutes flashed by like seconds as he fought in the growing melee. He wasn't used to fighting like this in the slightest. Too often, he was stuck behind his friends, just healing them and buffing them with his essence-stealing powers. But this, this let him be a force to be reckoned with. Not to mention, the scythe was classified as a dexterity based weapon, which helped increase his damage because the majority of his stat points were placed in dexterity.

Another swing of his arms saw the scythe tear through another zombie.

A gurgling growl came from his left. He turned and swung to deal with the next monster. But the zombie had already gotten in closer than he'd realized. Its boney fingers reached out for him, as gore dripped from its open maw. Riley's eyes widened. The voracious creature was inside his attack range and he couldn't hit it before it would reach him!

Time seemed to slow as Riley turned, swinging his scythe in hope of miraculously managing to outpace the zombie.

A translucent orange tendril appeared in the corner of his vision and stabbed the monster in the chest. The impact of the impaling blow cut the creature's momentum and gave Riley the precious second he needed to finish his swing and decapitate it. The gaunt-faced head landed on the ground with a thud, before its body slumped and became glittering particles of light.

"Watch your back, Reli!" came a male voice from behind him. "Why is it I'm always saving your ass?"

Riley tensed as he was chastised by one of the newest members of their group. He turned and spotted Amber Impaler.

Riley had first encountered the orange-tentacle wielding player during an invasion event, when the powerful monster known as Saros appeared. At the time, Amber Impaler had been tier-one. Riley didn't actually know Amber's real name. But what he *did* know, was that—

"Thanks Amber!" he said quickly.

—Amber Impaler *hated* being called just Amber.

A mix between a groan and a growl emanated from Amber Impaler. "Say the whole thing, or don't say it at all!" the orange-haired guy spoke.

Riley watched as numerous orange tentacles protruded from the player's back and lashed out with stabs and swipes at the oncoming horde of zombies. Amber was uniquely suited to deal with numerous enemies in melee range. Since Amber had become a paragon, his tendrils could extend further and do even more damage. He could also combine them together into one large tentacle, which did superior damage to enemies.

Riley diverted his attention back to the task at hand. He knew that even with his empowered scythe, he wasn't as good at dealing with enemies head-on as the rest of his friends who were actual damage dealers. At the end of the day, he was still a support class.

Something exploded nearby. But it wasn't like a gunshot or a bomb. It was more like… something wet, popping.

Riley spotted black and red gore being flung into the air as zombies exploded, their body parts flying in every direction.

"What's going on?" Amber Impaler shouted.

"What are they doing?" came Red Shotgun's voice.

"Don't let the stuff touch you!" Laura shouted from further away.

More and more of the zombies exploded around them. At this point, Riley and the others were retreating towards the bunker door, as the mass of attacking zombies rippled and exploded.

The sound of grinding stone came from all around them. Thin sheets of concrete were pulled up around them at various angles to shield the players from the airborne gore.

Numerous thick vines cracked through the asphalt below their feet and shot upwards to tangle around the concrete sections. The vines wove together, creating a loose mesh above their heads. This protected them from above, as the concrete slabs protected them from the sides, creating a makeshift dome around them.

The zombies clambered at the newly constructed barricade. Todd had made the walls thin so he could create the enclosure quickly. Sections of it were breaking away as the monsters bashed into it. Inevitably, the creatures exploded before they could do serious damage.

For an entire minute, there was nothing but meaty 'pops' coming from outside the enclosure. Then, everything went silent, save for their heavy breathing in a confined space.

Riley stood beside Amber and Red. He swallowed and looked from one to the other.

Laura was the first to speak up. "What

a nice way to remember our guild creation day, huh?"

CHAPTER 3:
THE BBS

"What the hell?" said Riley. "What kind of event was that?" He turned around and faced the others.

"They swarmed out of nowhere," said Red Shotgun.

"Was it an invasion event? I've never seen zombies like that in Sigil," said Brenda, whose paragon name was Crossbolt. She wielded a steel crossbow resting on her shoulder. She was a girl with blonde hair down to her mid-back with gray denim pants and a black long-sleeved blouse with a ruffled hem. She looked to be around the same age as Riley, in her teens.

"A hundred credits says that it was one of the new monster-players," said Erica. She had dark skin and looked to be in her late twenties or so. She wore a black skirt and an olive-green corset, along with a black jacket with neon green trim. She lifted her hands and slowly retracted the vines from around the sheets of stone encompassing them.

"Did anyone get hit?" asked Red Shotgun.

"Yeah, Chase did," said Laura. The copy maker held out her hand and one by one, she absorbed her duplicates.

"Where is he?" asked Riley.

"I'm over here," came a man's voice.

Riley stepped between several of the gathered players. Some had already started heading back into the bunker, now that the threat was over. Most of his friends remained outside.

Riley caught sight of the man he was looking for, seated against the side of the bunker. He had dark skin and was dressed in gray slacks, a black blazer, and a white shirt. As part of Chase's powers, he had a single cybernetic eye in the right socket of his skull. The eye had a silvery metallic glint with green lines running through it, that then coursed down through the man's body, like neon green veins.

Riley also spotted Carla beside him. She had bright pink hair and a blue zipped-up jacket, and looked to be of native American descent. With a moment's concentration, she created a green lotus out of thin air and let it fall to Chase.

The lotus fell and dissolved into a green glow as it was absorbed by Chase's body.

Chase's hand was up in the air, his eyes staring at something unseen. This was a telltale sign that the other player had his status-screen opened, and he was probably checking his ailments.

"Doesn't look like it's going away," he said. "It's really sapping my stats."

"Well you shouldn't have gotten hit, dummy," Carla murmured. She turned her head to Laura, who had walked up beside Riley. "Laura, you got any strong curative items?"

Laura thought for a moment. "I might, lemme head inside and check my storage. Be back in a minute. Make sure everyone else is in good condition." With that, Laura walked over to the bunker doors and went inside.

"Riley, you still wearing that curative belt?" asked Carla. "See if you can heal him."

"Right, good thinking," said Riley. "Nobody ever gets poisoned or diseased, so I keep forgetting that it has the curative effect." He walked over and looked between

Carla and Chase. "Well, I'm going to volunteer you for offering your essence," said Riley as he aimed his palm at Carla and launched his spike at her exposed arm. A moment later, the spike shot out and lodged about half an inch into her arm, causing a tiny bit of damage to her health.

"Yeah yeah, fight's over, I'll just heal myself," said Carla.

The glowing multi-colored essence rushed towards Riley's hand, streaking almost like a rainbow. For a paragon with the name 'Chromatic Lotus,' he didn't expect anything less from Carla's essence.

Riley's eyes took on the glow of a myriad of colors, but he didn't hesitate to launch the glob of essence at the seated Chase. The liquid smacked into his chest and was absorbed through his clothes and into his body.

Chase kept an eye on his status screen as the seconds passed by. He shook his head. "Nothing," he said. "Must be too strong for the belt to cure."

"This belt is useless," Riley grumbled. "Think I'll replace it as soon as I see anything remotely better."

"Maybe we can talk about trading belts later," said Chase. "I could always have half my bots on healing duty… but I'd rather stay a damage dealer. We'll have to see what works out the best. You looked like you were having fun with your new weapon."

Riley nodded. "Yeah, I could get used to being a melee damager. And with all the stay-alive items I've collected, I won't be too squishy if something tries fighting me. But I won't be causing as much damage as the rest of you, sadly. I really want to find a new item that'll boost my damage output."

The young man with the orange tentacles on his back, which had receded to a bulb-like shape, stood nearby. His arms were crossed against his chest as he looked around. "What are we doing now?" he asked, his voice less than enthusiastic. "We going to—"

A woman's voice cut him off. "Damn, I got hit too," said Marcella, who worked at the bunker. She had bright purple hair and darker skin. "Chase is right, this ailment is no joke. I'm barely going to be able to use my powers with this disease. I'm at about twenty percent capacity? This is really strong. Says it lasts for eight hours."

"Yeah, I noticed that too," said Chase.

"I doubt I have much," said Seth. "But

let me check my storage too, I might've held onto something that can cure it." With that, the white-haired player dashed into the bunker.

Riley couldn't help but smile. Seth definitely had an interest in Marcella. It was blatantly obvious; not that he ever tried hiding it, of course.

"Is it contagious?" asked Amber Impaler. "How'd you get infected? Did one of 'em bite you, or scratch you? Or just touch you? Did you touch any of the blood?"

Riley shook his head as Amber pestered Marcella with questions.

"I um… one of them got in close and swiped at me and snagged my arm," said Marcella. "So, I'm going to guess that they have to cause damage to you in order to infect you."

"I brushed up against one of them when I was fighting," said Todd, who was moving his hands and retracting the concrete sheets back into the ground. The sound of grating stone could be heard all around them as the stout man lowered the barricades. "But I don't have any detriments. So I bet Marcella's right."

"Do we know for sure if this was some game-induced event, or a hellion?" asked

Riley. "Did anyone see a monster?"

"Red and Green were on their way here," said Chase. "Everyone else was inside. Then, all of a sudden, Red comes in and tells us there's zombies everywhere. We all came outside to get some experience and maybe some loot, and things just kept getting worse as more of them flooded into the area."

"Yeah, there sure wasn't any loot from those things," Brenda grumbled. "And I doubt we got much experience for killing them."

As everyone continued to converse about what had caused the situation, Laura came through the bunker doors. She walked over to Chase, and without a word, she stuck his shoulder with a syringe.

"What're you sticking me with?" he asked.

"Should cure most ailments. It's all I got," said Laura, as she watched the red liquid in the vial empty into Chase's arm.

"Kinda weird for a half-cyberized player to get infected by a disease," said Amber. "You'd think you'd have higher resistances, or something."

"I don't think things work that way," said Chase. "Buuut, it looks like that did the trick, thanks Laura." With that, Chase dispersed his status screen and stood up. "Now I need to eat something to regain my stamina."

Todd and Erica finished deconstructing their makeshift defensive dome, which let them see the area around them. Red and black ichor covered their surroundings. It was on the nearby structures, and all throughout the streets.

"Eugh, I'm starting to wish they hadn't enhanced the sense of smell in this game," said Brenda, covering her nose with her arm.

"It shouldn't last too long," said Chase. "But we might as well head inside, don't you think?"

"You all go ahead," said Red Shotgun. "Melter and I will patrol the area, make sure nothing else is going on. We'll be back in ten minutes at the latest." The red-haired woman looked to Riley. "Can you head up the building and take a look around before we head out? If there's other players around engaged with leftover zombies, I'd like to help 'em."

"Uhh," Riley murmured at first, before he remembered his ring that let him climb any surface. "Right, sure thing!" Riley turned and headed to the side of Bunker 7.

He placed his hands to the wall and slowly climbed up, as if his fingertips could easily get a handhold by just pressing to the wall itself.

"Alright," said Laura. "Everyone else, let's head inside and get things started. Riley! Join us when you get back down," she called up to Riley, before looking to Red and Green. "Don't take too long, we've got work to do after the guild creation."

"We won't be long," said Red.

Through it all, Laura had become the de facto leader of the group. Among the group, she had the most connections to everyone. She knew Red and her friends, as well as Snow and her people. She'd also been the one to encounter Riley, and had already been loosely familiar with Seth's group. It made sense for her to take charge of things, when she already seemed to be a natural leader, despite how she never voiced wanting to lead a guild until everyone started saying how much it'd make sense for her to do so.

One by one, the players on the street slowly went inside, Riley ascended the wall of the bunker. The wind began to whip around a bit more freely the higher he went. The first floor was the main part of the bunker, but above it were offices and apartments. Most of the cityscape was filled with apartment-like structures, to give the city a more filled-in appearance.

Riley climbed up a good seven stories before reaching the roof. He hoisted himself up and sat on the edge of the stone railing. He looked down at the streets below and into some of the nearby alleys. The ground was still littered with red and black, and from his current vantage, it looked like some sort of macabre painting. He didn't see any movement, NPCs or players. The area around the bunker seemed pretty… dead.

He turned around and descended the side of the building. It took him less than a minute to get to the bottom, where Red and Green were waiting.

"You see anything up there?" Red asked.

"Nothing," said Riley. "Just the bloody remains of those zombies. I doubt you'll find anything out there, but it might be worth a look around."

"Alright, we'll be back in a few," said Red, who reached over and patted Green's arm. "Let's get going, don't wanna hold everyone up too much, but I wanna take a look around."

"Right behind you," said Green.

With that, the two women headed up the

street at a run.

Riley turned and opened one of the heavy doors to the bunker. The music was still playing inside, and people who weren't part of his core group of friends were already seated in their usual spots around the lounge area.

Marcella stood in front of a large vault door, inlaid into the wall itself. "Lemme finalize permissions on the door," she said as she reached out and touched the handle. A screen would appear before her that only she could see. She tapped in the air for about half a minute before stepping away. "All yours, Laura."

"Thanks," Laura said as she walked over.

"So this is going to instance us off from the rest of the building?" asked Carla, whose hands were on her hips as she stared at the door.

"Yep," said Marcella. "The owners gave me rights to set permissions, and you guys are paid up to use it. We'll setup a new lease contract for the room, once you form the guild."

"You decide if you're gonna join us?" asked Chase.

"I might as well," she responded. "If you guys don't have any requirements for attendance. I love monster hunting, but I like taking it easy, too. Working here at the bunker really suits me."

"I can understand that," said Chase. "And regardless, we'd be happy to have you."

Just then, Seth came up from the stairwell that led down to the player-owned apartments. "Sorry Marcella, but I've got nothing to cure ailments, unless it was freezing or fire."

Marcella turned to him and shot him a smile. "Don't worry about it. I'll just let it fade naturally after the eight hours, but I guess I'll have to sit out the after-guild-creation activities."

Seth frowned and sighed. "Damn, I was looking forward to you joining us. Your powers are fun to watch."

Marcella winked at him. "Is that the only reason you wanted me around?"

Seth's lips curled even more. His hand lifted as he scratched at the side of his scalp. "Ah, well. You know…" he spoke, without actually saying much of anything.

Laura took hold of the thick metal lever on the vault door. She pulled it up, causing a large metal 'thunk' to sound from inside.

"This door is serious business," she murmured as she pulled it open, showing off the room within.

Chase, Carla, and the newly arrived Riley all leaned in to look into the room as it was revealed.

A large wooden square table was the only furniture, save for the chairs around it. The table was easily four times as big as any of the ones in the bunker's common area, and even possessed a fresh pine scent. It could easily seat twenty-five or so people.

Laura pulled the door fully open and peered in. "Yeah, I think that'll do for now," she said as her lips curled, seeing the room for the first time. It wasn't much, but it would be the first room they owned as a guild. Once the guild was formed, that is.

"Let's start heading in," said Chase.

"Right," said Laura, who stepped to the side and turned to face the gathered group of players. "Everyone take a seat so we can get this started."

One by one, everyone filed in.

Riley lingered back near Laura.

"Aaron isn't coming, is he?" she asked.

Riley shook his head. "No, I think he's happier doing what he's doing. I think he also feels that he'd make us more of a target if he hung out with us too much. There's also his shop that he has to deal with, and the friends he's made in his area."

"I figured that'd be the case," said Laura. "He's a nice guy, and it's nice to have him around at times, but I definitely get the feel that he's on edge around us."

Riley and Laura watched as the last person passed by to enter the vault room.

"After you," said Riley, gesturing to the room.

"Let's do this," Laura said with a smile. She went into the room, noticing that the seat closest to the door was still available. She sat down and looked at the assembled players, as Riley took a seat nearby.

All in all, there were fifteen people there, including herself, but excluding Red and Green. Once the other two paragons joined them, they'd be seventeen strong.

"Glad everyone could make it, despite the ordeal we just went through," said Laura, speaking to everyone at the table. "Red and Green will be with us shortly, but it looks like everyone else is here." Laura gestured over to Marcella. "And everyone knows Marcella, but she's decided to join us as well, being our seventeenth member."

Several claps were heard around the table, causing Marcella to smirk. "Can't guarantee how useful I'll be to you all, but I'm happy to join up with you," she said.

Laura turned her head and looked to the open vault door. She wasn't sure how long it'd take Red to come back, but she could at least get some minor discussion topics out of the way. She looked back to everyone in the room.

"So, next topic on the list," said Laura. "Communications. Up until now, we've only been able to speak to each other in shouting range. Once we form a guild, we'll have access to the communicator devices that got put in with the last patch."

"'Bout time we got something like that," Snow grumbled. She was a paragon with power over snow, sleet, and ice. She had tanned skin and short frosty-blue hair, with a matching outfit. She was seated between Constructor, who was always dressed in a nice gray suit, and Shell, who had shorter red hair and very pale skin.

"Agreed," said Laura. "I'm sure plenty of people in the community were complaining, despite how the developers told us that they wanted a system that prevents spam. So, guild-based communicators is what we get. Essentially, they're cellphones. So, nothing special going on there."

Laura then thought for a moment as her eyes scanned the gathered players. "Oh! And of course, let's congratulate Todd on hitting paragon the other day. I think I lost a hundred credits on that bet, sadly. I was rooting for Erica hitting tier-two first."

Several people clapped, while a few laughed.

"Congrats Todd," said Chase.

"My money was on Erica too," Carla huffed.

"Now you can tank!" said Seth, prodding Todd's arm from beside him.

"Thanks, thanks," said Todd with a loose smile. Despite the congratulations, he found himself meekly looking over to Erica.

"Don't worry, I'll get paragon soon and

totally be better at everything again," Erica teased.

Todd chuckled.

"And of course, I'd like to remind everyone how Seth is still considered a cheater, for going with a pact power," Laura said with a small fake cough into her arm.

"Hey! I thought we were past that?" said Seth.

"Buying pact powers is totally cheating," said Laura. "You have at least another month of us complaining about it, especially since you already hit tier-two, and before me!"

"I wish pacts were around when I first started," said Snow. "But I'm happy with the powers I have. I feel like I earned them."

"Hey, I still get a ton of detriments to some of my stats because of my powers, thank you very much," said Seth, trying to defend himself as best he could.

Laura rolled her eyes. "Yeah yeah," she murmured. "Let's see, what else to talk about before Red and Green get here."

"What's the plan for after the creation?" asked Constructor, the middle-aged man with a nice suit.

Laura looked over to him. "On our guild's behalf, I've been in discussions with The Vanguard Alliance. It was formed when the monster-players in the city started organizing into clans and causing more trouble. We're coordinating patrols and raids with them, to help keep the city clear of nests. So we're going to break into teams and coordinate a strike on a nearby nest. At least, where we think a nest probably is."

"Sounds good," said Constructor. "This hellions expansion has really pushed me to change up how I use my powers."

"Same for a lot of us," said Shell, who sat on the other side of Snow. He didn't tend to speak too often, unless it was with Snow or Constructor.

There were several nods of agreement around the room.

"As a new guild in the city," said Laura, "we'll try and create strong ties to the other guilds, and work towards joining their alliance. It'll help the city, and it'll help us. Part of that will be to keep the city clear of nests and roaming monster-players. Of course, we also want to keep up our regular monster hunting."

"Do we have any plans for some of the NPC and low-level player features?" asked

Brenda, her crossbow set on the table in front of her.

"Uhh, which ones?" asked Laura.

"Well, there's the new stuff they did with guilds and player housing," said Brenda.

"Yeah, we won't be able to afford our own place for a while," said Laura. "But you're talking about how some of the bigger guilds are essentially giving new players a place to store their items and valuables, which are owned by the guild, but if the player dies, they still have their stuff, right?"

"That's what Warcry and her guild are doing now," said Riley.

"Yeah, that and the power-loan system," said Brenda.

"Power loan?" asked Amber.

"Power loaning is a new feature from the expansion," said Laura. "Guilds can buy special equipment to give powers to non-powered players. Usually it's simple stuff, like fireballs, or lasers coming from your hands. It only lasts for a specific duration, like a day or week, but it gives some of the more well-off guilds a method of recruiting non-powered players, to help them fill their ranks and get the new players leveled."

"Makes sense, bet it's expensive," Amber murmured.

Laura nodded. "Yeah, most of that stuff is out of our reach for a while, until we collect more funds. We're going to have to work out a tax system for that as well, one that doesn't hinder any of us too badly. But we can save that for later."

"Did we decide on a name?" asked Blue Mist, a younger man with blue hair who had mostly kept quiet until now. Blue Mist tended to keep to himself, and usually only spoke up if he felt it was really necessary.

"We did!" said Laura. "We will be known as The Bunker Brawlers, or BBs for short."

"I still hate it," Amber grumbled to himself.

"You've hated every suggestion that was made," said Carla. "I think it's good."

"I think it's ok," said Snow with a shrug. "But names are hard to come up with."

"I think it fits," said Seth.

"Well, not all of us are from Bunker 7 as our start location," said Parviz, the portal-maker that Riley and Laura had become familiar with after a particularly bad invasion event. Parviz had half-blue and half-red hair split down the center. His clothing matched.

"But we're at a bunker now," said Shell, the pale redhead. "Better than some of the other suggestions."

"Well, we had a vote," said Laura. "And you all voted, except for Marcella, sorry Marcella. But regardless, Bunker Brawlers won by five votes, so… that's what we're going to be."

"Fine, fine," Amber murmured. "I guess the name sorta makes sense."

Red's knuckles rasped against the vault door. "You guys create it yet?" she asked, walking in with Green behind her.

"Nope, you're just in time," Laura spoke, glancing back to the last two arrivals. "Close the door, and we can wrap this up."

Red glanced back, but Green Melter was already pulling the door shut with a resounding 'thunk.'

The two women grabbed adjacent available seats and relaxed into them.

"I think that's it. Communicators, guild perks, the name, guild politics with other guilds… and the attack we're about to make," said Laura.

"Sounds good, let's get this going," said Red.

"How does it work?" asked Riley.

"Like this," said Laura. She reached out and tapped the table twice with a single digit. When she did, a screen appeared before her that only she could see. Her eyes scanned the screen and tapped at different times. She then took about half a minute to tap out something rather long, probably the name of the guild itself. With a final press of her finger, numerous holographic images appeared in front of everyone.

Riley looked at the one before him. It read 'Guild Invitation From: The Bunker Brawlers.' Below the message were two buttons. One read 'accept,' the other, 'decline.'

"First!" Carla said, and immediately pressed 'accept.'

One by one, everyone at the table pressed 'accept.' Riley reached up and pressed the button as well. When he did, the message 'Thanks for joining!' appeared. Several seconds later, the screen dissipated.

"And that's seventeen," said Laura. She slowly rose from her seat and looked around the room, a smile on her lips. "Congrats everyone. We've just formed The Bunker Brawlers."

CHAPTER 4:
KNOCK KNOCK

Water dripped from overhead pipes. A musty smell permeated the air, which was better than some of the alternatives when you were in the Gargantuan City Underground.

Riley cautiously approached a T intersection. He hugged the right side wall and slowly peered around the corner to check right, then left.

His scythe was out, but unpowered. His shoulder was flush to the concrete wall, as he peered down the next corridor. His heartbeat throbbed in his ears. All he could see in the next passageway was emptiness and the dull white lights that were connected to strips of wire running along the edges of the ceiling.

"Looks clear," he said in a whisper.

"We've been down here for almost half an hour. Why haven't we found anything yet?" Amber Impaler grumbled. "This is a huge waste of time. Is this really the only way for The Vanguard to let us into their exclusive little club?"

"Yes, it is," said Laura, just a few feet behind, with Shell a few steps behind her. "There are tons of guilds in the area and plenty of them are the same size as ours. The alliance is mostly made up of the most active ones, but they don't want guilds joining them that aren't helping the city. So that's where we come in."

"Still seems like a waste. There has to be other alliances we could join," Amber murmured. "We're down here doing the hard work of searching for monster-players that probably aren't even down here."

"Well we might've found one by now, if you weren't alerting them to our presence every time you complain," said Riley.

Amber stepped in closer to Riley. "I'm sure I'm not the only one who thinks this is a waste of time. We could be leveling up in a group in some of the nicer zones, but instead, we're down here. I'm sure those other guilds in that alliance aren't spending all their time hunting monsters."

"Give it a rest, Amber Impaler, " Shell sighed from the back of the group. "I doubt we're going to be doing this all the time. Right Laura?"

"That's right," Laura confirmed. "This is just a good-will gesture, to show that we're willing to help out and do our part. So let's keep moving. I'm surprised one of the other groups hasn't found anything yet either."

"These tunnels are huge," said Riley, as he crept around the corner and headed down the next passageway. He kept his eyes forward, with his grip tight on his weapon.

"Hopefully we don't get lost," Amber murmured.

"I'm tracking our progress," said Laura, who held a flat and rectangular device with a lit screen. "These cells they implemented give us a few different features. We can track our movements, call our guildmates, and a few other things."

"Why didn't I get one?" asked Amber.

"'Cause we only had enough guild funds to buy four, which meant that there's only one for each group. You're welcome to buy your own when we get back to the bunker."

"Didn't the underground used to be smaller?" asked Shell, who looked around warily. "We haven't found any regular monsters yet either."

"The developers expanded it in the expansion, and then they've been modifying it in the last couple patches," said Laura. "It now has various layers and this layer is sort of a sandbox area, where the monsters can create small lairs and form nests."

"So we have to hope to randomly come across one of these player-monster nests?" asked Amber.

"Something like that," said Laura.

Riley led the small group of four down the passageway. He did his best to ignore Amber's constant grumbling about every little thing. He wasn't sure why a guy like Amber would bother even joining up with them, if he didn't want to do group stuff.

Perhaps he just liked to complain all the time? Regardless, he was a somewhat decent player, with powers that let him deal with a number of enemy types, especially the monster-players.

Laura had split the guild into four groups, minus Marcella. Marcella was still under the detrimental effects of the disease ailment from the zombie encounter. Which still left sixteen of them to break into groups of four. Laura placed a healer in each group, and then combined damage dealers and support powers throughout.

Riley was more suited to small-increment healing. Players were more likely to dish out a lot of damage in short amounts of time. He felt that he excelled as a support and hybrid healer class in regular monster fights, but so far, from what he's seen from the monster-players, he felt that he might not be fully suited to dealing with them, especially not one on one. Hopefully this excursion would prove him wrong. It was also why he already had his weapon out, prepared to fight.

"What's that there?" asked Amber, pointing to the wall near the ceiling. "Some kind of grate? Maybe it's a tunnel? We should try removing it."

"You wanna go crawling through air

shafts?" asked Riley, turning around to the orange tentacle user.

"Yeah, we might as well," said Amber. "Quicker we find something to kill, the quicker we can tell those alliance snobs that we did their work." He then walked over and without further discussion, he extended several of the translucent amber tentacles that protruded from his back.

From what Riley knew, Amber was able to manipulate the tendrils with his thoughts. He watched as the tentacles conformed to the corners of the metal grate.

A soft hiss filled the air, as if water was being poured over an incredibly hot surface.

"You're melting it?" asked Laura, who watched from nearby.

"Yeah, it'll be the easiest way to get rid of it. We should all be able to fit in a duct that size, don't you think?" Amber commented as the metal slowly dissolved under the attention of the gelatinous tendrils.

When the grate had fully disappeared, Amber withdrew his tendrils and reached up and clutched the side of the now-open duct with his fingers. He pulled himself up, and crawled inside.

"I'm not a fan of this idea," said Shell. "Seems like a good way to get trapped, or actually lost."

"I'm not big on crawling through air shafts either," said Laura, who was the next to head in after Amber. "But Amber might have a point. For all we know, the nests that monsters create might only be accessible this way."

"Ugh, I'm not sure I can bear the thought of Amber actually being right about something," said Riley, who waited with his hands on his hips, until Laura was fully inside the vent and crawling behind Amber.

Riley looked over to Shell and gestured to the duct. "Go ahead. I'll take the back this time."

"Right," said Shell, who then hoisted himself up into the vent.

Riley was left all alone in the passageway. He looked around and listened. He didn't hear or see anything. It was probably safe. Well… unless someone was watching them. Someone that could be invisible. He hated invisibility.

He finally crawled up into the duct and followed after Shell. There was a dull orange light coming from up ahead, which seemed to be emanating from Amber's tendrils. In the dark duct, it was the only source of light, albeit minimal, much like a night light.

The four of them crawled through the vents for several minutes before Amber slowed to a stop. He shifted to the side in the vent, but managed to have just enough space to look back to see the others behind him. "There's another grate up ahead," he whispered. "I'm going to check it out."

"Alright," said Laura from behind him.

Amber crawled forward and neared another metal grate, which was inlaid to the base of the vent. The duct continued past the grate, and seemed to end at a T intersection a bit further down.

Amber kept his movements slow, easing along quietly through the vent. When he got to the metal grill, he peered down through the slits.

A dull yellow glow ebbed out against the concrete floor in the room below. No matter what angle Amber tried to look from, he couldn't actually make anything out. He looked back to Laura behind him. He could only partially see her, thanks to the glow from his tentacles. He pointed down to the grate and slowly shifted back to give himself some room in the vent. His tendrils came out and slowly pressed to all the edges of the grill.

Instead of dissolving it quickly, as he'd done with the grate in the passageway, he melted this one slowly, to prevent any added noise. It took four times as long, but it also allowed him to listen in for any sounds in the room below.

When the grill was sufficiently melted, he reached out and clutched it at the edges. He then used his tendrils to softly push it over to the other side of the vent, without making even the slightest sound.

With the grate removed, he peeked his head down into the room below. First, he found where the yellow light was coming from. There was a mass of organic material against the wall, with small yellow globs that were brightly lit. The surface of the substance seemed to glisten in the light. There were thick tan veins running throughout it. It seemed to be some sort of… pod? He could only imagine that it was some sort of nest structure, the kind the monster-players used. It was easily the size of a car, but proportioned strangely against the wall.

He moved a bit more urgently now, with less silence. He leaned up and crawled forward, before he slipped his legs down into the opening and dropped into the room. He took several steps away from the drop-point in the ceiling, and looked around.

There was a single metal door, which didn't look substantial by any means. The only other thing in the room was the pod itself.

A few seconds later, Laura dropped into the room. She looked at the pod, then around the room as he had. She crossed her arms and looked the pod over. "That's got to be a monster nest," she said.

"What if it isn't, though?" asked Amber. "Maybe it's like… a tool bench for all we know?"

Shell dropped into the room, followed by Riley.

"Is this our target?" asked Riley, while Shell kept quiet.

"We should destroy it regardless of whether it's an actual nest, or some sort of monster workstation," said Laura.

She then pointed over to the door. "We also need to see where that door leads."

"Probably the same place that weird cord goes," said Shell, who pointed to the edge of the floor.

The other three looked to where he pointed. There was a cord much like an enlarged vein running from the pod-like structure, all the way to the wall that the door was on.

"Do these things need power?" Riley asked.

"I think we need to check the other room," said Laura, who walked over to the door.

Riley gripped the staff portion of his scythe as he stood nearby, his eyes on the door. "Should we contact the others first? Let them know where we are?"

"Yeah, one sec," said Laura. "Let's just see if there's anything important here first. Else, there's no reason to bother."

Laura turned to Amber. "Can you deal with this door?"

"Yeah, yeah, I got it," he said as he walked over. His tendrils extended from the orange pods on his back. Once again, the tentacles lined the edges of the door and slowly began to eat into it.

"This is gonna take a minute," he said. "Unless you want anyone on the other side to know what we're up to."

"Best to keep quiet," said Laura. "Might as well contact the others now, just in case."

She held the cell device and tapped at it several times. She brought it to her ear and pressed a button on the side. "This is Laura. We've found an organic mass about the size of a car. It seems to be some sort of pod-like construct. We're not sure what it does, but we're in an otherwise empty room and proceeding through to wherever this pod might be linked up to. You can track us on your cell. I recommend heading to my location."

"Heading to you now," said Parviz, the leader of one of the other groups.

"On our way, we're a bit far from you now, though," came Seth's voice.

A softer female voice sounded from the device. "A pod?" asked Snow.

"Yeah, we're not sure what it does, though," said Laura. "Any ideas? Should we destroy it sooner rather than later?"

There was a bit of silence.

"No idea," said Snow. "Information on the plethora of monster devices and furniture has been severely limited. Just see what else is there and make your best call on how to destroy it."

"Of course," said Laura. "We're going to go silent for the time being, we'll let you know if anything changes."

A series of confirmations came over the cell. With a few button presses, she slid it into her pocket.

"How's that door coming?" she asked.

"Almost got it," said Amber. His tendrils were moving against the edges in such a fashion that he'd be able to hold the inside of the door after melting it out of the frame.

"So, you can determine whether there's an acidity to your slime… appendages, or not?" asked Shell.

"Something like that," said Amber. "By default, they work like any of the slime monsters, but most of those monsters will cause either poison or acid damage to you. I have to mentally think about poison or acid if I want the tentacles to do one or the other, as opposed to neither."

"I gotcha," said Shell.

"How much longer?" asked Laura.

Amber grumbled. "I've got it," he said,

as he'd just finished melting through. "Ready to pull the door out. You all ready?"

Riley chewed his lower lip. "Mind if I take some essence first?" he asked, his sights on Amber Impaler.

The tentacle user narrowed his eyes back at Riley. "Can't you just steal some from any monsters inside?"

"What if they're all armored? If I can't steal their powers, and if I can't empower my weapon, I'm going to be useless. So do you wanna lose a percent or two of health and have me help in there? Or I can just chill in here and watch you guys go up against whatever's in the other room."

"Fine, fine I get it. Just do it," Amber grumbled.

Riley lifted his hand and launched the spike from the slit on his palm, letting it lodge into Amber's back. A second later, orange glowing essence rushed through the air back to Riley's palm. Then, with a squeeze of his left hand, he sent the essence into the staff. A curved orange blade formed at the top. If he was lucky, it'd be able to cause poison or acid damage.

"Thanks," said Riley, who then left his spike in Amber's back, just in case.

"Yeah, yeah, you owe me," Amber murmured as he directed his attention back on the door.

"Let's do this, open the door," said Laura.

Amber Impaler used his tendrils to slowly ease the door towards them. As he did, the room beyond was revealed. He stepped forward as his tendrils moved on their own, setting the door aside. His jaw dropped as his gaze went up and up.

Laura, Shell, and Riley all crowded around him to look into the room.

Dozens of dark organic pods littered the floor of the room, each the size of a car, but unlike the one in the room they were currently in. None of the ones in this much larger room had yellow glowing orbs on them, or any lighting of their own. But the most prominent structure was a glistening fleshy spire that created a sort of pillar in the center of the room. There were yellow bulbs all along it which cast an eerie yellow glow. The room was easily three times the size of the lounge area of Bunker 7.

Half a dozen dark shapes moved around amongst the pods. They were humanoid with dark gray skin and red spikes protruding out of their bodies at all sorts of angles.

Their heads were bald, save for the spikes.

As the four players stared into the room filled with all these things, one of the dark gray monsters turned its head and looked in their direction, seemingly alerted to the yellow light that was now spilling out from a room that had been closed off a few seconds prior.

The monster's red eyes stared at them, and a second later, its maw full of crimson fangs opened and released a terrible roar that echoed all around the large chamber.

CHAPTER 5:
PAIN

Laura grabbed the cell from her pocket. It was still set for instant-communication. She pressed a button on the side and spoke quickly. "This is Laura, they know we're here. Get to our location, now! Crawl through vents, break walls, just get here!"

"How we doing this?" asked Amber. "Wanna lure 'em to a bottleneck in this room?"

"What if they have a way to poison-gas the room or something?" said Riley. "They don't look like players, they all look the same. I think these are NPC watchdogs."

"You sure about that?" asked Amber, as he watched the numerous spiked monsters collect together and move towards them. "There's a bunch of them!"

"There's a lot of pod things in there," said Shell, who was slowly backing away from the entrance to the other room.

"Well, let's see how strong their guards are," said Laura. She pocketed the cell again and pulled her pistol from its holster. She spun the chamber and took aim at the closest monster. Her pistol was unique. It had a special added effect of doing increased damage if all the chambers were loaded.

She pulled the trigger and a shot rang out. The round smacked into the creature's head, making it recoil and fall back. A moment later, it burst into gray particles. "One down," she said with an exhale. "Get out there while I spawn copies!"

The only problem with using the special attack on her pistol was that it used all six rounds in the process.

"These guys look easy," Amber chuckled as he ran out of the room and went to intercept the monsters.

Two of the creatures were passing by the closest pods and coming out into the open. There was about fifty feet between the door and the nearest pods.

Amber focused and created two large tendrils from his back. He lashed out with them and knocked the two monsters in opposite directions. Then, the tendrils broke apart into five tentacles each, and began stabbing the fallen monsters.

Riley stepped outside the door, his weapon ready. He watched as Amber engaged two of the monsters, while another one charged the Amber Impaler.

One of the monsters that hadn't been close to the others headed for him, its arms pumping and its maw gaping open.

Riley's lips curled as he drew his weapon back. The creatures were fast and had wasted little time before attacking them. If he was right, which… he was sure he was, then these monsters were simply guards to protect the nest. He'd only spotted six. One was killed. Three were now engaged with Amber, and one was headed for him, with another not too far behind. It was unlikely that they'd even need Laura and her clones.

The growling monster got ever closer, and when it reached Riley's striking range, he swung with the orange-bladed scythe. The orange energy cut into the monster, but the creature didn't stop. It kept moving and lashed out at Riley. He knew he didn't have the kind of stopping power that a true damage dealing paragon could boast, but he still knew how to fight and deal some damage.

As the monster swung at him, he pushed off and lunged at the creature, smashing his elbow into its soft stomach region. At least the monster shared some similarities to human physiology, which made the stomach a weak point.

The creature grunted from the sharp blow. Its growling had stopped as it seemed somewhat stunned, its maw dripping viscous strands of saliva.

Riley pulled back from his attack and immediately swung again with his empowered scythe. The blade cut through the monster again and again as Riley renewed his attacks. The creature barely had enough time to pull its arms up to attack or even defend itself, before dispersing into a brilliant display of glittering gray particles. The second creature didn't seem fazed by the death of the first. It ran for Riley, and reached him sooner than he would've preferred.

He was just recovering from his final attack on the first monster when the second lashed out at him with its claws. Riley pulled back just in time to avoid the creature's attack, but it swung its other arm immediately after. Its sharp claws tore into Riley's sleeve and cut into his arm.

Riley's vision flashed red momentarily as he took damage. It didn't seem to be much, as these creatures were nothing substantial. If he had been a real damage dealer, he probably could've dispatched both of them with ease without taking any damage at all. But that wasn't the case.

Just as he'd done with the first, Riley swung his scythe to slice the monster. He used the scythe's range to keep as much distance between him and its claws as he could. The creature had been able to reach him quickly initially, but it wasn't all that fast in close combat.

Thanks to his high dexterity stat, he could dodge every follow up attack and managed not to take any further hits.

He sliced and cut, and soon enough, the monster dispersed into particles as well.

"'Bout time you killed yours," said Amber from a short distance away.

Riley looked over to see Amber standing with his tentacles protruding from his back, his hands resting on his hips. The other monsters were gone—he must've killed them without any issue at all.

"Yeah, I'm a slow damager, I know," Riley offered begrudgingly.

Without warning, Riley's vision went black.

Then, the world reappeared. At first his vision was hazy, but only for a second. Then, everything was crystal clear again.

"What the hell was that?" asked Amber.

Riley blinked and looked over to his guildmate. "Did… that just happen for you too?"

"Yeah, did your vision just black out?" Amber questioned.

Riley nodded. "Yeah, what was it?"

"I think the game just updated," said Laura, who was just now leaving the room they'd been in a minute ago. Her copies flooded out, one by one. The copy of Laura that had spoken was still holding her pistol. "That weird blackout, followed by hazy vision, is a sign of an update being pushed while the server is still live."

"I've never experienced that before," said Riley. "I've been in the game since the start. Have they ever pushed a live update before?"

"It's really rare," said Laura. "I experienced it once. Usually it's when they need to rollback some code without taking the servers down."

"So something was changed, or fixed?" asked Riley.

"How should I know?" asked Laura, who then lifted a brow at Riley. "There wasn't any news about it. Usually for something like that, there must've been something really bad that they needed to fix, and they needed to fix it before the usual server maintenance window."

"Wonder what it was," said Amber.

"I guess we'll have to wait till we get—" Riley's vision suddenly flashed red. When it did, a streak of pain rushed through his arm.

"Ah!" he gasped, jumping in surprise from the actual pain in his arm. He grabbed his arm with his hand. A dull throbbing pain emanated from where he'd been cut by the creature.

"What is it?" asked Laura. "What's wrong?"

"I… my arm! I felt it!" said Riley as he grabbed his arm through his sleeve.

"Huh? Felt what?" asked Laura.

"Pain!" said Riley, his voice haggard. "It hurt! It just… came out of nowhere!"

"The devs said they weren't implementing pain till two weeks from now," said Amber. "Are you sure?"

"Yes I'm sure!" said Riley. He pulled his sleeve back and looked at his bleeding arm as his hand trembled. He then gestured to bring up his status screen. He looked under the section labeled 'ailments' and saw that he'd acquired an effect called 'bleeding.'

"Why am I feeling pain?" he asked, and looked back to Laura and Amber. The other Laura copies had fanned out around them, creating a barrier of bodies between them and the pods.

"How should I know?" asked Laura, with a shake of her head. "Maybe that's what the update just now was?"

"They just updated and put pain in the game?" asked Riley, his eyes wide. "Why the hell would they do that? Why now?"

"Maybe they screwed up," said Amber. "Maybe it was a mistake. The devs have been doing a lot of crazy stuff lately since the hellions expansion."

"I need to get rid of this effect," said Riley. His focus centered on Amber. "Sorry!" he said as he reached out with his right hand, and willed a glob of orange essence to rush out from the end of the spike.

"Ah!" Amber grunted. He reached back and felt at his back. His fingers wrapped around the spike and pulled it out immediately. "Damn, you're not joking! I mean… it didn't really hurt that bad, but I wasn't expecting… I don't know, that!"

The orange glob flew through the air and smacked into Riley's hand. A second later, his eyes glowed red, and his hit points were restored.

"I told you," said Riley. "That was just me taking a little essence. Just imagine what a real attack would feel like."

He checked his status screen again, and the bleed effect was gone. Well, at least the bonus effect on his belt was still useful for the time being. His belt specifically allowed his healing abilities to cure one detrimental effect. It had been useless in trying to heal Chase's disease, but at least it still cured bleeding. Usually stealing essence from another player wouldn't give him a lot of health, but all he wanted to do was cure the bleeding. Plus, he had bonuses to his healing power. Not a lot, but enough to have him back to a hundred percent health at this point.

"I thought they were supposed to slowly increment pain into the game," said Laura. "But it'd only ever be like… I dunno, a minor annoyance? Like someone flicking you. They said they didn't want to make it actually hurt people."

"The bleed effect didn't feel like someone flicking, or even pinching me," said Riley. "It felt like being stung or bit by something like a large bug or a small animal."

"I'm really hoping it's just some glitch," said Laura, as she looked between them. "And I better not get pain feedback through my copies."

Amber walked over to the closest copy

of Laura. He reached out and pinched her arm.

"Huh, interesting," said the Laura that was holding the pistol, as her copy was pinched. "I got the usual feedback that the clone had been touched, but… that's it. Sweet."

"Must be nice," Riley grumbled. "Let's just wait a minute and see if they revert the change. I'm sure they have to know that they screwed up. This can't be how they plan to test pain, right? And there's no way it's supposed to hurt this much!"

Laura shrugged. "Who knows? But you're right, let's just wait here a minute."

"The others will be here soon, right?" asked Amber. "But you know, we're sorta right in the middle of a monster-player base. I doubt we have a lot of time. What if the monster-players spawn into their pod nests… or something?"

"I'm sure we have a minute," said Riley. "We don't get any sort of alarm systems when our homes are attacked. I doubt they have anything that warns them."

As the three of them discussed the possibilities of what a monster lair was capable of, one of the pods in the middle of the room began to slowly open. Various flaps of organic red and brown flesh pulled away, revealing a dark purple mass within. A glistening dark purple arm slowly rose from the pod and grabbed onto the side and pulled itself out.

But this pod wasn't like all the others around it. Instead of being the size of a car, it was the size of a freight truck, easily four times as large as most of the others in the room.

The movement caught their attention. All the copies of Laura turned at the same time.

"Shell! Get out here, we've got something big," said Laura.

They watched as the seemingly armored monster rose from its pod. Its head was pointed, like a shark's. But it had no neck, as the head was attached directly to the top of the narrow torso. Its arms were thick, with five clawed fingers at the ends. Its eyes glowed a dull yellow as it turned to scan the room, quickly centering its sights upon the gathered players.

"You think that's a player?" asked Amber.

"I hope it's just another guard," said Riley.

Laura turned to look back to the room they'd come out of. "Shell!" she called again, but got no response. She turned fully and quickly stepped to the doorway. It took only a couple seconds to look inside before she turned back to Amber and Riley. "We have a problem! Shell's gone!"

CHAPTER 6: SCRAPING BY

Riley and Amber turned to Laura at the same time, but Amber was the first one to speak. "What do you mean he's gone?"

"He's not in the room!" Laura exclaimed.

"Did he ditch us?" asked Amber. "He's not hiding behind the pod in there, is he?"

Laura glanced back into the room briefly, then shook her head. "He's not there!"

"His shields would've been nice, but we can take this thing without him," said Riley.

The monster lumbered towards them, easily twenty feet tall. Its arms were segmented, like the sections of a centipede, but whereas a centipede was rounded, each segment had rough and jagged edges. Its arm lifted and its sharp fingers pointed in their direction as its feet found available space to walk amongst the pods.

"What if it hits us? Laura can't fight it by herself!" said Amber.

"Then don't let it hit you!" said Riley.

"It's still coming, we need to engage it," said Laura. She checked her revolver and then looked back to the monster. It was almost at the edge of the pods. Its other arm came up and five pointed fingers aimed at them.

Tsssss.

A hissing sound echoed around the room, but it seemed to emanate from the monster's hand. Tiny jets of air billowed from beneath the tips of the creature's fingers. A moment later, the tips of its fingers shot off like rockets. The spikes streaked across the room, but were still attached to the monster by thin cords, just narrower than the spikes themselves.

The three players only had mere moments to dodge as ten spikes shot across the room.

Amber, Riley, and Laura all dodged and managed to get out of the way, just in time.

Several of Laura's clones were not so lucky. The individual intelligence on each of Laura's clones was limited. They would attempt to dodge and fight, if threatened, but their reaction times weren't anything close to the original Laura.

Five of Laura's copies were hit. Two were impaled in their arms, while two more only suffered a glancing strike, leaving cuts on their torso. One was struck in the heart and stumbled back, clutching at the spike in her chest. She burst into white particles and disappeared. One of the twenty copies had been eliminated in a single strike.

Amber was staring wide-eyed at the fallen duplicate. "Not good, not good," he muttered.

The spikes suddenly retracted. The two impaled Lauras were pulled toward the monster, but only for a few feet before the spikes were freed from their bodies.

The tips of the monster's fingers connected back into place. Its arms lowered and it began to head towards them again at a steady pace.

"I should've put a ranged damager in our group," Laura murmured, before she lifted her revolver. With a squeeze of her finger, she shot off a single round. Upon impact, the round made a spark as it glanced off the monster's tough organic armor. A moment later, the name 'Mauve Dire Guardian' appeared above the creature's head, along with a health bar.

"It's definitely not a player!" Laura said, as the name appeared. She then fired again and again until all her rounds were expelled. Now she had to wait for the chambers to reload. With her next thought, she willed all her duplicates to charge the monster.

"Not sure if that's better or worse," Riley murmured under his breath. He kept a careful eye on the large monster, making sure to spot any special movement that might allude to an attack.

Laura's nineteen remaining copies charged at once. Each one carrying a different melee weapon. Some held swords, others axes and maces.

"Amber! Do you think you can trip that thing?" Riley called over, as he started running to the right, so that they weren't all grouped up.

"It's too bulky! There's no way I have the power to topple it!" Amber yelled back as he went in the opposite direction, taking the same idea that Riley had.

As Laura's copies ran through the numerous pods, they struck them as they went. Deep gouges were ripped and torn into the tough, leathery ovoids.

"If you can't hit the guardian, go for everything else!" Laura shouted.

Riley reached the nearest pods on the right side, and without hesitation, he slashed with his scythe. The orange blade tore into the egg-like constructs. There was no way of knowing what they were for, other than the fact that the solitary large one had spawned the Mauve Dire Guardian. Perhaps there was some information online, but they'd have to go back to the real world and search forums and wikis.

The guardian's yellow eyes darted around, taking notice of Laura's charging duplicates. It was slowly passing by the outer pods, and Laura's clones had surrounded it. Its arms lifted and came crashing down, one after another. The copies managed to dodge the slow-moving arms just in time. They struck with their various weapons, but the natural armor of the monster was tougher than that of the eggs.

Laura sent her consciousness out to her duplicates, taking direct control of the ones that were in the most danger. It took its toll on her as she constantly jumped around. She was essentially taking direct control over a different body again and again. It was easy to lose sight of things around her as she was constantly changing her place.

The guardian's arm smashed down with greater force, rocking the floor and knocking back the clone that Laura was controlling. When she fell to the floor, she winced from the rough landing. In that moment, she realized that wherever her consciousness was, despite it being one of her clones, she'd feel their pain. With this sudden understanding, she pulled her consciousness back to her original body for some measure of safety.

The moment she did so, the monster's other arm smashed one of her clones flat into the concrete floor. When its hand lifted, there was a brief display of white particles. The weapon that the duplicate had been carrying had disappeared as well. This was a common occurrence when she lost her duplicates—the weapon would return to her inventory automatically. Laura's maximum stats would be lowered for each clone she created, and if a clone died, those stats were gone until she was able to rest or use a special item to regain the stamina that the clones took to make. But those items tended to be pricey, especially ones that you could use during combat.

"Amber! I'm not going to be able to solo this thing with my clones, I need you to get in there!" Laura yelled, as she brought her revolver up and took several shots at its pointed head. Each shot only seemed to glance right off, doing little damage. The monster's health wasn't falling very far.

Amber shook his head as he darted through the pods and got behind the guardian. He was hoping that the monster didn't have any abilities that allowed it to hit enemies behind it.

Without responding to Laura's call, he willed the tips of his tendrils to become like spikes. They extended out, and then shot forward, impaling the back of the guardian's leg. As soon as the tentacles stabbed in, they'd pull back out and jab again.

The guardian turned, one of its arms lifted. Its fingers curled and several aimed right at Amber.

His eyes widened. "Crap, of course it could easily aim at me!" he said as he rushed to the side, just as a loud hiss came from the monster's fingers. A couple seconds later, the pointed fingertips shot out and smacked into the ground. There had only been three, instead of a full barrage of all five finger spikes.

Riley was closing in on where Amber was retreating to. The guardian was slowly turning. Its attention was constantly being garnered by the Laura duplicates.

Riley looked past Amber as the spikes retracted. There were deep gouges in the concrete where the spikes had hit. He glanced around at the various pods around him. They were unscathed and the guardian was moving amongst them, as if it was being careful not to damage them.

Amber had gained a couple dozen feet of distance from the monster, but Laura's clones were still running in and scoring hits before running out of the way. Laura had to keep them moving, else they'd be easy targets.

Riley looked at Amber's tendrils. He'd seen how they were able to pierce the monster's tough armor, which meant that they were easily strong enough to pierce into the eggs.

"Amber! Come over here! Help me with something!" he yelled.

Amber glanced over and saw Riley heading for him. "What?" he asked, perturbed.

Riley stopped and swung his scythe at the base of one of the pods. The pods themselves were only loosely attached to the floor by some sort of hard but organic material, which was different than what made up the individual pods. Riley could easily cut into it with his scythe, which caused the egg to wobble. There were several cords hooked up to the base of the pod, which connected it to the other pods. He promptly cut the cords with his scythe. They split easily and leaked a strange yellow glowing liquid, which held the same glow as the bulbs he'd seen on the first pod in the other room.

"What do you want?" Amber asked, as he reached Riley. He noticed the glowing yellow liquid pouring out onto the floor, both from the pod and from the organic cables. "What are you doing? We should focus on the monster!"

"We are!" said Riley. "Use your tendrils and throw this pod at the monster, aim for its head. We can try and blind it with the goo these things are leaking."

"You want me to lob this thing at the guardian?" Amber asked, looking over to the monster, which was still engaged with Laura's copies.

"Yes, quick! If it notices what we're doing, it might use those spike-fingers on us," said Riley, as he considered how it might feel to have one of those spiked fingertips lodged in his chest. What if it hit his heart? Would it one-shot him as well? What the hell would that feel like? His teeth clenched. No, he didn't think he wanted to find out.

Amber's tendrils struck the leathery hide of the pod that Riley had dislodged. Like a catapult, he hoisted and lobbed the pod from the ground.

The dark ovoid construct flew through the air, leaking yellow glowing goo as it flew.

It smashed against the monster's left shoulder and released the golden liquid to splash against its dark purple exterior.

None of the slime managed to cover the guardian's head or face. In fact, the egg-smash hadn't really caused much of any damage.

"That didn't do anything!" said Amber.

"Of course it didn't!" said Riley. "I told you to hit its head! Try again! Now it knows what we're up to!"

The guardian turned, its body shifting so that it was slowly coming around to face the two paragons that had attacked it, despite the insignificant damage.

Riley's eyes widened. He had hoped that the monster wouldn't have directed its attention to them so quickly, but he supposed there wasn't any way around it. Without thinking, he turned to the closest pod and cut with his scythe. Once it was free, Amber didn't waste any time in grabbing it with his impaling tendrils.

"Second try!" Amber yelled as he hurled the pod at the monster, which was now facing them and lifting its hands in their direction. "It's aiming at us!"

The pod broke against the guardian's torso, causing the yellow goo to splash around its chest and up at its face.

"What are you guys doing?" Laura shouted from across the chamber, as the goo rained down on her copies.

The slime ran down the pointed face of the guardian, just as a hiss filled the air. A second later, all ten spikes shot at Amber and Riley.

Riley ducked behind one of the nearby pods. Amber didn't have a good angle on taking cover, so he threw his tendrils up as a shield, diving away.

Two of the spikes pierced his orange slime-tendril wall, but didn't so much as touch his actual body.

The rest of the spikes clattered and grated against the stone floor, causing no damage to them. The guardian retracted the spikes and immediately clawed at its own face in an attempt to clear its obscured vision.

"Amber! We need to hit it again!" Riley

grabbed the pod and used it to pull himself up as he gripped his scythe and renewed his attacks. The blade cut swiftly in a wide arc. He was getting quicker at freeing the pods.

"We're still not doing any damage to it!" Amber growled as he reluctantly went along with the plan. His tendrils sunk into the meaty interior of the pod and threw it at the guardian. At least they were destroying pods, even if they weren't hurting the monster all that much.

The egg smashed into the guardian's raised arms. It exploded like a melon falling on the floor. The pulpy innards fell to the concrete below, where Laura's copies desperately dodged to avoid it. The yellow goo splashed onto the monster's arms and hands, and more of it splashed against its chest and face.

"It's fully blinded!" said Riley. "Can you tear an opening in its armor, so I can spike it?"

"You want to get closer to that thing?" asked Amber, who watched as the monster swung and flailed its arms at the ground, trying to hit Laura's copies, even though it couldn't see them. It had moved out of the confines of the mass of pods, which let it fight more effectively now that it didn't risk damaging them.

"I can't buff you guys if I can't get the spike under its armor!" said Riley.

"If I get hit, I'm taking it out on you!" said Amber, as he ran toward the monster.

Riley shook his head and followed after.

As the two of them weaved through the pods, the orange blade on Riley's scythe disappeared. "Damn," Riley muttered. He knew that Amber wasn't going to let him steal more essence. Not if it meant he'd have to stick him with his spike again. Which meant that the only essence he could steal was from the monster itself.

Amber passed the outer pods, his sights locked on the Mauve Dire Guardian. It stooped and swiped its arms across the concrete, knocking the duplicates away, but luckily not killing them outright.

Along with the two copies she'd lost earlier, Laura was down four more. She wasn't used to having to fight a monster mostly by herself. It was large, but it wasn't big enough that it couldn't move easily, which meant that if her clones were the only ones damaging it, all the monster's aggression would be on her duplicates.

Her hand came up to fire off one of the renewed bullets in her revolver's chamber. In the corner of her eye she spotted Amber rushing towards the monster. She held her shot, waiting to see what the other two paragons were up to now.

Sweat ran down Amber's cheeks. He didn't have a huge amount of stamina to be keeping up with all this moving. He was used to fighting his enemies in melee range and keeping them there.

As soon as he reached the guardian, his tendrils formed into one large one. He turned it into a lance and drove it into the monster's side. The orange tendril pierced the dark armored hide of the monster and sunk into the softer meat beneath.

The guardian's arm swung down, quicker than Amber had expected. He hadn't saved any of his tendril capacity to help him dive out of the way. The monster's fingers swatted him away, sending him flying back against a pod.

"Ah!" Amber cried as his back smacked into the pod. His body crumpled to the concrete, but he wasn't defeated. His fingers grasped at the floor as he pulled himself up to look at the wounded guardian.

Riley's spike shot through the air and

sunk right into the wound that Amber had created. Yellow glowing liquid gradually leaked from the wound, which made Riley think that somehow everything was powered or made up of the stuff.

With a single thought, he willed the essence to flow through his spike, and streak to his palm. He absorbed it, and quickly switched his scythe into his right hand, as he used his left to throw the essence at Amber.

The yellow essence glob smacked into Amber's back as he rose from the ground. The paragon's eyes went yellow and some of his health returned to him. "There we go," he grunted, his lips curling as he righted himself and ran for the monster.

Riley drew more essence from the spike. He dropped his scythe for the moment, and only focused his efforts on empowering Laura's remaining copies. Some of them were injured and barely standing. At least this kept them fighting a little longer.

The monster continued to swipe at the ground with one arm, while it sought to clear its gaze with the other. Every time Amber jabbed his single large pointed tendril into its body, the guardian would spike out at him, but Amber kept a closer eye on the creature's movements, staying one step ahead of its swings.

With one essence drain, Riley picked up his scythe and empowered it. With the next, he empowered himself and gained the same yellow-glowing eyes everyone else had. Now that he was a damage dealer—thanks to the weapon—his hits would be stronger if he was also empowered. Riley had spent a great deal of time testing what he'd gain from various essence sources, whether they were players or monsters. There wouldn't have been a big increase in his damage if he'd taken Amber's essence for his body, but his essence did allow his weapon to function, which was all he'd needed originally. But now, with the monster's power coursing through him, his allies, and his weapon, they were ready to turn this fight around.

CHAPTER 7: CLEANING UP

With scythe in hand, Riley rushed in to join the melee with the guardian. Laura's copies had been taking the brunt of the attacks. Even though many remained, the overall health of all of the copies surely wasn't great, as far as Riley could tell. Some of them looked banged up and bruised, which was the game's way of letting you know that a person had lost some health.

The monster's attention was still mostly upon Amber, as he was the one causing the majority of the damage to it with the sharp jabs from his tendrils. But for a paragon like Amber, the more he went on the offensive, the worse his defensive capabilities became.

Riley focused on the opposite side of the guardian, to help try and pull some of its attention away from Amber. He swung the scythe and cut into the monster's tough hide. The gouges weren't nearly as deep as he was hoping, but some damage was better than none. He certainly wasn't going to be on par with Amber, as far as damage was concerned.

The Guardian's health was starting to dip. With its vision obscured, it was having trouble landing hits on them, which allowed them to take more chances with getting in close and causing damage.

Riley could only manage a couple hits at a time, before he had to look and make sure that those deadly harpoon-like fingers weren't aimed at him. The monster hadn't displayed any other attacks other than the corded spear fingers and regular attacks with its hands. Even though the monster was a guardian for the nest they were in, Riley was keenly aware that it was still a boss-level monster and could still change up its behavior at a moment's notice.

The monster's left hand turned towards him, which made him immediately tense and back away. His feet kept moving, taking him behind one of the many eggs that were still standing. Almost immediately after taking cover, its sharp fingers shot off and clanked off the concrete floor. The attacks had all missed him by several feet.

From behind the egg, he could see the guardian's head turn in his direction. Its face tilted and shifted, as if looking around for him through its muck-covered eyes.

Riley was still on the monster's left, while Amber was on its right. Laura's clones were spread out, making whatever attacks they could.

The guardian turned and looked away from all of them, over to one of the nearby walls. Its attention remained focused upon it, even as Amber drove his sharp tendrils into its armor.

A second later, Riley felt it. A dull rumbling and vibration, coming from the wall the monster was focused on. Both of its arms lifted, its fingers pointing to the rumbling wall.

A crack formed in the concrete wall, roughly eight feet high. The crack got bigger and bigger, before the concrete shifted and pulled away as the fissure became wider until it finally opened several feet.

A figure rushed into the room through the gap. From that distance, Riley could only make out the vibrant pink hair that the young woman had, but that was all he needed to know that it was Carla, The Chromatic Lotus.

In the brief moment that it took her to leave the artificial passageway, the guardian's fingertips shot off with a loud hiss.

Carla came to an abrupt halt as the sharp fingers streaked past her. Some of them ricocheted off the wall and floor, while two disappeared into the passage behind her. She didn't waste a moment as her hands whipped up. Orange lotuses appeared in the air and rushed toward the behemoth.

Two sharp cries came from behind Carla as she engaged the guardian.

In seconds, her orange lotuses reached the monster's body. One by one, they exploded against the guardian's tough exterior, pummeling it with damage and even driving it to stumble back for more secure footing.

Its fingertips withdrew, causing another series of shouts from the opening that Carla had come through.

One of the voices continued to yell as another form exited the passage, drawn out at the end of one of the guardian's fingertips.

Riley caught the brief blur of Parviz, the portal maker, being pulled out of the passageway. It was only when he was halfway towards the monster that he released his grip on the cord and let it pull free from his shoulder.

"Ahh! Why does it hurt so much?" came Parviz's strained voice as he grabbed at his shoulder while turning back and forth on the ground.

Riley shook himself from the distraction of the arrival of his guildmates. He gripped his scythe and rushed back into melee range of the guardian's leg. He swung again and again, cutting gouges into its armor while it remained fixated on the new arrivals.

A red bolt streaked out of the passageway and smacked into the monster's face, creating a micro-explosion on impact. The guardian brought one of its hands up to shield its face, as three more bolts exploded against it.

Carla had taken the opportunity to rush to Parviz's aid and get him standing again. Once he was on his feet, she ran to the side, keeping a safe distance from everyone else. Then, she started deploying more and more of her lotuses, which promptly blanketed the guardian with explosions.

With their aid, Riley could see the monster's health dipping by the second. It had proven a tough opponent for the four of them, but its armor didn't seem as resistant to the explosive damage that Carla and the hidden-away Brenda were able to muster against it.

With the still-hidden Todd in the passageway, the guardian was now confronted by a total of seven opponents, plus all of Laura's duplicates. Its fingertips clattered around the room, digging gouges into the stone floor and walls. It only managed to graze a few of the actual players, but ended up destroying several more of Laura's copies.

In just a few short minutes, the guardian's health dropped to zero, as it stumbled back from another of Carla's lotus barrages.

Its body burst into a myriad of colored particles, as it was defeated.

"Boss down!" Carla called, as her hands went to her hips triumphantly. But the smirk on her lips quickly faded as she looked at the place where the monster had just been standing amongst some of the remaining eggs. "Wait, it didn't drop any loot?"

Riley and several others looked to the ground, but there wasn't any loot to speak of. In fact, the lesser monsters from earlier also hadn't dropped anything. "I guess the guard monsters don't drop anything," said Riley. He quickly gestured in the air to bring up a screen for his stats. "We got some experience though, but not as much as a usual boss would give. Better than nothing though."

"Total rubbish," Carla groaned. "Did you guys find any loot when you came in? Looked like you were all having some trouble with that thing."

One by one, Laura's copies walked over to her 'core' body. She would take their hands, almost like a handshake, only for them to disappear as she absorbed them. She turned her head to Carla. "We didn't find anything useful. Just more weird… structures, like these egg things."

At this point, the short and stocky Todd made his way out of the passageway. There was a red mark on his side, which he had a hand over. "Can I get a heal? This really hurts," he groaned.

"I'd heal you… but it might be easier, and a little more pleasant, if Carla gets you," Riley called, as he had to 'stab' people with his spike in order to heal them.

"I got you," said Carla. She threw out a green lotus which floated in the air and disintegrated upon contact with Todd's body. When it did, the red spot on his clothes dissipated.

Todd let out a slow but deep sigh. "Ah,

much better. But seriously, what's with that new pain feature? Did you all get that weird black vision earlier too?"

"Yeah we did, just before we had to fight this guardian," Amber called back, as he shifted his attention on the nearby eggs. He started slashing them with his tendrils. "So we just going to wreck the rest of what's here, right?"

"Probably for the best," said Riley. "We should—"

Riley's voice caught in the air, as a form suddenly appeared in a dull flash of light, right amongst their spread-out group.

The figure was notably male, as it was unclothed and flat-chested. It was of humanoid appearance, but its skin was a deep gray. A series of short horns protruded from its hairless skull, creating a sort of'crown. Its feet ended in talons, and its fingers weren't clawed, but appeared sharp nonetheless. A single series of spikes ran down its spine.

Its head whipped around, as if taking in its surroundings. All around it were the destroyed remains of many of the pods. Along with the gathering of seven players.

His deep red eyes focused on Riley, then went to several of the other members.

It had only appeared for several short seconds before it spoke. "You idiots," it hissed. "I'll remember this."

Then, just as quickly as it appeared, it vanished. There was no light, just a sudden absence of its form.

Riley had been so stunned by its sudden appearance and ability to speak that he hadn't even thought to act. Of course, no one else had either.

"What the hell was that?" asked Carla.

"I think it was a hellion," said Riley.

"One of the monster-players that lived in the nest, probably," said Amber. "He sure didn't look happy to see what we'd done. We should probably finish up and wreck the rest of the place, and then move on. Don't want him alerting anyone else that might be online."

"How'd he disappear like that?" asked Laura, looking around.

"Some item? Maybe his power?" said Parviz. "Hell, I can portal around if need be. Of course, I can't do a whole lot else."

"Maybe that's all he does, is teleports around," said Carla, now crossing her arms against her chest. "I agree with Amber though, let's finish destroying this place, and then get out of here. We did our job for The Vanguard and they better be appreciative."

Riley slowly looked around the room. He looked at the pods, then the pod in the center of the room that had spawned the guardian. He looked back to the room that they had entered from. There weren't any other doors, or other rooms, for that matter.

"Guys, I think we might've screwed up on this one," said Riley.

"What do you mean?" asked Amber. "We killed their guardians, and there's no one here to stop us. We went out to kill monster nests, and that's what we did. Job done. Victory. What could we have screwed up?" His eyes were narrowed, focused on Riley.

Riley shook his head. "Yeah, we were sent to find nests. You know, groups of monster-players. It's only really the groups of monsters that are focusing on hunting hero-players like us, along with the NPCs in the city. I don't think this is a nest. I think this was a lair."

"Lair, nest, who cares? We're killing hellions," Amber countered.

"Oh, crap, I get what you're saying,"

said Laura, looking to Riley. "You think that hellion… the gray guy, was a neutral?"

"Yeah, he probably hunts hellions AND paragons. He's probably just… free-for-alling this whole game. Which, well, kinda in an odd way, put him on our side. Since most monsters are against us. And well… we just wrecked his lair. I have a feeling we just turned him against hero-players for good. And if he was able to build this whole lair by himself, and get a guardian like that, I bet he's pretty strong. No telling what any of this stuff does, but there's sure a lot of it for a solo player."

Amber shook his head. "Whatever. He was just another hellion. We kill 'em all." With that, he walked over to the next closest egg, and sliced it in half.

CHAPTER 8:
POWER

After decimating the monster hideout, Riley and the others met up with their other squads, which had been too late in joining in on the monster-fighting festivities. Once everything had been destroyed, the assembled guild of heroes made their way out of the depths, and back to the street level, returning to Bunker 7.

Theories were shared on what various members believed the hideout to be. Whether it was actually a lair, or a nest. And if it was a lair, what did that mean? Surely a single monster was no greater trouble than they were up against before.

Regardless, congratulations were shared and victory was claimed.

With the arrival of 'pain' in the game, it was decided that they should all call it a day. Most of the Bunker Brawlers headed back to their rooms to log out, while a few, like Red Shotgun, Green Melter, and Parviz, decided to remain and stick around in Bunker 7's lounge.

The idea that they had made a new enemy was still heavy on Riley's mind as he went back to his apartment in Bunker 7. He had barely spoken to anyone else after the fact, as all he could think about was the lair and the single hellion they'd encountered. What was his power? What was he capable of? He'd seen all their faces. Would he try and hunt them down? Currently in the game, hellions boasted a bit of an advantage when they were solo. It meant that most hero-types would usually group up. This meant that the game was somewhat "imbalanced" as far as players were concerned. At least, the hero-centric players. The developers were adamant to stress on social media that the game was always evolving, and changes would be made if they felt that things were significantly unfair, but with a game like Sigil Online, things might sometimes be unfair depending on a person's powers and situation.

Riley lay in his virtual bed and closed his eyes. He brought his hand up and made several gestures to initiate the logout sequence. Within seconds, his consciousness was pulled out of his avatar, and his senses in the real world returned to him.

He pulled his headgear off carefully and set it aside.

He reached over to the nightstand beside his bed and grabbed his cellphone. He flipped it on and quickly found Aaron's name on his contact list. He sent him a text, asking if he'd want to hit up Paragon Cafe, since there was a problem with the pain setting in Sigil Online.

Riley pulled himself out of bed and did a few stretches to help work his muscles. It had only taken about a minute, but before he could do anything else, Aaron had already responded to his text. He grabbed his cell again and read the message over. It read: 'I think it's better if we meet in-game, actually. There's something I need to show you, and now's a good time. Can you get to the Neon Nest quickly?'

Riley sighed and shook his head. He quickly texted Aaron back, and told him that he'd head right over, if it was that important. He set his phone back on the nightstand and laid back in bed. He wasn't feeling too hungry yet, but the idea of eating was sounding better by the moment. Oh well, he'd just meet up with Aaron quickly, and then see if he wanted to grab a bite of food after, since it was about lunch time.

He pulled his headset back on and got

comfortable. He initiated the login sequence and waited.

Once the countdown reached zero, he was back in the game.

It had only been a few minutes since he'd parted ways from his guild members. It felt a little strange to just walk right back up to the lounge of Bunker 7. When he entered, he didn't see any sign of his guildmates. In fact, there were very few other people around. A couple of other players were watching the televisions in the bar, but that was about it.

It didn't take him long to go over to the computer-like terminal against the wall and queue up a taxi to take him to Mega City and the Neon Nest—the place that Aaron called home.

Riley made his way out of the lounge area and onto the streets of Gargantuan City. There were numerous NPCs wandering around.

He waited for his vehicle to arrive, and when it did, he didn't waste any time getting in.

On his way to the Neon Nest, he saw various banged up and partially destroyed sections of the city. When he passed into Mega City itself, he noticed that things didn't look as bad as they were in his own city. It appeared as though Aaron's peers had a better hand on the hellion situation in the region than his city did. But it could also mean that there was just a bigger concentration of them in Gargantuan.

All Riley could do on his journey was stare out the window of the vehicle. He could've taken a faster means of travel. There were air vehicles, but they were more expensive. He wasn't in 'that' much of a hurry. There were also players who had the means of quick travel, but they were few and far between.

Finally, his destination was in sight. The vehicle pulled to a stop just outside the Neon Nest. He'd noticed on the way that there weren't too many players out on the streets. At least, as far as he could tell. Usually players were dressed a little more extravagantly than the NPCs that littered the streets and buildings.

He got out of the vehicle and made his way over to the doors of the Neon Nest. He'd been there a handful of times, and with all the glowing lights outside, it was true to its name.

There were about a dozen people around the lounge area. There was a tender behind the bar, and a couple groupings of people.

Off on the far side of the room was Aaron, seated by himself. No one paid Riley any mind as he went over to his best friend and sat across from him.

He let out a heavy sigh and relaxed in the seat. "So here I am," he said. "What's the big secret that I had to meet you in-game for?"

Aaron sat across from him in the small booth, his hands clasped in front of him. He looked over to the other patrons in the lounge, then to Riley. "Well, I figured I shouldn't keep putting it off. I wanted to tell you back when you discovered that I was the weevil, but… I just couldn't really get the words out. Like you said, it's kind of a big secret."

Riley blinked at Aaron. "Alright," he said, unsure what to expect. "Is it bad?"

Aaron shook his head immediately. "Oh no, it's not bad. It's really good, but… complicated, I suppose?" he said. "You see, there's this item—"

A blaring siren sounded over the televisions in the lounge. It only lasted about two seconds, but everyone who'd played Sigil Online for more than a month knew what the sound meant. It was an alert for breaking news that specifically dealt with

Sigil Online.

Their attention was drawn to the nearest television, where a woman with red hair and a black blouse sat behind a desk. Her hands were folded on the table as she looked into the camera. The name 'Susan Graff' was displayed at the bottom of the screen.

"Just a short while ago, reports came in of a sudden change that took place in Sigil Online. Out of nowhere, players reported that pain had been enabled, without any warning from the developers. Many players have responded saying that pain in the game felt just like it would in real life. From stabs, to punches, or even falling from a several story building. Pain was going to be an added feature to the game that the developers wanted to introduce in a very minimal amount. They had hoped to make it so that at worst, you might feel a pinch in-game. But in the past hour, we learned that something far worse has happened."

On the right side of the television, a blurry silhouette appeared. It didn't look like anyone, just a nameless image that was supposed to represent a person.

Beneath the blurry silhouette read the name 'Jennifer, AKA Jade Hornet.'

"According to witnesses, Jennifer, who also went by the name 'Jade Hornet' in-game, was hit by a powerful attack by a boss monster. Her character was flung across the room, where she smashed through a wall. By the time her friends got to her, her body was gone. It was assumed that her character was killed due to her name disappearing in group. But it wasn't until her friends logged out that they learned that something even worse had happened. According to Jennifer's sister, who she lived with, Jennifer was found dead, lying on her couch with her headset still on. Even with limited information, it's being hypothesized that Jennifer suffered some sort of traumatic event that somehow ended her life. No autopsy has yet been performed, but players are advised to be incredibly careful. It's recommended that if you're currently in-game, you should find a safe place immediately. And better yet, you should log out so that there is no further risk to your health. We are awaiting comment from the developers of Sigil Online, Apendia Studios. But they have yet to comment on the sudden introduction of the pain feature, along with the death of Jennifer. When we have more information, you'll be the first to know."

The television ran a small 'breaking news' media clip, and then started playing the same message over again.

Across the room, people began to converse amongst themselves, but Riley and Aaron were left speechless. They looked at each other, eyes wide.

"We should probably log out," said Riley. "What did you want to show me? I should probably head back to Bunker 7."

Aaron held out his closed fist, and Riley looked down to it. "Take this," he said.

"Alright," Riley murmured, as he reached out and held his open palm beneath Aaron's clenched fist.

Aaron opened his hand to deposit a small white orb on his palm.

"That's it," said Aaron. "Go ahead and put it in your inventory. It's not like anyone who sees it, is going to know what it is, but I wouldn't go holding it out for very long, else people may get curious. You shouldn't tell anyone you have it, either. It could complicate things."

"Well, what the hell *is* it?" Riley asked. After having touched the item, its name appeared above it. It read: 'White Orb of Transcendence." He used his other hand to open his inventory. A screen appeared where all the icons for items he was carrying were displayed. He tapped some of the holographic buttons, and a moment later, the orb disappeared from his hand, and a new icon was added to his inventory. "I just see its name, but no details," he added.

"It's how I turn into the Weevil," Aaron said. He kept his voice low, but it was highly unlikely anyone could hear him, even if he was speaking at a normal tone.

"It allows you to transform?" Riley asked. "I thought the Weevil was part of your paragon powers?"

Aaron shook his head and leaned back in the booth. "My original power was the ability to control small and mid-sized monsters. My paragon power allowed me to control boss-sized monsters for a limited time and also use them to… kind of portal around? Only some of the monsters let me do that, so it's not a sure thing. But the Weevil is something else entirely. It's… well, it's a temporary tier-three."

Riley's eyebrows lifted. "What? I didn't know tier-three was attainable."

Aaron looked over to the television, where the news clip was repeating. He looked back to Riley and nodded slowly. "It's a little pricey to make, and not many people know about it. Me and some of my crafter friends learned how to make it a while back, so they're aware of it, and it's likely that there's other methods to attain tier-three. So there's probably other people out there that can do it. They may even be able to do it with a different item, or some sort of natural mechanic. I don't know. All I know is that with this, I can turn into the Weevil, and I have some pretty strong physical powers. I was on the edge as to whether I wanted to even tell you about it. It's hard to make, and I have to end up using it a lot to even keep up with all these damn hellions around. I wasn't sure if I should give you one. It can be really easy to use it, thinking you're going to need it in order to prevent a death. But with what's going on with that sudden update, and what they just said about that girl dying, well… I wanted you to have one. If you help me collect some of the materials, I can try and get you some more, but it takes a lot of time and resources to make. Just… thought you should know."

Riley had remained quiet all through Aaron's revelation. He looked at his inventory, and then up to Aaron. He dispersed the screen and lifted his brows again, then let out a sigh. "So all this time… You were fighting at a level above all of us. I can kinda understand the secrecy… but I'm not sure why you didn't tell me weeks ago."

"It's not exactly my secret to just go telling people," said Aaron. "There's four other crafters I work with. We all agreed that we'd keep it a tight secret. I don't know if they've told anyone yet, but if more and more people start doing crazy stuff that they weren't doing before, then… well, the secret is going to get out, and other crafters are going to start theorizing on how to make items like these and figuring out the recipes. It took a lot of time and effort for the five of us to do it. So we've been trying to reap the rewards while we could. But… I don't know what I'd do if you ended up actually dying somehow from the game, when I could've helped prevent it. So… yeah, I don't want you to die, alright? I know I was keeping another secret. I'm sorry. But that's everything."

Riley watched Aaron's reaction, and nodded slowly. "Thank you," he said. "I really appreciate it. I have no idea how expensive it is… but seriously, thanks. I'll try not to use it, unless I absolutely have to. And I'll try not to die on you," he said, managing a half smirk.

Aaron slowly smiled as well. "You better not. After everything that happened with my mother, I don't think I could take it. So don't you go doing anything stupid, alright?"

Riley chuckled and slowly looked to the television. It was on the third run of the breaking news release. "Don't worry," he said. "I have no intention of rushing to my death. I just hope they fix the problem soon."

CHAPTER 9: GET SOME SLEEP

With little left to discuss, Riley and Aaron parted ways. Despite the fact that being in-game was still hazardous, Riley called up a taxi to return him to the bunker. He could log out anywhere in the game, even in Aaron's apartment, but he figured that it would be better if he logged out in his own apartment, so that he could make full use of the rest bonuses that he would accumulate while logged out of the game.

Luckily, nothing of note occurred on his way back to Bunker 7. His thoughts were full, even more so than they'd been before. There was a lot to digest. There was the hellion from earlier, the advent of pain in the game—which had yet to be rectified—along with this new item that Aaron had introduced him to. Even if he used it, what would happen? Would he turn into some sort of insect like Aaron did? Aaron had later told him that the duration was different from person to person, but usually when the item was used, the user had somewhere between thirty minutes and an hour until it would wear off.

He hoped that he'd never have to use it, but he really wished he knew what bonuses or powers it would grant him beforehand. It was strange to have an 'ace in the hole,' as the saying goes, when you didn't know what that ace was capable of.

The return to Bunker 7 seemed far shorter than his trek across to Aaron's city. He quickly made his way back into the safety of his apartment in the bunker. He hadn't seen any of his guild friends. They were probably playing things smart and safe, and were most likely not even in the game.

Riley laid back down on the bed in his in-game apartment, and gestured to log out.

Ten seconds later, his eyes opened in the real world. He pulled his headset off and checked the time. It was just after three in the afternoon. There was still plenty of time in the day, but what was he going to do if he wasn't playing Sigil Online? He could head to the cafe, but he wasn't too hungry yet, and he had food he could eat at home. Even though he had the money, he shouldn't eat at the cafe all the time.

Riley slid out of bed and went over to his computer. He turned the monitor on and sunk down onto the office chair at his desk. He opened a web browser and started looking for information related to current events about what had happened in Sigil Online. There was a lot of talk about the girl who had died. People were unsure if they should even be playing the game, if there was such a risk. There were people who said they knew Jennifer, and that she had some health problems which could've led to what had happened. Then, other people would comment on those posts on the online forums, saying that the game's End User License Agreement, or EULA for short, stipulated that only 'healthy' people should play a mentally intensive game like Sigil Online, or any 'full immersion' game, where the player's consciousness was essentially taking form in virtual reality.

Riley's eyes scanned post after post as he digested everything people had to say on the matter. People were referencing clinical studies about the headgear that was used for full immersion games, and how it could put a strain on the mind and body. There weren't a lot of documented deaths from its use, as far as Riley could tell. But several users on the forums were bringing up good points, that full immersion technology and its features, were evolving faster than any trials that could take place. Especially with what had happened with the developers implementing pain out of nowhere.

In the blink of an eye, several hours had passed. Riley noticed the time was now after six and he decided to get up and stretch, and fix a microwave dinner.

As it was heating up, he thought back to the monster nest, and the monster that they'd encountered there. The player that had called them idiots.

When his food was finished, he took it back to his desk and let it cool while he started scouring the forums for any information he could get on hellion nests or lairs.

Unfortunately, with how new the hellions expansion was and just how diverse things could be for hellions, there was very limited information. He figured he wouldn't be able to find much, since the game had a dynamic system that could change on the fly. Technically, each and every monster-player in the game could have different looking structures with different functions. Some of the monster-players had gone on forums and spoken about the types of facilities they could build, but each of their answers was quite diverse, and any imagery supplied was different than what others were showing.

The best guess Riley could make was that the pods they'd destroyed earlier were somehow powering the lair itself, and were somehow used as a method of increasing the hellion's power. There was no way to know if it was some sort of flat bonus, or over-time bonus that slowly built up. And what about the guardian they'd fought? It seemed similar to the other pods, but came from a larger one. How was it made? What sort of work went into spawning such a creature? Had the hellion worked on that lair for a week? Two? Or had they been working on it tirelessly since the expansion launched? Without speaking to the actual player, there was really no way to know.

Riley had finished his meal during his search for information.

Several more hours passed and he felt that any answers he'd obtained were still incomplete and probably incorrect. He ran a hand up through his hair and scratched his scalp. He just wished he could play. Even if he had to play solo, he just wanted to be doing… something, anything. Sitting around reading forums was fine, but if the game wasn't fixed by tomorrow, he'd probably start to go crazy. Sigil Online was… well, his life. He played it every day. It was his main form of entertainment, and his only source of income.

He navigated back to the main Sigil Online forums to see if there was any update on the pain implementation.

It was now just after nine, and the only update that the developers had given was made two hours prior. It read, 'We are working diligently to resolve an ongoing issue in Sigil Online. Thank you for your patience.'

There was no reference to pain, or an estimate on when it would be resolved, or even what they were trying to resolve exactly. It was… essentially a non-response. All Riley could think of was that if the pain update was responsible for that girl dying, then perhaps the developers couldn't admit to anything without legal repercussions. But, who knew?

Riley stared at the screen. Well, there wasn't much else he could do tonight. Best to just go to bed and hope everything was fixed in the morning.

CHAPTER 10: SPIDER CITY

Sleep hadn't come easy. The state of Sigil Online was on Riley's mind for almost two hours before he finally found sleep. Even in slumber, he was restless. Nightmares assailed him. Large ominous creations from the worst areas of Sigil Online stalked him and chased him through a darkened city. He couldn't log out, he couldn't escape. Rending claws would rake at his back, only for him to turn around and see nothing but shadows.

The terrors only ended when his alarm went off.

He didn't feel particularly well-rested. He leaned up in bed and thought about the nightmares he'd had. Then, he thought about the girl who had died the day before.

He pulled himself out of bed and immediately went to his computer to look up information about potential updates regarding Sigil Online.

There had been no new updates from the development team. Pain was still in the game, just as it had been the day before. But luckily, there were no newly reported deaths. There were even larger media outlets that were reporting on the fact that the girl had prior medical issues, which could've led to her death. But the pain update could've still been the cause, due to the circumstances of her health.

Riley didn't waste much more time on the news. He went about his morning routine. He jumped in the shower, went to the bathroom, brushed his teeth, and then grabbed a snack bar for breakfast. Despite the fact that pain was still in the game, Riley was starting to think that now would be the best time to actually gain some ground in Sigil. There could be a lot of PVP (player-vs-player) centric players who were keeping out of the game. If that was the case, then there was a good chance that he and anyone else in the guild could try and make some headway with assaulting other lairs. That would increase their chances of getting in the good graces of the Vanguard Alliance.

In no time at all, Riley had finished his morning activities and was laying back in bed. He shifted around, seemingly unable to get comfortable, but eventually he managed. He pulled his headset back on and initiated the login sequence. He closed his eyes and waited for the game to accept him.

When his eyes opened, he was once more in his apartment in Sigil Online. His real life apartment now traded for the virtual one.

He didn't dawdle in his room and went straight for the door.

Once out in the hall, he headed for the stairwell that would lead up to the main floor. Just as he was reaching the steps, he heard the sound of a door opening in the hall he'd come from. He glanced over and saw Parviz, with his notable half-red and half-blue hair.

"Morning, portal guy," Riley greeted him, in the usual manner that most of the guild did. It had been sort of a running joke that no one actually ever used his real name, unless things were serious, in which case they tended to use his actual name for the sake of speed.

"Morning," Parviz murmured with a yawn as his hand came up to cover his mouth. He then waved and slowly closed in on Riley. "I didn't check the news, but I guess they still haven't fixed pain, huh?" he asked, as he reached over and pinched his own arm. "Hmm. Yep, still kinda hurts."

"Not yet," Riley answered, even though Parviz answered his own question. "If a few more guildies are already upstairs, we can probably form a quick group and go hunting. If we're careful, we can avoid… you know, getting hurt."

"Well, I don't have to worry about it too much," said Parviz.

As Parviz reached him, Riley started heading up the stairs, with the portal maker right behind.

"Yeah, you're able to keep a safe distance, usually," said Riley.

"Yup, that's the plan. But I still gotta be in sight of where I'm throwing my portals. Not totally safe, but mostly."

Riley reached the top of the steps and pushed open the doors to the lounge.

There were only a handful of people around the bar and lounge. They all had solemn and dreary expressions as they watched the televisions, which were on different news streams.

Riley was about to watch one of the televisions when he realized that someone was standing near the door. He spotted Laura staring at one of the TVs.

"Morning Laura," Riley called over to her, as he walked in closer. It was a little strange for her to be standing just inside the door as she was.

"Morning Laura!" Parviz greeted as well, from right behind Riley.

Laura seemed fixated on the television, then, after several seconds, her head turned towards them.

"Riley! Parviz! Get outside! Giant robot! Now!"

Riley's brows furrowed. "Wait, right now? Where at?"

Laura seemed to go dormant again, as if all expression left her. She just stood there, much like a statue.

Riley and Parviz exchanged looks.

Laura's eyes widened. "What are you still doing here? Get outside! Invasion event! We're getting owned!"

In that moment, Riley realized that the Laura in front of him was merely one of her copies and not her 'core' body. "Let's go!" he said to Parviz, as he ran for the door.

"Right behind you!" came Parviz's quick response.

Laura's copy remained standing, having gone emotionless again. Riley rushed past her, and pushed the door open.

Riley's eyes narrowed as he walked out into the daylight. But within seconds, the light became shadow as darkness enveloped the street. Riley looked around, then up into the sky.

"Crap! Run!" he shouted as he turned to the left and started running.

Parviz looked up into the sky as he hurried after Riley. A tall metal leg as wide as a van was long descended into the street. It was made of some type of dark bronze metal and came in at a strange angle that made it hard to determine where it was going to end up. Within seconds, it smashed into the street, kicking up debris and quaking the area.

Riley was pelted with tiny pebbles, but now that the metal leg had landed, he turned around and looked up into the sky. The air was thick with dust that filled his nostrils. The metal leg was somewhere around fifteen stories high, since it towered above the nearby structures, which were only around ten stories. There were a dozen other metal legs, all slowly lifting and descending in the area. The legs held aloft an enormous disc in the sky. It was slowly moving away, which allowed Riley to discern that the disc was made up of compartments and sections, almost like a tiny city itself. It was like some sort of mechanical tiny-city spider. Riley had never seen anything like it. Was it the monster? Or was it somehow terrain?

In the distance, Riley made out the faint signs of various things flying up toward the spider-city. Beams of red. Streams of fire. Dark purple orbs. Tiny black specks, which he couldn't discern due to the distance, but they were firing what looked to be some sort of munitions at the nearby legs.

"What the hell is this thing?" Parviz muttered. "What do we even do?"

"We have to find Laura and whoever else is fighting it," said Riley. "I don't think we're going to be able to do much down here.

I can see small explosions up in the top portion of it. So someone has to be up there already."

"Yeah, I see that too," said Parviz. "I can try and get a portal up there. It's moving kinda fast, though. Might be a bit of a hard fall."

"I think I can climb the leg with my ring," said Riley. "But it'd take me a while, and I have no idea if it's capable of throwing me off, or doing anything to defend its legs. I think portals are going to be the best option."

Riley looked around the area. The metal leg was still planted in the middle of the street. He ran around it, so he could get a better look. Dozens of NPCs were running around terrified. Or at least, they were mimicking terror. Riley supposed that if he was only a virtual construct that could be deleted when killed, that maybe he'd be terrified too.

"There!" Parviz said, pointing. "Here!" Parviz threw his right hand out, directing it down the street. Then, he gestured right in front of them with his left hand. "Go!"

"Um, alright!" Riley said, and with little hesitation, he hopped into the portal on the ground.

Riley had only traveled by portal a few other times in the past, and it was never a pleasant experience.

The world rushed around him. At first, he was falling, and then he was floating up, only for gravity to seize him again and drag him back down, a foot away from the exit portal. The world around him seemed to be spinning. He felt to his knees, catching himself with his hands on the concrete. He could feel the hard concrete against his knees. He felt sick, his vision blurred and darkened. "I…" he muttered. "Ugh," he grunted. He felt as if he might actually vomit in-game, but nothing was forthcoming.

Parviz followed him through the portal, and dissipated them immediately after. He knelt beside Riley. "Dude, are you alright?" he asked. "Riley?"

Riley shook his head, blinking rapidly. "I don't… I can't…"

"Riley? Man, what's wrong?" Parviz reached out to help Riley up.

Riley accepted the assistance as his vision started to return to him and the sick feeling ebbed away. "Ugh, why… why are portals like that?" he asked. "Every time I go through a portal, it's just… I dunno, agony."

"I've never seen anyone have a problem with them but you," said Parviz. "Are you good now?" he asked, looking Riley in the eyes.

"Yeah, it's passed," said Riley. "Where are we?"

"'Bout time!" came Carla's voice from nearby. "Parviz! We need you, like, bad!"

The two of them looked over to Carla, who was standing a few feet away from Laura. This Laura was holding her iconic revolver. Which told Riley that she was the 'core' Laura.

"You alright?" Laura asked, noticing how Parviz was helping Riley stand.

Riley nodded, easing away from Parviz. "I'm good. We're here. What's going on?"

"This thing showed up, like twenty minutes ago," said Carla, pointing up to the sky. Riley looked up, and noticed they were more directly under the machine monstrosity. He turned his head and saw the leg that had almost crushed them. They were about a block away.

"Here, join our group." Laura hurried over and shook both of their hands, quickly inviting them to the group she had already formed earlier.

Riley could now see their names and health. Then, he looked up at the monster and saw its name as well.

"Dread Fortress Alpha," said Laura, even as Riley was reading the name. "As best we can figure, it's either on par with, or stronger than that Saros thing we killed not too long ago."

"That was a tough fight, and we had a lot of people around," said Parviz.

Riley then looked at the monster's health. "Wait, is that right?" he asked. "It looks like it's at a hundred percent."

"Yeah," said Laura. "We don't know how to hurt it yet. Occasionally, smaller machines come out of it and fall down into the city. We've fought some of those, but its health hasn't budged. We saw a few paragons head up to the city portion, but we're not grouped with them."

"There's probably something inside that we need to hit," said Riley. "Parviz can get us up there."

"That's what we were hoping," said Laura. "There's not a lot of people online, with pain still enabled. Not sure what's taking the devs so damn long, but it's getting real old, real fast."

"Have there been any hellions?" asked Riley.

Laura shrugged. "I don't think I've seen any. There could be. Technically, I imagine they'd want to fight this thing as bad as us. They can't PVP us if this thing kills us, right?"

Riley managed a half smile. "Yeah, I guess you're right. So, is it just the four of us then?"

"I'm going to keep one of my dupes back at the bunker, in case anyone else logs on, but we didn't have anything scheduled for today," said Laura. "So I'm going to be down one of my copies, but I've got plenty of stamina for the rest. But yeah, it looks like it's just us four."

"Might as well just be the three of you," said Parviz. "I can get you all up there, for sure, but… I'm probably going to be useless up there. We don't know how to hurt this thing."

"But Laura said there were smaller machines coming from it, right?" Riley asked, looking to Laura. "Are the machines small enough to fit through one of his portals?"

Laura nodded. "Yes, they're about human size, so… yeah, they'd fit."

Riley looked back to Parviz. "Then you can be on robot cleaning duty."

Parviz's brows lifted. "I see what you mean, yeah, I can do that."

Riley diverted his attention to Carla, who then met his gaze. It took only a couple seconds for Carla to realize what Riley was about to say.

"At least hit my arm," she told him. "Anywhere else, and I'm sending an exploding lotus your way, and I'll be aiming for your face."

"Thanks," Riley said, trying to smile, even though he knew he was about to cause Carla a little harm. "You've got the best essence, so you're the best choice."

"I know," said Carla. "Which is why I'm telling you to just go ahead and do it and get it over with. We gotta bring this giant metal spider down. Things are bad enough with the hellions, and now we got this bastard. So hurry up!"

Riley lifted his right hand and shot his spike at Carla's left arm. She winced as it stuck into her skin about an inch. Her eyes narrowed sharply at Riley, which made him feel all the worse as he then pulled multicolored ribbons of essence from her to imbue himself. When he absorbed the essence, his eyes took on a multicolored look, which changed fluidly every few seconds. He then willed the spike back to his palm, and freed it from Carla's arm, causing her to grunt.

"I'll be so happy when they fix this pain crap," Carla grumbled.

"Sorry," Riley said, as he then brought his hand up and quickly gestured to bring up his inventory. He didn't have many things on his person. He'd only really planned on doing some light questing, or maybe even just some socializing. At least, that was before he knew that there was an invasion event going on. He tapped at the icon for his scythe, which made it materialize in his hand. He could see that Carla's health had taken about a one percent hit due to him stealing her essence, so it hadn't caused much damage. Next, he empowered the scythe, which caused the actual energy blade to appear. The blade itself was made of various shifting colors, which was probably the coolest it'd ever looked. "Good to go," he said, and looked to Parviz.

Carla and Laura diverted their attention to the portal maker as well.

"Oh, I'm up?" Parviz asked. "Right, let's see here," he murmured as he looked into the sky. The metal spider-like fortress was slowly moving overhead, its long legs lifting one after the other, propelling it far above the cityscape beneath it.

He lifted his right hand and tilted his head from side to side. "I think I can get us on the top of its city section. But… it's gonna be the very top." With that, he deployed the portal from his right hand, then made a nearby portal in the ground with his left. "I'll go first," he said. "In case I need to alter it. Otherwise, one of you might go splat. Give me… I dunno, ten seconds? I'll know if I'm plummeting too far by then." With that, he walked right over and hopped through the portal.

"Who's next?" Riley asked.

"I'll go," said Laura. "Wait ten seconds, then follow me in."

"Got it," said Riley.

"We'll be right behind you," said Carla.

Laura waited the intended amount of time that Parviz would need before she hopped into the portal.

"Damn," Riley whispered. "I hope this time is gonna be better for me than a couple minutes ago. I felt like I was going to vomit."

"You really do have some weird problem with portals, don't you?" said Carla, giving Riley a strange look. "Might as well get it over with." She then walked over and hopped through the portal, after several seconds had passed.

Riley was left alone in the street. He looked up to the fortress, but couldn't make anything out from that distance. He couldn't even see the portal that Parviz had created. He shook his head. "Here we go," he whispered, and walked over and jumped into the portal.

CHAPTER 11: DREAD FORTRESS ALPHA

Riley came out feet-first from a portal attached to a nearby metal wall. He stumbled and fell forward, dropping his scythe as he caught himself on his hands again. The world around him seemed to spin.

"You alright?" came Parviz's voice from beside him, as the portal maker knelt down, placing a hand on his shoulder.

"Just… a minute," said Riley. He could hear strange grinding sounds, as if larger gears were crunching and turning. There was a dull hum all around him. At first he thought it was just his messed up head, but the sound persisted. The nausea wasn't as bad this time as it had been a few minutes ago. He looked around, seeing numerous copies of Laura all around him, with Carla just a few feet away.

"Hurry it up," said Carla. "We can't wait around here."

"Yeah, yeah," Riley groaned and with Parviz's assistance, managed to stand. The world around him seemed to grow clearer, but it was still moving. Probably because they were on top of an enormous *walking* fortress.

He took a few moments to retrieve his scythe before paying closer attention to their surroundings.

They were surrounded by what appeared to be tall gray and bronze metal walls, welded together like some sort of makeshift contraption. Some of the walls rose for several stories. The center of the walking fortress appeared to have taller areas than the outskirts, which was where they were now.

"What's the plan?" Riley asked, looking over to Laura, who would've had more time to scope out the situation. Not to mention she probably hadn't doubled over upon exiting the portal, as he was prone to do.

"Now that I can see better, I could try and get us up in the center of the fortress," said Parviz. "Or should we search around?"

Laura's core body stepped back from the mass of duplicates to join in the discussion. "My dupes are keeping a close eye on everything. This fortress is just like a tiny city. Streets, walls that make it seem like there's buildings, but no sign of any other players or monsters yet."

"The whole fortress is a monster," said Carla. "We need to take it down."

"It has to have a weak point," said Riley. "Could be something located deeper in the city, or it could have multiple points we have to hit."

"And they're probably going to be guarded," said Laura. "There's only four of us. I hope we can deal with any mini bosses that might be littering the area. The fortress hasn't tried shooting at us yet or anything, but its legs are damaging the buildings down in the city."

"Let's just search the area and check the streets," said Riley. "I don't see any windows or doors, so we're just going to have to run through the streets and hope we come across something."

"Sounds good, my clones will take point," said Laura, as she began to move them all at once, quickly giving them minor-AI controlled behaviors to circle the group, while also placing more of them at the front.

Riley gripped his scythe. He was starting to wish he had some sort of ranged weapon, if pain wasn't going away anytime soon. There had been a few options as far as ranged weapons went, but none of them were in his price range. A scythe seemed practical enough, and that was what he'd had crafted. But with pain enabled, he was starting to wonder if he shouldn't have spent a bit more on the luxury of hitting things from a distance.

"Moving out," said Laura, as her clones began to walk forward briskly.

There were a dozen clones in the front acting as a shield, while the rest were spread out in a loose circle around them. Carla was walking beside Laura's core body, while Riley was behind them, and Parviz behind him. Even though Riley had a melee weapon, he was still a support class. Carla could heal with her lotuses, but it took a lot of her stamina to do so, which was more of a detriment to her damaging abilities. It was going to be up to Riley to keep them alive, if he was able to steal anything's essence.

"I shouldn't have logged in today," Parviz murmured from behind Riley.

Riley glanced behind him. "You can still leave," he said. "But you'd be abandoning us up here. But it's still your choice."

Parviz shook his head. "No way. I'm not going to pull a Shell on you guys. Abandoning you when I can actually do some good. It's crappy that all I can do is mobility related, or helping everyone access places. I'm like… a support class that can't heal or buff anyone. Sure, I can move around really quickly, but… in combat, I feel a bit weak."

"You're not weak," Riley told him. "The game isn't well-balanced, we've known that from the beginning. The devs said they never wanted a precisely balanced game. So this is just what we have to deal with. If you're ever tired of your powers, you can always go the same route Seth did."

Parviz scoffed. "Pact powers? No, I think I'm good. I may feel underpowered, but at least the type of power I have is super rare. I'll stick with it."

Riley smiled and looked forward.

They were heading down a street that ended in a T intersection.

"Which way we going?" Laura asked. "Should I navigate us closer to the center of the fortress?"

"That's probably best," said Riley, as his eyes scanned the surrounding area.

"We need to watch out for traps," said Carla. "So far, there hasn't been anything, but this place totally seems like it's going to have traps."

"I really hate being out in the open like this," said Parviz. "Who knows what could be hunting us up here."

Riley looked into the sky and checked the rooftops. He couldn't see anything. He hadn't even spotted any of the mechanoids that Laura and Carla had mentioned seeing. Perhaps they'd been thinned out? Or maybe most of them had been deployed to the city below already. With a new invasion boss like the one they were facing, there was no way to know. Most invasion events in Sigil Online were one-time situations that the game's AI devised, so that each one would be different and unique. Which also made it incredibly problematic for players trying to take it on. If an invasion event got out of control, large portions of the city could be damaged, which would put an economic strain on the surrounding players who would then have to spend time and resources on repairing buildings and services that they normally used without worry.

"I'm going to scout ahead a little," said Laura as one of her duplicates ran straight ahead across the intersection. There didn't seem to be any particular order or symmetry to the buildings around them. There also didn't seem to be any way inside the structures themselves.

In the blink of an eye, a metal wall rose on the left and on the right of the T intersection, closing them in against the wall they'd been facing. The metal sheets jutted into the sky, preventing their trek deeper into the city-like fortress.

Everyone froze in place. The sound of grating and groaning metal surrounded them, along with the constant droning sound they'd heard since they arrived.

"What's happening? The walls can move?" Parviz yelled. "Are we trapped?"

"I hate mazes!" Carla hissed. "Screw it, I'm making my own hole in this damn wall!" She turned to the wall they'd been heading towards. Her hands came up, but before she could create even a single lotus, the tall metal sheet before them plummeted into the ground.

Thirty feet away stood a bulky construct. It was roughly eight feet tall, with a square metal head on top of a cubed torso. All the segments of its bipedal body were made up of squares. Its legs and arms were square segments, ending in larger boxy feet and fists. It looked like some sort of child's block toy.

Without warning, the blocky metal construct marched toward them. It didn't seem to possess any ears or eyes, but moved with intent and purpose.

"We got an enemy!" Carla was the first to speak.

Everyone was looking at the machine, but Riley noticed that just as prominent was the device sticking out of the metal floor behind it. It seemed to be some sort of… well, Riley really wasn't sure what it was. It was about the size of a car, with levers and buttons all over and an orange glowing sphere in the center, which was connected to transparent tubes carrying fluid around the generator and down into the floor. It reminded him of some kind of generator.

To Riley, it definitely looked like something that needed to be destroyed.

"We need to take out the generator behind it!" Riley called, knowing that the machine stomping towards them was their primary concern, but who knew when the walls would rise up around them again. Would they even be able to create a hole through them? Carla's lotuses were powerful, but could they do the trick? Even Parviz couldn't create portals where he couldn't actually see, so navigating around them could prove problematic.

"Screw it!" Carla yelled, her eyes wide, seemingly ready to get into the heat of battle. "I'll destroy it all!"

Carla's arms moved, her fingers flexed. Lotus after lotus appeared in the air and shot towards the robot and the generator.

"Parviz!" Riley called, turning his head to the portal maker. "Send it through a portal, to fall on the generator!"

Parviz was still watching the machine march toward them when Riley called out the order. He saw Carla's lotuses already moving through the air, but regardless of where the robot was, she'd still be able to destroy the generator. If he was quick enough, he could have the robot land on the generator just as the lotuses reached it.

Which was just what he set out to do.

With one hand, he created a portal just barely large enough for the robot to fall into. With his other, he created a portal in the sky.

He timed the portal creation with the robot's movements, and as the tall machine took a step, the portal opened up as the robot's weight came down, which propelled it into the portal, only to disappear and then suddenly appear about fifty feet above the generator.

Carla hadn't let up, despite the change in position of her quarry. She'd heard Riley's strategy, but it didn't matter to her. Everything was going to explode in her path. It was just going to take a couple more seconds until the boom.

Her lotuses raced through the air. The robot fell.

Almost as if it had been timed perfectly, the robot enemy smashed down onto the generator, just as Carla's lotuses met with it. A loud crunch echoed against the nearby walls, as a multitude of explosions detonated against the crushed generator and fallen machine.

They could all see the machine's name and health pop up, but it was only visible for a span of seconds, as with each explosion, it lost chunks of its health. Its red hitpoint bar went down roughly five percent per explosion, and Carla had thrown at least twenty-five explosive lotuses at it.

Interestingly enough, the 'Fortress Generator' itself had a name and a health bar. But its health didn't last nearly as long as the 'Lesser Fortress Minion' which had been guarding it.

The smoke from the explosions lifted and abated. Laura hadn't even moved any of her duplicates into combat range, and Riley just stood with his weapon in hand, watching.

The fortress minion and generator were both gone, having dispersed into glittering particles.

Riley didn't bother to check his status screen to see how much experience he'd gotten for being in the party that made the kills. His attention had risen higher up, to the fortress's actual health bar in the sky.

It had gone down roughly five percent.

Riley's lips curled. "We can kill it," he said. "We need to find more of these generators!"

"Easy pickings," Carla said as she

swiped her hands together, as if cleaning off imaginary dust.

"We need to be careful of our positioning," said Laura, who looked around at their surroundings and the metal walls. "We might get separated. I'm going to reduce my copy count, else I might end up losing dupes to walls going up." With that, she quickly set out to absorb a large portion of her copies, until only her core and four others remained. "This is good," she said. "Let's move back the way we came. Probably an alternate route now."

"Yeah," said Riley. "We might not even have to go to the center, depending on how many of these generators are spread out across the fortress."

A sudden explosion sounded in the distance. It sounded almost like a muffled gunshot due to the sound being absorbed by the metal walls. Everyone looked around. It was hard to pinpoint the exact direction it came from.

"Someone else killed a generator?" asked Carla.

Riley looked back up to the fortress's health. It had gone down a little more, maybe close to another five percent. It looked like it might be close to about ninety percent, give or take. It was hard to guesstimate just by looks alone and no concrete numbers, but that was just how Sigil Online was.

"Well, if this event is performance based, we're going to want to kill as many generators as we can," said Riley. "Remember how the Saros fight was?"

Laura's eyes widened. "Let's move! I want more stat points!"

"Let's get that sweet loot!" Carla shouted, before turning and darting back the way they'd come.

The rest of the group followed her, with renewed vigor now that they had some idea of what they were up against.

The party, which had lowered in number now that Laura only had four other copies out, was able to make its way quickly through the streets. The walls would occasionally move, rising and falling seemingly at random. Again they encountered a generator, but this time, it was guarded by two of the blocky minions. Laura and her copies, along with Riley, managed to focus their damage on one, while Carla dealt with the other. Parviz had attempted his portal trick again, but couldn't get the machines to step into his portals. Either he'd gotten lucky earlier, or they'd already adapted to what he had done to the first one they'd fought. Regardless, they neutralized the minions and destroyed another generator, causing the fortress's health to decrease to roughly eighty-five percent. Then, they went on the move again to find the next generator.

While they ran through the streets, the fortress's health dropped another five percent, and then another. Apparently, there were at least two other teams out in the fortress, unless it was a single team that had eliminated two generators back to back in the span of a minute.

It took five more minutes for the group to come across another generator, guarded by five robotic minions. Riley took the liberty of assuming that as the number of active generators went down, the number of enemy minions would go up.

In this encounter, Parviz was able to slam two of the bulky machines into each other, while Riley and Laura dealt with another. Carla didn't have any issue with disposing of the last two before destroying the generator herself.

Again, the fortress's health dropped. They were on the right track, and the anonymous other groups elsewhere on the fortress were also making decent headway from what they could tell.

The group encountered another generator and more minions, but had little difficulty in dealing with the slowly increasing number of robots.

They moved on to the next, and the next, and the next.

It under an hour, the fortress's health had dropped to somewhere between fifteen and twenty percent, as best as Riley could guess.

They ran through the streets, heading closer towards the center now. They'd started having difficulty finding new generators, and it seemed as though the other groups were also running into the same problem.

For ten minutes, they searched for the next generator to no avail. They delved deeper towards the center of the fortress.

Riley ran behind three of Laura's copies. So far, he hadn't had much difficulty with avoiding painful combat. He was being careful, as were the others. Parviz and Carla had the least to worry about, being ranged combatants, but Laura and Riley were both melee. Riley knew that if the pain 'feature' was toned down, he could probably up his damage output, whereas right now, it was hard to run head first into something that could really hurt you. He couldn't imagine what it'd be like to actually die in the game, or have something broken or severely burned.

Unfortunately, he had a feeling that there were already plenty of players who were already acutely aware of such things.

Their small group was heading down yet another fully enclosed street. Riley kept his attention ahead of them. The walls hadn't moved recently, so they were just following the only paths available to them, which seemed to take them closer to the fortress's center, but it was hard to tell from a ground level. Everything around them was pretty tall.

They were coming close to another T intersection.

"What do you think?" asked Laura. "Left? I think that'll get us closer to the center."

"Sounds good," Riley said from right behind her.

"Feels like this is just dragging on at this point," Carla huffed. "Just show us another generator already!"

Four figures darted out from the right side of the intersection and headed toward the left.

Laura's copies slowed to an almost immediate stop, along with everyone else.

They all watched the four figures, but Riley's attention was fixated on the figure running behind the other three.

She had long silvery hair, a pair of black pants, and a shimmering silver jacket.

Riley would've recognized the outfit and hair anywhere. Probably because the person was closely tied to his memories of the day he gained his paragon powers.

It was Glint, one of the player-killers who had been in Glasser and Shadow Witch's group when they'd encountered them in the Crystal Fields. It was the day Riley had reclaimed one of his lost items and gained tier-two. Glasser had been killed, but Shadow Witch, Glint, Aurora, and Crimson Spear had all fled from that fight, only to reappear later when they fought with Aaron, when he was still masquerading as the White Weevil.

Riley didn't recognize the other three figures she was with. They were dressed strangely like NPCs, in plain clothes with no distinguishing features. Usually, players dressed rather showy, sometimes for preference, and sometimes due to the items they found.

"That's Glint," Riley spoke, as she and the three others kept running. He hadn't spoken loud enough for Glint to hear him, but despite this, her head turned and spotted them.

She and her companions came to a quick halt and turned to face them there in the street.

There was only about a hundred or so feet to separate them now, but it wouldn't be difficult for Glint and her group to just keep running and get out of sight of them. But that wasn't what they did.

"Long time!" Glint had to yell to be heard, her naturally flirty voice echoing slightly off the nearby walls. "Same friends, I see?"

"What are we doing?" Laura asked, looking to Riley.

Riley stepped forward. "Where are the others?" he called back. "Are you PK-ing people up here?" he asked, referencing the shortened term for player-killing.

Glint crossed her arms against her chest. "We've parted ways," she called back.

"I don't run with them anymore. I was never into the whole killing bit. I'm just after loot. That's all I've ever been after, but things kept getting out of hand with them. So I'm done with them."

"Who're your new friends?" Riley asked, unsure if he should trust what Glint was saying about having parted ways with Shadow Witch and the others.

Glint turned her head to the three figures near her. One of them looked back to her, but Glint just returned her attention to Riley. "Just friends," she replied. "You hunting generators?"

Riley was quiet for a few moments. It didn't make sense to hide that information. "Yeah, you?"

"Yep!" she replied. "I smashed two, but I haven't been able to find any others. You wanna group up?"

"Looks like you already have a group," Riley claimed. "And you know we can't trust you after what happened."

"I don't trust her one bit," Laura murmured.

"I bet I could take all of them out, since they're grouped up really nice," said Carla, her lips curling at the idea.

"We're pretty close to the center of the fortress," Glint called back. "If we're going to fight this thing, we'd be better off doing it together. Don't you think?"

Riley's gaze seemed permanently set on Glint and her companions. He was contemplating the situation. What should they do? Usually, he'd defer to Laura in situations like this, since she was essentially the guild leader. But since it was someone he used to know, Laura was apparently letting him take the lead.

Riley shook his head and spoke in a low voice. "Parviz, can you—"

The area around them shook. The ever present droning sound became more of a screech as the metal walls around them began to move once more. Riley tore his eyes from Glint and looked at their surroundings to determine how things were going to move, and if they needed to push forward or retreat.

"We're getting closed in!" Laura called, as she saw several of the thick walls move up behind them.

Riley turned his head and looked around. "But these are lowering!" he said, as all the walls to their sides, and ahead of them, plummeted into the ground.

The metal whined and groaned, but

several seconds later, the walls came to rest.

Just to the left, a few hundred feet away, was a house-sized orb. It looked both gelatinous and electric, perhaps more like plasma than anything. It had been hiding behind several layers of wall, but now, they, along with Glint and her friends, were trapped in a large arena with this orange-glowing orb.

"The hell is that?" Carla said as she and the others stared at it.

"Looks like the core of the fortress," said Riley. "I bet if we take it down, we defeat the world boss."

"Uhhh," Parviz murmured. "Quick question! If we destroy that thing, what happens to the fortress?"

Riley, Laura, and Carla all turned their attention back to Parviz, and in a mere moment, they realized the significance of his question.

Parviz looked to each of them. "Scenario one is the thing dissolves like everything else in the game, and we plummet to the city. I can't do a portal that fast, especially at those speeds, it'll be really tough to manage a safe landing. Scenario two, this fortress falls into the city and smashes a large part of it, which hurts the city, and… well, it'll probably hurt us a little but we might survive it."

"Maybe there's a scenario three," said Riley. "We can't worry about what we don't know. Who knows how much time we have to kill this thing, let's just nail it before anymore of the city gets destroyed."

Laura turned and pointed. "Looks like your old friend is beating us to the punch."

Riley glanced over and saw Glint and the three others running towards the globe.

"She can't damage that thing, but the others in her group might be able to," said Riley. "Focus on the orb, but keep an eye on her and those she's with. We can't risk that they still might be interested in PK-ing us if they get the chance."

"Let's do it!" Carla yelled, and ran ahead to close in the distance on the globe.

"Time to spread my copies out," Laura said, as she began to create more of her duplicates, totaling nineteen including her core, and minus the one back at Bunker 7. One by one, they started running for the orb while she stayed back.

"Carla, wait!" Riley shouted. "We don't know its attacks yet!"

Almost as if on cue, the energy within the gelatinous orb began to swirl. Dozens of lengthy ropes of energy shot out from the center. They stretched all the way to the walls enclosing the arena. Then, the orb began to rotate, swinging them around.

"Watch out!" Riley said, taking a few steps back to better prepare for the sweeping energy cords.

The nearest rope of energy slid along the floor. It didn't seem to damage the metal ground, but it was coming right for them at head-level.

"Duck!" Riley yelled, before falling flat to the ground.

Carla and Parviz followed suit, while Laura did the same, but it took longer for her to command her copies to follow her orders. Some of them were closer to the orb, which put them nearer to the energy ropes.

The closest Laura copy got caught in the torso by the rope of energy. It smacked her to the side, sending her falling. She hit the ground and stopped moving. Little arcs of orange electricity zapped around her.

"My copy is paralyzed, and pretty hurt," said Laura. "She won't take another hit!"

Riley stood up, but looked to see how long he had until the next energy cord. He then spotted Glint, who was jumping over lower ropes and diving under higher ones, as she was much closer to the orb than they were. The closer any of them would get, the more frequently they'd have to deal with the ropes, as there was less room to maneuver.

"There's nothing for me to do!" Parviz called. "Should I set up two portals to dodge between? I think the tendrils might disperse them if they hit them."

Riley glanced around quickly. "I have an idea!" He looked to Carla, then to Parviz. "Make a portal for Carla to throw lotuses into, and put the other portal right over the orb. That way she can blast it while being all the way back here, else those cords are going to intercept all the damage."

Parviz's eyes widened. "On it!" He quickly created both portals. Carla was a little ways away, but he could still create a portal just in the floor for her, because he could still see it.

Riley looked to Carla. "Carla, just—

"I know how to use my damn powers, idiot," Carla shot back, and within a moment, she was creating orange lotuses to throw into the portal, just a second after Parviz created one directly above the orange orb, where the ropes didn't appear to reach.

"Crap!" Laura called, as one of the lower tendrils rushed toward them. They wouldn't be able to duck it, they'd have to jump it.

"Duplicating was a bad idea!" she said, as she quickly grabbed the hands of her nearest clones, summoning them back to her. She only managed to grab three before the energy rope was upon them.

She sent a quick command to each of them, trying to time it as best she could to have them jump over the rope, but there were so many of them to command at once.

The first duplicate that had been paralyzed was promptly hit by the cord and turned into particles.

Everyone else managed to avoid the energy rope, but five more of Laura's copies were caught by it, and tripped. She could see their health bars plummet in her vision, and the moment they hit the ground, they started to arc orange energy while laying immobile.

"Ahh! Dammit!" She had lost one clone, while five more were paralyzed.

"We're not even a minute in, and I'm getting wrecked!" she said, as she quickly withdrew her remaining clones. It appeared that she'd made a mistake in making her clones that quickly, which was usually the best option in most boss fights.

"We can do this!" Riley said, as he threw his spike toward the orb. It shot through the air and sunk partially into the gelatinous sphere. He didn't waste any time at all before he drew out whatever essence he could. He was actually glad the 'boss' fight, if that was what this really was, wasn't a machine with tough armor, else he'd be particularly useless.

Ribbons of orange energy flew through the air and into the slit on his palm. He directed it back out of him with his left hand, shooting it off towards Carla, who was once again their primary damage dealer. He had to avoid another rope of energy, but a moment later, he empowered Parviz, then started to buff Laura and the five clones she had on the ground. Unfortunately, he was only able to heal the paralysis on two of them before a low energy rope came back around and turned the other three into glittering dust.

Laura had been able to absorb the two, which allowed her to retain some of her stamina and stats. With just herself now on the field, she focused on shooting the orb with her revolver, as much as she was able to.

Riley didn't have much ranged capability, but every time a tendril of energy rushed past, he slashed at it with the now-orange energy blade of his scythe. It wasn't a lot of damage, but any damage would add up to be meaningful.

"Parviz, how's your stamina?" Riley called.

"I got plenty!" Parviz replied, as he kept his attention on the ropes, helping to call out which ones were coming and how fast and at what angles.

"We're making good progress!" Laura said. "It's down to about thirty percent!"

Riley looked around the arena. Glint had gone entirely around to the other side, along with her companions. Occasionally he saw flashes of light, but the sphere was so big that it kept her group out of sight. It was probably for the best, he thought. At least that way their groups wouldn't get in each other's way, and they wouldn't have to worry about getting killed by Glint.

Just as the sphere's health dipped a little lower, all the ropes of energy suddenly stopped.

"What's it doing?" Parviz called.

"Phase change! Keep your eyes on it!" Riley yelled.

There was barely any time at all before the energy ropes lashed around the arena. They curved and bent, no longer confined to straight lines. Now they were like whips, smacking around the arena wildly.

"This isn't fair!" Carla shouted as she dodged from side to side. The cords didn't seem to be 'aiming' as much as flailing around randomly.

"Keep hitting the orb! You're our main damager! Just watch the cords while you do!" Riley instructed.

"I know what to do!" Carla shot back, as she went right back to creating lotuses to throw into the portal.

Parviz focused all his attention on dodging tendrils, as the one mercy the boss was giving him was that it wasn't hitting his portals.

Riley caught glimpses of more flashes on the other side of the orb, but still couldn't discern what might be going on.

After another minute of constant explosions, the orb's health crept to zero.

In an instant, the cords stopped flailing and the orb stopped swirling. Then, bit by bit, it broke apart and dissolved into orange glimmering particles, which promptly dissipated within a couple seconds.

"We got it!" Carla yelled. "Thanks to me! You know, the person who did all the work."

Riley watched as the orb 'died.' His attention quickly shifted when he realized they were still technically on the monster. "Wait, what's going to happen to the—"

Riley blinked.

When he opened his eyes, he found himself no longer on the top of the fortress world boss. Instead, he was down in the city below. Near him were Carla, Parviz, and Laura.

He looked to each of them. They had equally bewildered expressions.

"Tell me I didn't just imagine us fighting on a giant fortress?" Riley asked, starting to feel woozy at the sudden landscape change.

"No, we were up there," said Laura.

White orbs, the size of basketballs, suddenly appeared before them.

"What are these?" Parviz asked, stepping back from the one that had appeared before him.

Riley's eyes widened. "It's loot!"

He reached out without a second thought and touched the white orb in front of him. World events had different ways of allocating loot to the players who took part.

"Mine better be way better than anything you guys get," said Carla as she reached out to touch hers. "I did soooo much more work than you all."

"Hope I get stats," Laura murmured.

Riley touched the orb, which immediately transformed into…

"A glove?" Riley murmured, seeing the orb become an item. It was a black glove, but at the center of it, there appeared to be some sort of plastic screen.

Above the item was the item's description.

-

Glove of Dispersion

Increase **Power** by **5**

Increase **Mind** by **5**

All the wearer's beneficial effects, cast from the hand wearing the glove, can be instantaneously sent to all intended recipients in a 180 degree arc from the glove.

-

Riley focused only on the description of the item. The wheels in his head turned as he realized the significance of what he'd received. Then, his eyes widened. If hitting paragon had streamlined his powers, then this glove was essentially going to streamline them further and allow him to do his job even quicker. His lips curled.

"What'd you get?" Laura asked, looking to Riley.

Riley managed to blink out of his stupor and look over to Laura. "Oh, uh… something pretty sweet, actually. I think I might be able to buff everyone a lot faster. What about you?" He looked over to Carla next, who seemed to be tapping away at her inventory.

Laura shrugged. "I got two stat points. Nothing major, sadly. I didn't do a whole lot of damage to the generators, or the boss… so I guess it's not a bad reward. Especially since the stats aren't tied to an item."

"I only got two stat points as well," Parviz said, stepping closer to Laura and Riley.

"What about you, Carla?" Riley asked, as he watched her continue to tap at her inventory.

"I got a bracelet!" Carla replied, but didn't look at them. "I'm just… ugh, I already had one on each arm. Not sure which to get rid of… bleh."

"What's it do?" Parviz asked.

Finally, one of the bracelets on Carla's wrist disappeared and a moment later, another appeared in its place. It was a multicolored beaded bracelet, with beads the size of peas.

Carla turned around and smiled down at her new item, then looked to everyone else. "It has an effect that lets me modify my powers. Instead of creating one lotus for one-hundred percent damage, I can create up to five at once, instead of creating a single lotus. If I split it into two, each lotus does fifty-five percent normal damage. If I split it into three, they do… it's something like thirty-eight percent damage, and so on. So basically, the damage is split between the lotuses, but each one gains a flat five percent, so the more the better, as long as they hit. It's a bunch of dumb math, but now I can make a ton of lotuses. I think my explosive ones are going to benefit the most." She then looked to Riley, noticing the glove on his hand. "What did you say yours did?"

The group's attention changed to Riley.

"So, this glove lets me buff everyone I can see," said Riley. "I absorb essence normally, then I expel the essence through my hand, like I've been doing. But the little screen in the glove somehow flashes the essence out to everyone I want to buff. I'll have to test it in the next fight."

"Speaking of which," Laura spoke up, turning her head to look around. "Where's Glint and those people she was with?"

Everyone glanced around, but there was no sight of them.

CHAPTER 12:
TRUST

It didn't take too long to get back to Bunker 7. One of Laura's clones had still been at the bunker, but she decided to have that duplicate run back towards them so she could absorb it, since the threat had passed.

"I was really worried that the boss was going to be harder than that," said Riley. "I think we lucked out. I'm surprised we were able to defeat it with just the four of us."

"Again, I did all the work," Carla said, with a smirk on her face. "But apparently you did 'something' since you got better loot than two stat points."

"I believe the rewards are somewhat randomized," said Riley. "And usually they calculate buffs and healing when they do the reward algorithm."

"Uh huh," Carla murmured. "I kinda want to blast some stuff now… but it doesn't look like they fixed pain yet."

"Not yet," Riley agreed. "Might have to deal with it for a long time. Or maybe they don't even intend to fix it?"

As they neared the entrance to Bunker 7, they saw a young woman toting a crossbow against her shoulder, with her other hand on her hip. As the group neared her, they all smiled.

"You missed the action," Laura

commented.

Brenda's shoulders slumped a bit and she lowered her crossbow. "Yeah, I figured. I just got online, but I didn't see the boss anywhere. Did you just defeat it? How'd it go? Is the damage severe?"

Laura looked around at their surroundings as they closed the distance on Brenda, and then waited outside. "I don't know how the city fared, but I don't believe the boss was alive for very long. We were able to take care of it somewhat quickly. It was kind of a pain, but we managed."

"*I* managed," Carla murmured, crossing her arms.

Brenda looked to Carla with a smile. "Did you guys have to deal with any monster-players?"

"We didn't encounter any," said Riley. "But it's likely that some might've been down in the streets. We were mostly fighting the boss up in the fortress… which was also part of the boss, apparently."

"Really, no hellions?" Brenda seemed to smile just a little. "Well, all for the better I guess. They would've just made things harder, I'm sure. But some of them probably want to defend the town from actual world events. But anyway, sorry I missed the fight. I saw it on the news and I rushed online, but too late, I guess. Brenda turned her head and looked to the Bunker 7 door, then gestured to it with her thumb. "By the way, someone just came into the bunker that said they wanted to speak to you, Riley. She looked familiar, but I couldn't place where I'd seen her."

"Her?" Riley asked, perplexed.

Brenda nodded. "Yeah, she's waiting inside."

"Um, alright," Riley murmured. "I was gonna hop over and visit Aaron, to see if he could craft something new for me, but I can spare a minute."

Brenda shrugged. "The rest of you down to do some monster farming?"

Riley made his way past Brenda while she spoke to the rest of the group. He pushed open the doors, which felt oddly heavier with the greater tactile feel since the pain update. He walked into Bunker 7 and looked around. Everything was just as they'd left it. A few more people were filling out the seats and bar. In the far corner, he spotted someone familiar. His eyes widened and all he could do was stand there for a few seconds before finally willing himself to step forward. He shook his head as he walked over to the booth she was sitting in. He was quiet, but frustrated. His frustration turned to mild anger as he took a seat across from the silver-haired woman, whose hands were clasped neatly upon the table. Her sights were already upon him as he approached.

"What do you want?" Riley asked, looking into her eyes.

Glint's lips curled. She shrugged and leaned back just a little. She was still wearing her iconic silver jacket with the zipper down a couple inches. "As I told your guildmate out front, I just want to talk. Not like I'm going to try to kill you in here, right?"

"How should I know?" Riley asked, still tense. "I've got things I need to do, so what do you want?"

"I want to make amends," said Glint. "I want to get back into the hero community. I never enjoyed tagging along with Glasser and Witch. And if you'll at least hear me out, I think I can help, maybe a little. When we fought you that day in the Crystal Fields we'd never PKed anyone before. At least, I was never in a group that had. I found out later that Glasser, Witch, and Crimson had all done stuff like that, but me and Aurora never had. Aurora was happy to jump into a fight, but after that day, it just didn't sit well with me. Especially after we went after you all in Death's Chasm. I ended up leaving the guild the next day. You'd killed Glasser, the leader, and then Shadow made a new guild and recruited most of the players who she thought were competent. I decided to join up with her, thinking that with Glasser gone, maybe we wouldn't be doing as much PKing. Well, that wasn't the case, as I quickly found out. I jumped ship about a week ago, and I've been running with some friends of mine."

"Like the ones you were with earlier?" Riley questioned, trying to measure the honesty behind her words.

"Uh, kind of," Glint said, glancing away for a few seconds before looking back to him. "But seriously, I was never into PKing. Sure, I was into it in the moment and I fought with them, but it just felt weird. So I bailed and never looked back. I want to get into a guild again, but running with Glasser and Witch really left me with a stigma. You knew me before I ran with them, and you didn't mind having me around."

"Sure, from time to time," Riley said. "Back when I was Radiance. And back before you ran with PKers."

Glint rolled her eyes and shook her

head. "I'm not going to defend my actions that day. Just know that it's behind me. As far as I know, Glasser never remade a hero character. But I think he might've made a hellion, based on some things I overheard from some people who currently run with Witch."

"What about Shade?" Riley asked. "Him and his guildies. We beat a bunch of them that day, but what happened to them?"

"I think some of them left," said Glint. "But the guild is still around. I'm not as familiar with the guild and their stats as I was with Glasser's, but I think their guild has grown since then. They're based in an area pretty close to monster-player nests. So I think they tend to have their hands full with PVP against hellions. Which is good for the hero players."

"Yeah, I imagine so," said Riley. "A lot less PKing has been going on since the expansion, now that players can fight other players… who are monsters."

"Which leads me back to the whole wanting a guild thing," Glint said, her gaze now on Riley's eyes. "I want to join a guild, and… I was kinda hoping I could try out for joining yours. What's it called? Bunker Brawlers or something?"

"Yeah, that's it," said Riley, his eyes narrowed. "Why do you wanna join us though? Sure sounds like you're trying to join us to spy on us. For all I know, you're going to feed information to Witch's guild. How can we trust you after what happened?"

Glint sighed. "I know you have no reason to trust me, I get that. Make me… I dunno, like, the lowest rank or whatever. Keep a close eye on me. Don't tell me guild plans until they're happening then and there. Give me a trial period where I can prove my worth, and if you still don't trust me, just always keep me in the dark about guild plans. I've heard it all before. You and your friends weren't the only ones Glasser and Witch crossed, and the people I know also know that I was running with them. Everyone I've approached so far won't even give me a minute to plead my case."

"It's not really up to me," said Riley. "I'll have to bring it up to Laura, and we'll probably have to vote on it."

"Speak to Amber," said Glint. "I ran with him a bit before the whole PK thing with you and your other friends. I know Amber's in your guild now, but I didn't feel like I should approach him about joining, and I know you and Laura are pretty good friends, right?"

Riley brought his hand up and scratched the side of his head. "Yeah, kinda, I guess."

"I understand if you're just going to tell me 'no.' I just want another chance. I love this game. I love everything about it, even the bad stuff. Hell, I even love the crappy pain feature that's in the game now. I love it! I just… want a group to call my own again. I screwed up with Glasser and Witch. They were just the people who were around. So… if you can bring it up to Laura, I'd really appreciate it. Maybe Amber will be my character reference."

"Amber doesn't usually like anyone," said Riley.

"Amber likes who he likes," Glint said with a half smile. "He's very opinionated."

"Yeah, I've noticed," Riley murmured. He then slowly slid out of the seat. "Look, I'll bring it up to Laura." He turned and noticed that the rest of his group hadn't come in yet. Perhaps they were still talking to Brenda, or perhaps they'd all gone off to quest. He turned his attention back to Glint. "But it'll be her call, as well as those of us that were attacked that day. So I'll bring it up, but I can't promise anything."

Glint slowly stood up and held out her hand. "Here, take my contact info, so you can send me a message either way."

"Alright," Riley said, and took her hand for a shake, which allowed him to gain her name on his contact list. He then withdrew it and sighed. "Was there anything else? I wanted to head somewhere else."

Glint shook her head. "No, that's it. Thanks for at least hearing me out. I know I screwed you guys over bad, but it means a lot to me that you at least heard me out. So, thanks."

Riley nodded and managed a smile. "Sure thing. Sometimes we all need a second chance."

CHAPTER 13:

POWERING UP

It had been several days since Riley had spoken to Glint. He'd talked to Laura about recruiting the ex-PKer. Laura was apprehensive about letting Glint join, and had told him that she'd speak to some of the others about their opinions on the matter.

Riley didn't blame her. He wasn't entirely sure he wanted Glint around either, but he knew that if he was in such a position that he'd want a second chance as well. He couldn't remember if Glint lived off what she made in Sigil Online. Most of his interactions with Glint, back when he was Radiance, had been in-game related. They'd never spoken on social matters or anything out of game.

With the release of Hellions, Riley and others had become more social in and out of game. All of the 'hero' players now had something in common. A common enemy to work towards defeating. A common foe that they each had to survive against. And for some, that survival meant being able to pay their bills, or buy actual food in the real world.

Sigil Online wasn't the only game that people made a living off of. It was just like any business that employed people. Some games had larger audiences, some had smaller ones, but the virtual reality games tended to have the biggest payouts as far as what gamers could make from them. At least for the players who played it more than casually, like Riley did.

Riley watched the tall structures slowly glide by. He once again found himself in a taxi, heading to Aaron's city and usual hangout in-game. He had visited Aaron the other day after speaking to Glint. But Aaron had needed a few days to work on a new item for him. Something to replace his scythe, but Riley didn't know much more than that.

Riley looked down to his arms resting on his lap. He reached over and pinched his other arm. There was a twinge of pain as he did so. It was strange. It wasn't like he was getting a perfect tactile sense of touching his arm, or the sense that he was even pulling his skin, but the sharp pain was certainly prevalent.

The developers didn't seem capable of removing pain from the game. They hadn't even dulled it yet. It was one-hundred percent, and a lot of players were still keeping their distance from the game, which made Riley think that the developers would probably try and come up with a solution soon. There was talk on the forums, and on the news, that the developers would try and reduce the pain factor down to only ten percent, so that the worst pain possible would only feel like a light pinch.

But what was taking so long? Surely they only had to modify a few numbers in a line of code somewhere. At least, that was what it seemed like to Riley. But apparently, it was more complex than that, else they would've already changed it, right?

Riley wasn't thrilled by the prospect of experiencing severe pain. At least the pain wasn't permanent, like it would be in the real world. There were no broken bones or lost appendages, just hitpoints. He had a feeling that most of the players currently in the game were in situations like himself. People who *had* to play, in order to pay their bills. But then again, maybe that wasn't the entire case. Riley knew that Parviz had a part-time job, as did Seth. For them, the game was supplemental. Riley shook his head and sighed. Maybe they just wanted the thrill of it all. Who knew? Maybe pain would be alleviated down to ten percent and then never get raised. It'd be 'the time that Sigil Online was as dangerous as the real world,' and people could gloat and claim that they survived when Sigil Online was truly hellish. For all he knew, it could all just be a publicity stunt that the developers were pulling for Sigil Online.

Riley managed a half smile and shook

his head.

It didn't take long for him to reach his destination.

He found himself on the curb, staring at the Neon Nest again. Riley headed inside. Nothing had really changed since the last time he'd been in there. Just some new faces, none of whom really looked at him for more than a couple seconds.

He made his way over to where Aaron was seated in the corner.

"I really wish you lived closer," Riley said, as he slid into the seat across from Aaron.

Aaron smirked and shrugged. "You're the one who lives far away."

"So what do you have for me?" Riley asked. "And how much is it going to cost? It's a new weapon, right?"

"It is," he said. "I'll need to dematerialize your scythe to get the power core out of it, but I guarantee you're going to love what I came up with."

"Sure," Riley murmured. He reached out and shook Aaron's hand, which prompted both of them with various options through the holographic interface window that popped up.

Riley released the handshake and tapped one of the icons from his inventory, and brought it over to a small 'trade' window.

"Here you go, what now?" Riley urged.

"In a hurry?" Aaron asked, as he took his time and lifted his hand to do the same thing Riley had.

"Well, kinda," said Riley. "I might as well make the most of the fact that the player base isn't as large as it usually is. So I want to hit some of the smaller hunting grounds, until my guildies get online to party with."

"Still hunting nests?" Aaron asked.

"Yeah, occasionally," said Riley. "We've gone on three outings so far. Only really found that one lair in the beginning though. But stop stalling! Show me what you've got for me."

"Alright, gimme a minute," said Aaron. He accepted the trade for the scythe, then spent a couple minutes tapping at his own inventory screen. "Almost… done," he murmured, before tapping a few more times. Then, he offered his hand back to Riley, to initiate a new trade. "Alright, one more time."

Riley nodded and took Aaron's hand.

They initiated a new trade, and Riley accepted the item Aaron was sending him.

"It's… a glove?" Riley asked, as he started to read over it, and its stats. The item itself was called 'Glove of Acceptable Power.' Which kind of sounded strange to Riley.

"It looks like it has a higher damage capability than the scythe, but it all kinda goes off the essence I steal anyway. So I'll have to punch things?" he asked, still reading the info on the item.

Aaron's lips parted to speak, but Riley spoke up again before he had a chance to say anything.

"The glove shoots?" Riley asked. "Like, a beam?"

Aaron smirked. "That's right. It'll fire beams of energy based on the essence you steal. Just like with the scythe, the stronger the essence, the stronger the attack."

Riley continued to read the description. "So, for each installment of essence, I get ten shots that fire a one-second long beam that has a range of five hundred feet? That seems pretty far."

"Yeah, but you'll notice that it has

reduced damage on structures," said Aaron.

Riley nodded. "Ah, yeah, it says that here. Ninety percent reduced damage, in fact. So, if I need to break down a building, I won't be using this. But on the other hand, I won't be wrecking the city every time I get in a fight."

"Exactly," said Aaron. "You'll have to let me know how you like it. I know that you were having trouble with the scythe."

"Yeah, I really loved the scythe. It was pretty awesome to use," said Riley. "But as a support class, I really shouldn't be in melee range that often. Especially after the pain update."

After a few moments of reading the rest of the information on the glove, Riley looked up to Aaron. "So, how much do I owe you?"

Aaron's brows lifted. "Oh, don't worry about it. It didn't cost me much, actually. Well, I suppose I could've made something else to sell with the parts, but it's not that big of a deal. The rarest part was the power core that was already in the scythe, so I didn't make another one of those. There aren't a lot of power cores out there, but there's also not much of a demand for power-imbuing items. So don't worry about it."

"Thanks, I really appreciate it," said Riley. He gestured to close his status screen. "So, I guess that's it then?"

Aaron smiled and nodded, before slowly slipping to the side to stand. "Yeah, that's it. I've got some stuff I need to take care of, but I wanted to make sure you got that. We can chat more at our usual meetup later."

"Alright, sounds good, catch you later then," said Riley, as Aaron headed towards the steps, probably to log out of the game.

Riley got out of the booth and went to a nearby terminal close to the exit. He queued up another cab and headed back outside.

While waiting for the cab, he thought about taking the glove out to test the beam. The only problem was that he still had to find some essence to empower the weapon. He couldn't take his own essence, and he wasn't about to attack any of the nearby NPCs.

Ever since Hellions released, attacking NPCs warranted steeper penalties towards a player's standing with the city. There was now an 'infamy' score that would build up, depending on how much damage a person caused to a city or its denizens, including other players who had low, or no infamy rating. It meant that if a player wanted to PVP other hero players, the city itself would actively be against them. NPCs would signal proximity sightings of bad players, that nearby guilds could then find out about. It made PVPing harder for hero players fighting hero players, but it also made it easier for people to take care of the city they called home.

"Wonder what it'd be like to play as a monster," Riley murmured to himself. He looked up and down the street, watching the various NPCs walking by, going about their digital lives.

Riley thought about being the bad guy. A monster that stalked around and killed everything in sight, while also picking fights with other players every chance he got, and then disappearing if things got too heavy.

Riley's lips curled a little as he found himself daydreaming, picturing himself as a hellion terrorizing the city.

A chime sounded from nearby, and Riley realized that his taxi had arrived, and had probably been sitting there for a minute.

He quickly got in and greeted the NPC driving the cab. Seconds later, he was on his way back to Gargantuan City.

CHAPTER 14:
NICE WEATHER WE'RE HAVING

The architecture between cities was mostly the same, but as the taxi neared the border between the two cities, buildings became shorter. There wasn't any sort of wall separating the cities, at least, not between Gargantuan and Mega City. But there was a train track, grass, streets, and a distinct lack of buildings for a narrow strip of area that separated the cities. It was about the width of a city block, and it didn't take long to drive right through it.

But as Riley's taxi driver neared the end of the street, just before entering Gargantuan, the taxi rolled to a stop.

Several seconds passed, and Riley looked over to the taxi driver. There wasn't any traffic that would've kept them from going on, but with just a glance, Riley noticed a distinct red-glowing message on the taxi's dash screen that read, 'No Safe Route.'

Before Riley could say anything, the driver turned his head. He was a thin man with graying hair and blue eyes. He offered a meager smile and a shrug. "Sorry, but I can't take you any further. Too much threat going on in the next city. You'll have to get out here. Half your fare has already been refunded. Sorry for the trouble."

Riley blinked. He'd never actually found himself in this situation before. "Uh, we… can't just drive a bit further? I don't see anything going on," he said, turning his head to get a better look outside the car.

"Sorry, but I can't go any further, you'll have to get out. My apologies," the man said again.

Riley looked to him, then back to Gargantuan City. He couldn't see any fires, or smoke, or anything.

"Um, alright," Riley murmured. "I guess I'll… get out then." He sighed, knowing he couldn't very well persuade an NPC to keep driving into a town that the NPC was forbidden from entering.

Whoever had control of the district that Aaron's hideout was located in could set 'NPC parameters' to dictate NPC behavior, such as entering hostile zones, or navigating around them. They could even set local NPCs to have weapons and defend themselves, or run away, based on a percentage of the population. On one hand, you could have your district's NPCs fight off low level monster-players with this method. On the other, if you had too many NPCs fighting potentially high-threat monsters, you could lose a large portion of the population with no real benefit. Generally, whoever owned a district would have to make those decisions based on the needs and desires and climate of the district itself.

The sun was high in the sky as Riley made his way into the outskirts of Gargantuan City. NPCs were milling about on the street. He could even see some of them up in homes or offices. NPCs didn't do much but they did add a vibrant life to the game. They dressed differently, looked differently, and could hold at least a mediocre conversation about various in-game topics.

With little else to do, Riley took in his surroundings as he made his way up the street. He didn't have any ability to move quickly, so all he could do was walk. He looked all around, trying to discern if anything was 'wrong' with the city, but there weren't any sirens. No smoke. No rumbles. Everything seemed… normal, as far as a city in Sigil Online went.

He didn't notice any other players around. Not yet, at least. No one in extravagant or unusual attire, to warrant being noticed as a player. He shook his head, wondering if maybe a fight had broken out closer to Bunker 7, which had been the destination he'd set the taxi to go towards. Maybe something had happened near the bunker which prevented the NPC from driving him in any further.

But with nothing else to occupy his time, all Riley could do was think about how strange that was, and that it didn't seem like something he'd heard of happening before. It was certainly possible, but usually NPCs only avoided an area after some sort of warning system was triggered, and the NPC he'd been in the car with had entirely avoided Gargantuan City.

Maybe he was overthinking things.

Which reminded him.

A smirk played across his lips as he gestured to bring up his inventory. With a few quick taps, he materialized his new power glove. It shimmered and glinted in the sunlight. He admired it and flexed his fingers. With the opening in the center of his palm, the spike wouldn't harm it. He could then just use his left hand to touch and empower it, much as he'd done with the staff. He hoped it proved as useful as he thought it should be.

He continued to head deeper and deeper into Gargantuan City, towards his usual hangout. As he walked, he glanced over his status screen, checking his stats as well as the glove's description one more time. Ten shots per imbue. Then he'd have to reload it again. Shouldn't be much of a problem with his quick essence draining paragon powers. And, with his left hand glove, he'd be able to buff everyone around him with a single blast.

He had to admit, he was feeling pretty powerful, as far as hybrid support classes went. Perhaps not as strong as Radiance had been, but Relinquisher was starting to feel pretty amazing.

He dismissed his status screen and looked into the sky. There weren't many clouds, which let the sun shine across the city. As he went towards the center, the structures grew taller, and shadows began to hide certain alleys and streets that the sun couldn't reach, even at its high angle.

He started to drift off in his thoughts. Who was online still? Would he be able to get a group? Would anyone be up for grouping? Had Laura and the others headed off, or stuck around the bunker? Hmm, they were probably off in some hunting ground, he figured. Carla and Brenda were a potent damage dealing duo.

Riley tried to remember what time various people usually got online, and as he did, he found himself ever deeper into the city. He glanced around to gain his bearings, to make sure he was taking the fastest route back to the bunker. He used several tall buildings as landmarks, and knew that he had another fifteen to twenty minutes of walking ahead of him.

Walking wasn't so bad, he figured. He was able to check out the sights, and see various structures he hadn't usually seen. It felt like a real city, but without all the anxiety he usually had when he was out in public in real life. It was similar, but also more… refreshing? Not to mention, it wasn't as if the people in Sigil Online were anything like the random people he'd find out in the real world. Some people could be so noisy. Yelling at each other outside, over the most mundane things. At least in Sigil Online, all the noise was usually a manageable level of conversation or meaningful shouts from one NPC to another. It was only when players were introduced to the mix that things became…

Riley blinked, and slowed to a stop in the middle of the street. He broke from his mild daydream and train of thought, and took a look around. He looked up the street, then to the one beside him.

There were no NPCs.

No moving cars.

He turned around and glanced behind him. He'd taken a few turns to get onto the street he was on now, but… there was no one. No movement whatsoever.

Riley's brow furrowed. He looked up at the nearby buildings to the countless windows around him.

He couldn't see inside many of the windows, but the ones that he had clear line of sight on, he noticed that there was no movement inside the rooms. He didn't see *anyone*.

He reached over and pinched his arm. He wasn't sure why he was driven to do this, but he had to make sure something weird wasn't going on in-game.

Sure enough, he felt the sharp sting yet again, just as he had earlier.

"Weird," he whispered as he started walking again. Were the NPCs somehow offline? They should be somewhere in-game. Even if they weren't moving or going about their daily lives. According to the developers, there were various parts of the game that were handled by different servers. Whether those servers were different blades on a server rack, or actually different machines in other locations, Riley had no idea. He'd never really known a lot about servers and computers, other than how to use one to access Sigil Online, and other games prior to it.

Riley couldn't shake the unusual feeling that something had to be wrong. If it was a glitch, then that meant that something was really going wrong in Sigil Online. First there was the pain issue, which had yet to be resolved, and now NPCs weren't spawning?

Riley continued to think about it as he made his way all the way back to Bunker 7. He didn't see any NPCs or players at all. He considered heading into one of the other hideouts, as Bunker 7 wasn't the only meetup place in the area, but all the places he could check would be out of his way. He might as well just get to the bunker and see if anyone was around.

It didn't take long to reach his destination. The area seemed as normal as it usually did. In fact, some of the damage from the fortress had already been repaired, probably by some civilian players or NPCs, trying to up their crafting and construction.

Riley pushed open the heavy door to

Bunker 7 and stepped into the lobby.

"I'm not heading into the sewers," came a woman's voice.

Riley glanced around and spotted two familiar faces.

"It won't be anything for us to check," came a gruffer male voice. "We tunnel down, you have your vines. I have my earth-moving. It'll be easy. Something's messed up, and the more we let it go, the worse it might get."

Riley smiled as he spotted Erica and Todd standing in the center of the room between some tables. In fact, they were the only two people in the entire place.

As the door shut behind him, Todd and Erica both turned their attention to him.

"Riley!" Todd spoke up. "What's going on?"

Riley glanced between them. "I… I don't know. I just walked here from the outskirts of the city. I just came from Mega."

"Do you know where the NPCs are?" Erica asked.

Riley shook his head. "No, I noticed there didn't seem to be any around. I wasn't sure if it was some glitch, or what. The taxi NPC from Mega wouldn't drive into Gargantuan. Apparently, the threat level is too high, but I haven't seen anything weird. Except for the fact there's no NPCs around."

"We just got online," said Erica. "And we didn't see anyone here, so we stepped outside to see if anyone was outside, but we didn't see anybody. So we were trying to figure out what to do."

"Yeah, luckily our powers help us avoid damage pretty easily, so we figured pain wouldn't really hinder us from getting some levels. Or, in this case, figuring out what's going on with the NPCs."

"So you haven't seen anyone else online, player wise?" Riley asked.

Todd and Erica shook their heads.

"So what was your plan?" Riley asked, looking between them.

"Well, I wanted to check the underground, as that's where the hellions are usually hiding out," said Todd.

"And I told him that it would be stupid for just the two of us to head down into monster territory," said Erica.

"Yeah, but now Riley's here," said

Todd. "Now we have a healer and a buffer. So that changes things, right?"

"I guess," Erica murmured.

"I'm down to investigate the underground," said Riley. He smirked and lifted his right hand, flexing his fingers in the new glove he'd gotten from Aaron. "I can do ranged damage now, got myself an upgrade. I'm itching to try it out, so I'm all for getting into some action."

"Then that settles it," said Todd. "If it's a glitch, then the NPCs will be back on their own and we'll have scoured some of the underground for lairs. That's what Laura wanted us to do in our free time, right?"

Riley nodded. "Yeah, as much as we could."

Erica sighed. "And if there's something going on, maybe we'll find a few hundred monsters down in the underground and get ourselves killed."

Todd chuckled. "No way. We've got this."

"We don't have a huge amount of damage," Riley mentioned. "All three of us are mostly hybrid classes." Riley looked to Todd. "You're utility and damage." He looked to Erica. "You're also utility and damage.

I'm healing, buffing, and a little damage. So if we do find something, we're going to be better off running away and trying to find help."

"I guess we'll decide on that when it happens," said Todd. "Who knows, maybe we'll find some other heroes along the way."

"If we're lucky," Riley murmured. "But I'm still concerned that there's so few players on."

"Well, we've got the pain issue. That's hurting the populace a bit," said Erica. "And it's just after lunch. So people are either eating offline, or they're already back and in hunting groups. But yeah, it's unusually dead."

"Well, I'm ready to get going," said Todd. "You good, Riley?"

Riley thought for a moment and then opened his inventory. He tapped across a few screens to check himself over. "Health is good, inventory has some healing items in it… uh, yeah, I'm good. Let's go."

CHAPTER 15:
UNDERGROUND SHADOWS

Riley sighed, glancing around at the nearby concrete walls, leaky pipes, and dusty floor. "I hate the scenery down here," he groaned.

"Yeah, I'll take a forest or any sort of plant life any day," Erica added.

"I dunno, I kinda like it. Very… earthy, and minimal," said Todd.

"You would like it down here," Erica scoffed. "You and your concrete apartment. I don't know how you stand it down there all the time."

"You don't seem to mind it too terribly," Todd spoke up, glancing over to Erica with a curious smirk.

Riley was following behind the two of

them, glancing between them as they started speaking back and forth. It wasn't lost on him that the two of them had started to discuss hanging out or being around each other in the real world. Riley didn't remark on it too much. What they did in the real world was their own business. People didn't really ask him about what he did, or when he hung out with Aaron, so he let the two of them be.

"I wish there was some way we could better track monsters down here," said Riley. "Feels like we're always walking around aimlessly."

"Yeah, it does feel like that, doesn't it?" said Todd.

"Do we know anyone with powers to track other players, or help in that regard?" asked Erica. She looked to Todd, then back to Riley.

"Don't think so," Riley replied. "I used to know a guy who could teleport people anywhere by just mentioning the destination. But that doesn't really help with finding the monsters. It was just a nice way to travel really quickly."

"And Parviz needs line of sight to teleport us around," said Todd.

"Maybe we should start digging

tunnels?" Erica asked. "Wreck our way down into some lairs?"

Todd slowed to a stop and looked over to Erica, then back to Riley. "Is that what we're going to do?

Riley stopped and glanced around at their meager surroundings. They hadn't managed to find any hint of hellion activity yet. "It might be our best move. It's likely that the hellions have some way of detecting us if we get close to their lair. They may actually know we're here right now."

"We don't know how many lairs are beneath the city," said Todd. "We could crash into one, and it could be a completely different group than one that's doing stuff to the NPCs above."

"Or, this is all for nothing anyway, and it's just a glitch in the game," Riley mentioned. "We have no way of knowing. We're grasping at air right now. It's like we're trying to solve a puzzle, but we're not even sure where the pieces are."

"Are you saying we should give up already?" Erica asked, crossing her arms against her stomach.

"No, not at all," Riley spoke up again. "I just think that we have to expect to make some mistakes, and be prepared for the possibility that we have no idea what we're getting into down here."

"Good, then we're all in agreement," said Todd with a slow smirk. "Let's smash our way down."

Riley sighed and shrugged. "Might as well. I guess if we all die, we can always make monster characters," he said, offering up a half smile. Of course, he wasn't serious in the least. Starting the game as a monster character would be a bit of a step back for him financially, even if he was able to be a pretty strong monster. Currently, the monsters had less of an economy than the hero players, since trading and crafting were a bit different. But each week, more and more money was coming into the game on the hellion side of things. It was only a matter of time until it caught up, or even surpassed the hero side.

Todd stepped forward. "Huddle up," he said. "Erica, be ready to catch us with vines if we start falling to our deaths."

"I got you," said Erica as she moved in closer. "If I could detect nearby plant life, maybe I'd be able to use that method to scan the area, but unfortunately, I can only beckon it and hope it's there."

Riley stepped in as well, so that the

three of them made a small triangle.

They were currently in a long hall but it was too dim to actually see more than a hundred feet ahead. The lights were interspersed to only allow vision on the nearby area.

Todd lifted his arms and moved them along with his hands. At his command, the concrete floor beneath them shifted. There was a wide circle they were standing upon that began to lower inch by inch. A few seconds later, the concrete that had been the floor was passing by overhead.

"So… does the ground get packed in, or something?" Riley asked. "Or are you making it disappear?"

"Unless the ground is diamond or something, I'm able to pack it in tighter, to allow space for us to move into," said Todd. "Sometimes I get stopped by too-tightly packed dirt or concrete that I might've already moved previously. But that doesn't happen often."

"I see," Riley murmured, really having no way to imagine how Todd's powers worked, since all he'd ever been able to do was manipulate the sun's light as Radiance, or shoot spikes and essence as Relinquisher.

Dust began to fill the air around them

as the ground was disturbed. A dull crunching and grating sound filled their ears as they made their descent.

Riley looked at his hands. His new glove on the left, and the shooting glove on the right. With just the three of them, he figured he wouldn't get a whole lot of value out of the left one.

The light in their hole quickly diminished, casting them mostly in darkness.

"And none of us has a light source, right?" asked Erica.

"I got nothing," said Todd.

"I guess I don't either," said Riley. "I don't think the glow factor of my buffs really illuminate anything. And I doubt either of you want me to stab you right now."

"Yeah, I'll pass on that," Erica laughed.

Suddenly, a dull white light appeared around their feet. As it did, the three of them plummeted.

But not very far.

Todd and Erica landed relatively gracefully about ten feet below.

Riley panicked as he fell and landed on his feet, but then promptly on his ass.

"Agh!" he grunted, feeling the sting of the landing.

"Another tunnel?" Todd asked, looking around quickly.

"Where the hell did you guys come from?" came a woman's voice.

At once, all three of them looked in the direction of the female speaker.

But even before they saw the figure, Riley realized he recognized the voice, and quickly scrambled to his feet. Standing roughly fifteen feet away was a woman with deep raven hair that went to her shoulders. She had on a form-fitting gothic leather outfit, with frills coming from the hips like a skirt.

Riley's eyes widened as he looked at the woman.

She looked between Todd and Erica, her brow furrowing. Then, she looked to Riley and her eyes widened.

"You!" she gasped.

Riley took in a slow breath, his eyes darting around to make sure she was alone.

Then, he looked back to her. "Hey… Shadow Witch."

Shadow Witch's fists clenched as she looked at Riley.

For several long seconds, nobody said anything. Shadow's gaze flitted to each of them. Then, she spoke. "Your city seems to be missing some NPCs."

"You're not somehow responsible, are you?" Erica asked.

Shadow scoffed. "Hardly."

Riley couldn't help but feel that this was somehow a trap. First Glint, now Shadow? Were they up to something? Both encounters seemed coincidental, but how much could be tossed up to coincidence?

"Why are you here?" asked Riley.

Shadow's gaze on him didn't falter. "You first."

"No reason to hide what we're doing, if she's not to blame," Todd murmured from behind Riley.

Riley considered their options. If they wanted, they could attack Shadow here and now, and try to eliminate her. But that wouldn't make them any better than the average PKer. For all he knew, she'd changed. It also didn't help that if they attacked her first, their standing with Gargantuan City would fall slightly, since they would be considered the aggressors.

"We're trying to figure out what's going on with our NPCs," said Riley. "We thought some monster-players might be up to something down here."

"I thought the same thing," said Shadow. "I'm not stationed here, I could care less about your city. But I was meeting up with… a few people. Our meetup was in Gargantuan, so here I am. The two people I was supposed to meet weren't where they were supposed to be. I figured there's something weird going on, and monster-players were the most likely suspect."

"And monster-players are underground," said Riley.

"Exactly," Shadow confirmed.

"So here we are. You came alone?" asked Riley.

"Well, I'd say that my habits tend to lead to having plenty of gear," she said. "Not to mention, I'm probably the top five percent as far as levels go. I can take a hellion, or two."

"You didn't do too well against us, and you had a level advantage back then," said Todd with a smirk.

Shadow narrowed her eyes at him. "You want to test me, down here in the dark?" A sly grin curled the corner of her lips.

It was in that moment that Riley remembered how Shadow's powers worked. She could manipulate shadows, and bend them to her will and cause them to damage her enemies, or entangle them, or many other things. In a lot of ways, her powers were very similar in functionality to Todd and Erica's, since she could manipulate things around her. And therein laid the current problem. Sure, they were surrounded by cement and earth that Todd could move, but it was low damage and cumbersome for all of them to navigate around in such close quarters. Erica could manipulate plant life, but again, these were all very physical constructs. Shadow, on the other hand, was able to move things without mass, but that could take a physical form. Not to mention, they were utterly surrounded by shadows, which made Shadow Witch far more powerful than she'd been in the last two engagements.

Riley also knew that Shadow had quite the level advantage on them. And just like how Riley had plenty of gear to augment his own abilities, it was even more true for

Shadow. She may have even found items that made her incredibly more powerful than the last time they saw her.

All of this led to his next decision.

"We don't want to fight you," said Riley. "But would you be willing to join us? Obviously we have no interest in each other's survival, but we're after the same thing. Let's call a truce, for now."

"Sure," Shadow said, without taking much time to think about it.

"Really?" Erica asked, looking over to Riley, then back to Shadow.

"It makes the most sense," said Riley. "We're fighting hellions. We need all the hero players we can get. Even if one of them is an anti-hero."

"I've been running around aimlessly down here," said Shadow, moving the conversation along. "Seems like you guys have a better method of travel."

Riley turned and looked back to Todd and Erica. Neither of them were wearing happy expressions.

"If you keep digging down, you might hit something, I guess," Shadow spoke up again. "I'd suggest heading through this wall over here," she said, gesturing to the one on her left. "I haven't been able to find any meaningful way to go in that direction, but I've heard some sounds coming through the wall. Not sure what sort of sounds, but sounds. That's the only lead I've got."

"Then let's do it," said Riley.

"Are you sure about this?" asked Erica.

Riley looked back to her. "We haven't much of a choice. Shadow knows we're here anyway, and the longer we wait, the more damage the monster-players can do to our city."

"And personally, I couldn't care less about what happens to you all," said Shadow. "This isn't my city, but I do want to find my friends."

"Then let's go," Todd said, in a less than enthusiastic voice. He turned and without wasting a motion, he manipulated the earth and concrete and started forming a tunnel.

Riley turned his attention from Todd to Shadow. "After you," he said.

Shadow shrugged. "Certainly."

CHAPTER 16:
HEROES IN THE DARK

The group of four moved at a slow pace through the tunnel. The darkness seemed to envelop them, which made Riley uneasy with Shadow Witch in their party. Thanks to the above level that they'd just come from, there was a little more light than there had been when Todd made the hole in the ground. But with each step they took, the light stretched thinner and thinner.

Crch.

Thmp thmp.

"You hear that?" Erica asked.

"Sounds like it's coming from ahead of us," said Riley.

"Told you there was something this way," said Shadow. "Sounds like it's still some distance, though. Crazy to think that there's as much underground down here to equal the city above."

"What do you mean?" Erica asked, glancing over to Shadow.

Shadow Witch kept her gaze forward as she walked a couple feet behind Todd, Erica and Riley behind her.

"The underground almost mirrors the city," said Shadow. "As far as how much space is available for monsters. They can't build anywhere they want. At least, not yet. They can only build in certain areas underground. But in those areas, they can make their lairs and nests. They can't build outside the cities yet. Oddly enough."

"There is a lot of blank space outside the cities," said Riley. "I keep hearing that the devs plan to do something with it, but the Hellions expansion practically ignored it. So I take it you've been researching what hellions can do?"

"More or less," said Shadow. "I just wish I could make a hellion and keep Shadow."

"If you were a hellion, would you fight other hellions?" asked Riley.

Shadow turned her head and glanced back to Riley, the corner of her lips curled. "I think you know the answer to that." She turned forward again, just as more dull thumps could be heard coming from straight ahead.

"Have you fought many hellions yet?" asked Erica.

"Of course," Shadow responded, as if the question was absurd. "What about you three? Still sticking to fighting the in-game monsters?"

Riley grit his teeth a bit from the way Shadow spoke. "We've fought and killed our fair share of hellions."

Erica glanced over to Riley. The darkness was encroaching further and further around them, obscuring their vision.

"Wouldn't suppose you have something to light the area?" asked Riley.

"Like I need the light to see," Shadow snickered.

It took Riley several seconds to realize Shadow's meaning. Did she have some sort of dark vision? If so, that would certainly put all three of them at much more of a disadvantage than he'd thought. Of course, it only made sense that someone who

PVPed so much and whose powers were literal shadows would be able to see in the absence of light.

"But you know who could really light up a place like this?" said Shadow. "Your old friend, Glint. Has she started running with you yet?"

Riley's brow furrowed as Shadow mentioned Glint.

"What do you mean?" he asked, trying to play dumb, but it was apparent that Shadow knew something.

"Well she's not with us anymore," said Shadow Witch. "I figured she might've hit you up, like she has a bunch of other guilds. She's a tricky one, for sure."

Riley listened carefully to the words Shadow Witch chose. He didn't get the feeling that Shadow and Glint were working together, to get Glint to spy on them. If anything, it sounded as though Shadow was suspicious of Glint for some reason. Perhaps he needed to speak to Glint a little more and find out what she might know, or at least, what she could do. Had she gotten some items that helped make her more of a threat to Shadow? He had no way of knowing. "Well, she's not running with us," he said. But he didn't allude to the idea that maybe she would be in the future, since it was still up in the air if Laura and the others would be welcoming of her.

They continued to walk for several minutes in relative silence, except for the sound of the ground moving as Todd manipulated it at will.

The sounds they were able to hear were gradually getting louder.

Without warning, blueish light streamed into the tunnel as Todd pulled the dirt away from ahead of them. The opening widened further and further, now that they had reached… something.

Erica went to the right side of Todd, while Riley and Shadow stepped around him on the left.

"Really?" Erica muttered under her breath, as each of them stared at the sights before them.

"It's… trees?" Riley asked, blinking.

Standing before them was a forest of trees. The trees ranged in height—some were only a couple stories high, while others stretched even further. The dark blue leaves created a glimmering canopy that prevented them from seeing any sort of roof or ceiling to the chamber they were in now, as surely they were still underground. The blue light they were seeing was from numerous apple-like fruits hanging off the branches. The 'apples' were translucent blue, emitting plenty of light around them that then reflected off the leaves. The trees themselves were made of a deep black bark, almost like pillars of obsidian.

But it wasn't the tops of the trees that held their attention, it was the base of the trunks.

At the base of many of the trees were several large sections of blueish amber. The sections were easily as tall and wide as a person, because within each one of them was a body.

"Are those our NPCs?" Todd asked, pointing to the nearest tree, where four of the amber-like pods were situated against the base, seemingly nestled into the tree itself.

"Looks like it might be," said Riley.

"Hmm," Shadow murmured, as she walked right out into the forest. Her shoes crunched softly against the sharp dark blue grass.

"Shouldn't we be careful?" asked Erica, stepping forward. "Didn't you say there were guards in the last lair you went into?" she asked, as she looked to Riley.

"Yeah," Riley confirmed. "And a boss."

Shadow didn't stop moving until she reached the nearest softly glowing blue pod. She reached out and ran her fingers along the transparent cocoon. "Hmm," she murmured again. "I bet they're siphoning off energy, somehow. But… what are they producing?" she asked, as she tilted her head and looked up into the canopy above. "The fruit?"

Riley walked towards her, but his gaze was flitting around to the many trees around them. Was there a chance they'd already been detected? If so, what sort of monsters might come after them? If this was an actual lair, then it stood to reason that the hellions who owned it were probably around in full force.

"Maybe they use the fruit to gain experience, or power?" Riley mentioned. "Or, they're feeding the fruit to something else, like some sort of boss monster or something."

"Could be," said Shadow. With a thought, she drew the nearby shadows together and formed a spike, which she then drove into the nearest cocoon. The outer layer cracked like glass. With her next thought, the spike shifted and pulled apart, breaking the cocoon further, causing a wispy mist to flow out and fall to the ground, only to disappear.

Shadow reached in with her hands and shook the occupant of the pod. The woman had dull orange hair to her shoulders and wore a simple blue tank top and a pair of blue jeans.

"Hey, wake up," Shadow urged. She reached out and patted the woman's cheek. "Wake up."

The woman's blue eyes opened. She blinked rapidly before her gaze settled on Shadow. "Who're you?" she asked. She then glanced around some more. "Where am I?"

"What do you remember?" asked Shadow. "Are you a player?"

"I doubt she's a player," said Riley, who was now standing just off to the side of Shadow, attentively watching what was happening.

"I… I'm a citizen of Gargantuan City," the woman said. It was an in-game indicator that the woman was an NPC. NPCs never blatantly said that they were such, as everything had a sort of loose masquerade to it, to allow for a more engrossing experience in-game.

"How'd you get here?" Shadow asked, leaning up and giving the woman some room.

"There was an orange light," the woman said. "I was at my desk in the office, and an orange light emanated from behind me. Before I could turn around and see it, I blacked out."

"Orange light?" Riley asked, crossing his arms as he tried to think. "Some sort of energy weapon? Something that stuns or knocks out NPCs?"

Shadow reached out and helped the NPC from the pod. "That's all you remember?" she asked.

The woman nodded. "What… should I do now?" she asked.

"As an NPC, she probably has no way of getting back to the city," said Riley. "Unless we create a tunnel, we can't get her back either. And, well, there's nothing but pods all around us. This forest is probably large enough to allow them to abduct the whole city. We could be at this for hours, if not longer."

"I can try and make a tunnel," said Todd.

Shadow turned her attention to Riley, then Todd. "You wanna save all these NPCs, and send your ground mover off on tunnel duty?"

"Yes," said Riley.

"You realize that to abduct all these NPCs, there has to be either a pretty powerful hellion, or a bunch of them. And you think we can save all of them before someone notices?" Shadow countered.

Before Riley could reply, a loud crack sounded in the distance.

Bang bang.

Bang bang.

Bang bang.

The sound rang out through the trees and didn't seem to be all that far away.

"Red?" Riley muttered, hearing the telltale sign of the loud bangs that Red Shotgun's powers made.

"Is she here?" asked Erica, looking to Riley, then out to the direction the sounds came from.

"If she is, she could be with others," said Riley. "We can leave the NPC here for now. Let's go meet up with anyone else that might be down here, they might have a plan on saving these NPCs."

Shadow sighed. "Sounds like a terrible plan, but whatever. Your show, I guess."

Riley thought it strange that Shadow wasn't putting up more of a fight on the matter, if she didn't feel it was the best thing to do. But for the most part, it didn't really matter since there were more pressing concerns.

"Sounded like it came from that way, let's go," Riley said as he turned and ran off ahead, further from the way they'd come in through the tunnel.

"So I'm not making an exit?" Todd asked, as he quickly ran after Riley, with Erica right beside him.

"Not yet!" Riley called back. "We need to find out who else is here and team up with them!"

"Nothing about this feels right!" Erica said as she followed Riley. "How did they abduct all these NPCs in such a short time?"

"I'm sure we'll find out!" Riley said, as he raced between the thick trees.

After a minute of running, Riley spotted a partial clearing. It was the only clearing he'd seen so far, and most prominent were the three hero-looking figures standing in the middle. They were speaking to each other, but Riley was just a little too far to hear what they were saying. "Looks like some paragons ahead," Riley said to the three behind him, as he entered the clearing and headed towards them.

"Hope they're not anti-heroes," Todd grunted as he ran to keep up.

One of the three figures heard Riley running toward them and turned in their direction. "Who are you?" he called out.

"We're here to help! And find out what's going on," said Riley. "Where's Red? Is she with you?"

The person who had first called out to them was a man in his late thirties, maybe early forties. He had short blue hair and sharp, angular facial features, and a muscular physique. If Riley had to guess, he imagined the player had power over water, or maybe something to do with blue energy.

"Red? Who's Red?" he asked.

Riley stopped about ten feet away, giving him a perplexed look. "Red Shotgun," he said, looking to the blue player, then over to the other two.

One of them was a woman in her thirties. She had dark skin and smooth black hair to her chin. She wasn't dressed much like a player. She wore a pair of black pants and white shoes, along with a purple T-shirt. She had on several intricate bracelets and rings and also a necklace, but other than the jewelry, she appeared almost like an NPC. Perhaps she was one?

The other person in their group was a seemingly younger girl, probably in her late teens or early twenties. Her arms were down, her hands clenched into fists. She was fair skinned with blonde hair, but it was tied back in a bun. Most notable were her black boots, which seemed to crackle with prominent and visible electric energy.

"I… I don't think she's here," said the man in blue.

Riley glanced around. "But I heard a—"

Movement in the distance caught his eye before he could finish speaking. With the clearing they were in, he was able to see partially over part of the canopy around them. A dark shape rushed up above the treetops. It was then that Riley noticed the glittering cave ceiling far above. In a way, it was almost like a star-filled night sky. He wasn't sure how high above it was, but it was high enough to make the forest feel even more immense.

Regardless of the sight, Riley's attention remained on the dark shape, now plummeting towards them. "Something's coming!"

The group of three all turned their heads, just as the object slammed into the ground nearby.

"The hell is that?" Erica said from behind Riley.

The man in blue's eyes widened. "One of the hellions!"

The hellion had a lobster-like main body. It had a deep blue chitinous outer armor, like a shell. Two large pincers loomed on either side of it. But that was where its similarities to a lobster ended. It had four legs total, each one more like a bird's talon than a crab or insect leg. Its feet clutched the dark dirt beneath it. It had two beady eye stalks that shifted and turned, looking amongst the gathered hero players. Without warning, one of its pincers pulled back and swung out. It was too far to hit anything in melee range, but as its pincer came forward, it closed suddenly in a sharp *bang*. A burst of flame spouted from the space in front of the pincer. It shot out towards the gathered hero players.

"Get back!" the blue-clothed player yelled, as he swung his arms up. A sheet of ice materialized in front of him, and with another swipe of his hands, the ice sheet was thrown toward the oncoming flames.

Riley sidestepped and rushed off to the side to avoid the attack. The ice-powered player's sheet of ice smashed into the oncoming fire, creating a sharp hiss as it evaporated mid-air, creating a cloud of steam. Luckily, it was just enough to abate the flames, causing only a wave of heated air to assail the now seven-strong group of players.

"We need to beat him before any more show up!" said the more plain-clothed woman with jewelry.

Riley turned to face the lobster-like hellion. It wasn't too far away, but it was decently armored. He thrust his right arm and shot his spike, hoping to find purchase on the hellion's leg.

As the spike flew through the air, the hellion's right arm rose into the air and aimed at the sky. With another loud *bang*, a burst of flame shot up into the sky and rose above the canopy. A second later, Riley's spike sunk into the monster-player's leg.

Riley didn't waste a single moment, as

he willed the essence to shoot out the back of the spike and rush to his hand.

"He sent up a flare!" said the blue-haired player. "Ava, engage it! Aegis, focus on her!"

The girl with the electric boots ran toward the lobster. The other woman with the jewelry held out her arms and faced her palms towards who was surely 'Ava.' Which made the jewelry woman 'Aegis.'

A soft green field appeared around Ava, the girl with the electric boots. It looked very similar to a force field, but it wasn't repelling the blades of grass that she was running across.

The lobster hellion lowered its raised pincer and aimed it at Ava. With another shotgun sound, flames shot out in Ava's direction. She quickly came to a stop and with a jump-kick, a short electrical wave was expelled from her boot.

The electrical wave collided with the flame, but seemed to all but dissipate on the collision, while the flame rushed toward her.

"Crap!" she yelled. She held her arms up to shield herself as the flames buffeted the green field. As the flames assailed it, the shield grew more intense.

Riley was still in motion, using his new left-handed glove to expel the buff he'd gained from stealing the hellion's essence. With a flash of light from his left glove, the six other players around him all gained a soft blue glow to their eyes.

The fire had abated and Ava seemed unharmed, thanks to the shield.

"Did I just get a buff?" Aegis asked, glancing around before spotting Riley with his arms out. "Thanks kid!"

Riley really wished she wouldn't have called him 'kid,' but at least he was getting thanked, which was rare. Usually people just ordered him around.

"The buff increases your resistances to his attacks, while also empowering your damage to his element, which is fire, I guess?" said Riley.

Just as Riley finished speaking, movement caught his attention. He looked around, thinking there was someone moving on the outskirts of the clearing they were in. It was then that he noticed it wasn't a person, but the deep shadows of the nearby trees, all moving and swarming toward the blue lobster.

"Earth guy, plant lady, get ready to hit it hard!" said Shadow as she drew in all the surroundings' darkness. The shadows slipped up the hellion's legs and began covering every inch of it. Its eyestalks darted around as it shifted its footing, trying to see what was happening beneath it as the shadows enveloped it. Both of its pincers snapped toward the ground with a double *bang!* The sudden flames tore away the shadows coming from the front, and singed and carbonized the grass before it. But the shadows were coming from all angles, wrapping around the now-trapped hellion.

"Ugh!" Todd grunted.

Riley looked over to see a large chunk of the ground being hurled through the air. It looked to be comprised of both dark gray stones, dirt, and the blue grass.

The hellion crouched, taking a posture as if it was about to jump. But Erica was on top of the situation. Before the hellion could leap away, thick vines shot out of the ground beneath it and coiled repeatedly around each of its legs and seized tight.

The hellion attempted to leap, but only managed to slump to the ground. Its eyestalks were now covered in shadow. Its pincers opened again, about to fire. But before it could, the house-sized chunk of ground smashed down into it from above.

"Got him!" Todd called.

"Nice hit!" said the blue-clad hero player.

"It's still not dead!" said Shadow Witch. With one outstretched hand, she manipulated the shadows, causing them to draw back like elastic, then stab into the lobster like spikes. But she quickly found that the hellion's carapace was too thick to actually pierce, and it was resisting a sizeable portion of the damage.

The hellion was already shaking off the dirt that had landed on it.

"Erica, seize its claws!" said Riley.

Erica drew more vines from the ground and wrapped them around the hellion's pincers in an attempt to keep it from using its fire abilities. "I can only focus on so much here!" she said, in relation to keeping either its pincers or its legs down.

"I'm not getting through its armor!" said Shadow.

"Let me try!" said the blue-clothed player. He brought his arms up and in a flash, three long, narrow spears of ice formed in mid-air. He drew his hand back and with a swing of his arm, he launched them one by one at the trapped hellion. Each spear shattered against the lobster's tough hide, seemingly no better off than Shadow's attacks.

"Are we even hurting this thing?" said Todd.

Ava had resumed her dash for the lobster, apparently trying to get into melee with the beast.

Riley drew more essence from the still-spiked leg and reached over to specifically empower his beam glove, since the essence-flash wasn't able to buff his weapon as well. Once it was imbued, he took aim at the hellion and let loose a torrent of pale blue blasts.

The beams smacked against the hellion's armored hide, but it was difficult to tell if he was actually doing any damage. When players fought other players, whether they were paragons or hellions, they never saw the other person's health or name.

From off to the side, Todd continued to hurl smaller and more tightly packed clumps of earth, roughly the sizes of cars. He had to take more careful aim, since the electric-footed Ava had reached melee range with the lobster.

Ava rushed between the hellion’s two large pincers. She jumped into the air and stayed aloft for longer, as if being propelled somehow by her boots. She kicked rapidly at the hellion's chitinous face. Each impact made a sharp electric 'crack' and 'sizzle.'

One of Todd's larger boulders flew through the air, but a basketball-sized jet of flames cut through it and broke it apart with ease.

"What the hell?" Todd yelled, looking up into the sky, where the flames originated.

Flying above the trees was a sickly, pale blue creature with two sets of bat-like wings.

Riley looked into the sky, spotting the winged hellion. At least, it was likely that it was a hellion. He directed his glove into the air and fired off the last beam-round he had imbued.

The soft blue light streaked up and caught the gargoyle-like creature in the chest, but didn't seem to disrupt its flying in the least. The gargoyle flapped around and circled from high above. No health bar or name appeared, which meant that another player had arrived.

"Dammit!" said Aegis. "One of its friends arrived. Ice Block, can you deal with the one in the sky?"

"I'm on it!" said the blue-clothed player, whose name was apparently 'Ice Block.' He directed his attention on the sky, and in a flash, created several hundred marble-sized balls of ice. Then, in groups of ten, he fired them off into the sky, pelting the aerial hellion.

"We're not going to be able to handle many more arrivals with this group!" said Aegis.

The gargoyle hellion dove towards them. Its mouth opened and another jet of fire streaked out toward the ground. Except for Ava, Riley and the rest of the heroes were still gathered in a group. They weren't close together, but the long beam of fire headed right for Todd.

The moment it reached him, a green field appeared around him. It flashed intensely, bathing the area in green light. The second the flames were past him, the green field abated.

Next in line was Erica. She'd been close to Todd when the gargoyle dived toward them. Its fires reached her, but a green field appeared around her as well. The shield glowed more intensely. Then, with a sudden flicker, it shattered into green particles. Part of the fire broke through and caught her leg, causing a bit of damage that saw her health drop to eighty-nine percent.

"Ah!" Erica yelled. "Damn, that hurts!" She winced, only to find that the pain quickly alleviated. She hadn't been too badly injured since the pain update came out, but wondered if somehow the 'duration' of pain had been scaled back, since there was no lingering effect.

The smell of burnt grass filled the air, along with a low-hanging haze.

Riley stole another helping of essence from the lobster and quickly empowered his glove again. The buff that he'd given everyone would hold for plenty of time, but he needed to be on the offensive and help take down whatever hellions he could. With the lobster well-subdued, he focused his beams on the aerial hellion, which Ice Block was also attacking.

In between blasts, he looked over to make sure that the lobster wasn't a threat.

The crustacean-like hellion's claws were still tangled with vines, but with Erica's loss in concentration, it had managed to free its left claw. Erica was quick to draw new vines from the ground, but the hellion was faster. With a *bang* the blue lobster fired off another burst of flame at the gathered heroes. Riley, Todd, and Erica were forced to dive out of the way, in hopes of alleviating the flames that were about to engulf them.

Simultaneously, three green fields appeared around them, but the flames were too strong, and broke each field within a second.

Aegis was doing her best to keep threatened players shielded, but her shield was at its strongest if she could focus it on only one target at a time. Focusing it on several weakened its strength.

Riley, Todd, and Erica all took about fifteen percent of their health in damage. Erica took the most, as she had the least amount of defensive attribute points.

Riley's body had been buffeted by the flames, and while it definitely hurt to get hit by fire, the pain only lasted a couple seconds. He started to get to his feet when the ground beneath him shook. He quickly looked to Todd, assuming that the earth-mover was doing something with the ground, but Todd was also trying to get to his feet, and didn't appear to be using his powers.

A blue-gray tendril burst from the

ground.

Riley's eyes followed it as it rose into the air about ten feet. Another tendril broke through the ground, and then another and another.

"I think a third hellion just arrived!" he called out, as most of the tendrils seemed to be appearing between him, Todd, and Erica.

"We have to focus on the lobster!" said Aegis. "We can deal with the flyer, but the lobster needs to be eliminated first!"

Ice Block was still launching ice pellets into the sky, managing to hit the gargoyle from time to time and keep it moving. The gargoyle seemed more interested in dodging than attacking.

The tendrils that had burst from the ground lashed about, swiping wildly and randomly. Erica managed to duck, avoiding one of the tendrils, but just as Todd managed to stand, one of them hit him square in the chest and knocked him several feet, sending him back to the ground.

"Get away from it!" Aegis called, as she saw the tentacled hellion attack them.

Riley looked to Todd, who was scrambling back to his feet. He didn't seem to be in any trouble, but his health had taken a small hit from the lash of the tendril. Riley was still amongst the tentacles, so he decided to run towards Ice and Aegis, to gain a better defensive position. Aegis and Ice had moved in closer together. Every time the gargoyle let down a blast of fire, Aegis would be quick to shield herself, or Ice.

As Riley neared them, he made sure that he didn't create a straight line of the three of them, as he didn't want to make an easy target.

Bang!

The sharp sound cut through the air, causing Riley to look to the lobster. He'd thought the hellion had been decently subdued.

The deep blue crustacean's arms were now free of the entangling vines. It swiped and clawed at Ava, as the electric-footed young woman dodged and kicked, smashing her electric attacks against the monster-player's tough hide, seemingly going toe to toe with a foe much larger and perhaps stronger than herself.

But what Riley noticed the most was the distinct lack of shadows encompassing the lobster. He turned to find Witch, wondering what she was doing in the battle.

Erica and Todd were both weaving around the subterranean hellion's tendrils. They created makeshift barricades of dirt and vine, deflecting its attacks, but whatever form the hellion had beneath the ground, it was able to quickly demolish their constructs.

"Where's Shadow?" Riley called, looking all around.

"Who?" Ice Block asked from nearby, as he was still engaged with the aerial hellion.

"That shadow-powered player you were with?" asked Aegis, who was able to keep a better look on the battlefield due to her support powers.

"Yeah," Riley confirmed. "Did she run—"

In the corner of his eye, Riley caught movement. It was so quick that it broke him out of his train of thought and sent up numerous instinctive alerts in his head. He looked down and watched as a wave of thick shadows raced toward him, and a second later, up his body. His vision went black and he felt as if he was under water as the shadows encompassed him and started to squeeze.

A small indicator in his vision told him that he was suffocating and unable to breathe. The only reassurance he had was that somewhere in the pain update, they hadn't coded in anything to make him actually 'feel' as though he was suffocating. For that, he was immeasurably thankful.

Unable to see and barely able to move, he activated his beam glove. The blast tore away at the shadows around his hand and caused them to retreat, but since the shadows were covering his face, he wasn't able to see this. But he did feel a distinct lessening of intensity on his hand and arm after firing. Unfortunately, he wasn't able to test the beam glove any further, as something smashed into the front of his body. It was almost like something with a large hand or claw had punched him. Had the blue lobster closed the distance on him?

The shadows released him as the force of the hit caused him to fly across the clearing. His body smacked into the blue grass, leaving him face-first in the dirt. His whole body ached for several long seconds before the pain subsided. He sunk his fingers into the grass and dirt and pulled himself up. His vision was partly hazy at first, but what he saw was unmistakable.

Two fists loomed eight feet in the air, close to where he'd just been.

Beneath the shadowy fists stood a cloaked figure.

Riley didn't need to see the person's face, as he knew him easily by his powers.

It was Shade, the leader of the PKer guild 'The Dark Cloaks.'

CHAPTER 17:
CRASH

Riley managed to stand. "We have PKers!" he yelled. "Shadow turned on us!"

The rest of the group was still engaged with the hellions, but with the arrival of Shade, and the truth behind Shadow's intentions, they were now fighting a two-sided battle. Riley hadn't imagined that Shade and Shadow might be working with the hellions. Had Shade been nearby the entire time? Was he cloaked? Did Shadow wait for the most opportune time to turn on them? Riley couldn't believe how stupid he was. Shadow had fooled him, or at the very least, Shade had found them here in the hellion's lair and Shadow decided to take her chances at PKing them and stealing their gear. Because what other reason would she have for the deception?

Riley couldn't see where Shadow was. It was likely that she'd hidden amongst the trees. With her power over shadows, she'd be able to mostly conceal herself while still being a severe detriment to them.

Shade ran for Riley, his shadowy fists pumping in the air, mimicking his actual movements.

Riley lifted his right hand and fired off the remaining three blasts from his glove. The first beam missed, barely an inch from Shade's arm. One of those shadowy hands came down and shielded him as he advanced. The next two beams smacked into the dark palm protecting him. Riley couldn't solo

Shade, not with his powers.

A streak of fire cut across the clearing and buffeted Shade. He was knocked to the side, having taken a full blast of fire from the gargoyle above. There was no way for him to know how much damage it had done to Shade, but he could only hope that it was substantial, since he hadn't seen it coming.

Riley couldn't help but smile. It meant that the hellions weren't working with them. He quickly reached out with his other hand and stole more essence from the blue lobster that was still fighting toe to toe with Ava. Which was impressive, given the fact that Ava wasn't a paragon, and hellions generally were on par with paragons, whether they were tier-two monsters or not.

He didn't waste any time in directing his beam glove back at Shade. "I need help with this guy!" he yelled as he let loose a torrent of beams from his glove. The blasts smacked into Shade's body and fists, as he quickly took a defensive posture to protect himself from both Riley and the apparent threat of the gargoyle.

In the corner of his eye, Riley caught that dark movement. He turned his head and spotted the shadows rushing toward him from the treeline. They were further away this time, but they would be on him in seconds. He had just a couple shots left in his glove. He directed it at the encroaching shadows and fired.

The beams of light smacked into the ground, causing the shadows to disperse in a several-foot area around the impacts. It slowed the shadows, but by no means did it stop them. Luckily, those few precious moments were all Riley needed as the ground rose between him and the shadows.

The wall of dirt spanned at least a hundred feet and went ten feet high. It curved in such a way to block sight from the area of the trees that the shadows had come from. It didn't matter where Shadow Witch was, she'd have to take time to reposition to get sight on them.

"Thanks!" Riley called, as he quickly took account of everyone's position.

Todd was on full alert. "The underground hellion disappeared. I can't feel it moving or anything. We're fighting this guy and Shadow now?"

"Yeah!" Riley replied. "It looks like Ava can deal with the lobster, and Ice Block…" Riley looked over, seeing Ice Block still firing up at the gargoyle, trying his best to bring it down.

Riley quickly looked around for Erica, spotting her not too far away, as she was looking all around for signs of the subterranean hellion as well. "Erica, can you ground that gargoyle?"

Erica turned her attention to Riley. "I can try!"

"Todd, I'll need help with Shade," Riley instructed, as Shade was just now regaining his bearings, after having gone on the defensive.

Riley could actually feel his heart pumping in his digital body. The smell of grass was prevalent all around him, as he'd just been face down in it. It was only in this minute respite that he realized his health was sitting at fifty-seven percent. Shade had hit him hard, and might've caused bonus damage due to Riley being unable to see it coming. Just like with Shadow, Riley had no idea what sort of special equipment Shade might have to help boost his stats and powers. He looked just like he had back when they fought him previously, but that was only because Shade and his guild members all wore cloaks of concealment and kept their gear mostly hidden.

"Leave this guy to me!" Todd yelled. He swung his arms and lifted small boulders of dirt into the air and hurled them at Shade.

The boulders were much slower-moving than what Ice Block was doing. Riley knew Erica's vines could move quicker in mid-air, but only for a short time before the height would slow them down. This meant that only Ice Block would have a strong chance against the aerial hellion, while Todd was suited for this ground battle with the powerful PKer.

"I'm going to help Ice Block, the gargoyle's going to be a pain!" said Riley as he rushed over toward Ice Block, but he kept about ten feet away so that they wouldn't be an easy target for the gargoyle.

"No problem!" Todd replied. "Look out for vibrations in the ground, the subterranean one is still probably around."

"Right!" said Riley, deciding to leave Shade to Todd's capable earth-moving hands.

"This thing is fast," said Ice, as he noticed Riley's arrival nearby.

"We need to bring it down," said Riley. "Is Ava alright?" he asked, sparing a glance over to the electric-footed heroine who kept jumping and dancing around the lobster.

"Oh yeah, she's got that. Melee is her specialty," said Ice, as he continued to aim at the sky, focusing on small, sharp pieces of ice that he then launched. "I don't care what that hellion's stats are, she can beat it."

"If you say so," said Riley, as he stole more essence from the lobster, causing blue strands to rush between the distance of himself and the lobster. Once he'd regained his ten charges on the glove, he took careful aim at the flapping gargoyle, which was trying its best to keep out of range of Ice Block.

As Riley aimed the glove, there was no reticle or sight for him to line up the shot with. He reached over with his other hand and grabbed his wrist while he lined his arm up close to his head, wanting to be as accurate as possible with such a high and fast target. Not to mention it wasn't very big.

With careful precision, he fired once, only to miss. He shot a succession of three more times, only landing one of the hits.

"This is harder than it looks!" Riley growled.

"Tell me about it!" Ice replied. "Try and aim just ahead of it, as best you can. Your laser glove is almost instant, but it's moving really fast. I haven't been able to do much damage yet, but I don't think these guys have any way to heal the damage we've been adding up."

Riley decided that aim might not be as important as fire-rate. He had almost an unlimited capability of stealing essence from the Blue Lobster. So why not use it? He started firing rapidly, trying to unload as many blasts as he could, in hopes of hitting the gargoyle more often. The blueish beams lit up the sky, and were surely making their location visible to others, if anyone else in the enormous lair was watching.

Once the glove was depleted, he took more essence and tried again, managing to land about two or three hits out of the ten he fired. With his powers being added to the assault, the gargoyle's movements were becoming more erratic. Every time it tried to dive on them, Ice Block would pelt it with rapid hail, loading up a lot of damage with each dive attempt, which ultimately ended in failure as the gargoyle was forced to veer away, else it would take even more damage from the two of them. Before long, it darted off over the canopy and out of their vision.

"Guess that's good enough!" said Ice, who looked to Riley.

Riley glanced back to him. "As long as it's not going for reinforcements." With that, Riley directed his attention back on

Todd. He'd been sparing him the occasional glance, to make sure that Shade wasn't overwhelming him, but Todd seemed to be fully on top of things. The ground was cropped up in numerous spots, where Todd had constructed walls, as well as pillars that laid horizontal, which was a signature attack of Todd's, where he would pull the ground up at an angle and try to smash and crush his opponents for heavy damage.

Shade's dark fists were smashing through the makeshift pillars and walls. He was even striking out at the walls that Todd was constructing, which had been blocking line of sight for Shadow.

Riley took aim at Shade, hoping to push the odds in their favor and get this battle over with.

He held out his arm and lined up the shot, hoping to land some hits on Shade's head for critical damage while the PKer was distracted with Todd.

His vision started to shake and he narrowed his eyes and grit his teeth to compensate instinctively, but it wasn't getting any better. A moment later, he realized what was wrong, but by then, he'd already been standing still too long.

The ground burst beneath Riley's feet

as an ocean-blue tendril shot up and threw him back. The 'sky' entered his vision as he fell to the ground. His body landed hard, causing a whole percent of damage from the impact.

His head spun. He couldn't move his body at all. It was in that moment that he realized a small yellow lightning bolt icon had showed up at the bottom of his vision. He was under the status ailment of paralysis. The icon blinked and lasted an entire three seconds. When the icon disappeared, he quickly pulled himself up, but even then, his body was sluggish, as if it was still recovering from the hit he'd taken.

He scrambled to his feet and looked around. There were several other tendrils in the air, having sprung free of the ground. One of them had assailed Ice Block, while Aegis was already back on her feet, running from the one that had appeared near her. Her arms were held out, directed at Erica, who was actively drawing nearby vines up to create a tendril of her own to grapple with the one nearest to her. She even started to pull with it, as if to draw the hellion out of the ground, but her progress was slow.

"Help!" Todd called out.

Riley looked to Todd. He didn't see him

at first. Instead, he saw Shade punching and grabbing the nearby tendril that had attacked him.

Then, Riley spotted another tendril. It was curled, as if it was wrapped around something.

"It's got me!" Todd yelled, the sound coming from the direction of the tendril.

It was then that Riley realized that Todd had been grabbed and was being flung around by the tentacle.

Todd controlled the ground, drawing it up to smash into the visible tendrils, but when he managed to obstruct it partway, the tendril would throw him over to one of the nearby ones, which promptly grabbed him and squeezed. Riley could see Todd's health dropping in tiny increments.

Riley fired off a series of blasts, which smacked into the tendrils and singed them with hot energy. But even as he mounted what damage he could on the tendril that currently had Todd in its grasp, the tentacle would just throw him to another.

Riley had no idea if he was building up enough damage to actually harm the subterranean monster.

Spears of ice rushed through the air

and impaled the tendril that gripped Todd. But as Ice Block sought to subdue it, another one burst from the ground and took Todd.

"It keeps moving him!" Riley yelled. "Do we just keep attacking the tendrils?"

Aegis held her arms out and focused a shield on Todd. But every time he was thrown, the shield faded, causing her to have to re-adjust to shield him, which greatly diminished her ability to keep him protected from damage.

The tentacle curled down, as if it was about to release Todd, even though very little damage had been done to that appendage.

But instead of releasing Todd, the tendril sprung up and launched him into the air. "Ah! Guys, help!" he yelled, as he was hurled above the treetops.

"Don't let him fall!" Riley yelled, knowing the damage would be catastrophic from such a height. He knew that Todd didn't have anything to mitigate such damage.

"I've got him!" Erica shouted as she swung her arms around and drew a tangle of vines into the air. It stretched up quickly, rising five feet, ten feet, fifteen.

A stream of fire cut through the vines, tearing them in half and burning the stalk that had formed.

"No!" Erica shouted, as the flames tore away her lifeline to Todd.

Riley caught movement in the sky and spotted the gargoyle again. It swooped in and grabbed Todd with its talons and lifted him higher into the air, foot by foot.

"Help! I can't fight this thing!" Todd yelled from the sky, having no way to deal with an enemy that far from the ground.

"He's getting too high up! He won't survive that kind of fall!" Riley said as he looked around at their surroundings, trying to figure out who might be able to get to Todd.

Ava was still fighting with the lobster, having barely moved from melee range since she started. The two of them seemed to be trading blows. Ava would dodge, and the lobster would block, keeping their damages to a minimum and prolonging their fight.

"Ice, can you put down a bunch of snow?" asked Riley, looking to Ice Block, and hoping his abilities worked similarly to his guildmate 'Snow.'

"My powers don't work like that!" he said. "I can only do ice objects, not small ice particles. If he falls, I can't save him!"

"Aegis?" Riley looked to the shielding woman.

"I can try!" she replied as she directed her arms up, focusing on reaching out with her powers to protect Todd. A shield formed around him, but it didn't repel the talons that clutched his shoulders.

The gargoyle continued to rise, higher and higher. Riley was already doing some loose math in his head, knowing that each additional foot was adding damage that Todd would take upon landing.

Erica was surrounded by burning vines. "I can try again, if you can distract it!" she called, intent on saving Todd. She used her vines to coil up together, trying to construct a foundation of plant life that she could use to cushion Todd's fall and try and reach out to him again.

Riley managed to look over just in time, spotting two dark pumping fists heading for Erica. "Erica, look out!" He pointed to Shade.

Erica looked over to him, then quickly

spotted the oncoming PKer.

Riley fired his glove at Shade, trying to disrupt his attack, but the beams just smacked across the dark fists, not hitting Shade himself.

"I'll try to distract the gargoyle!" Ice Block called, seeing Riley engage Shade. He looked to the sky, only for his eyes to go wide. "He's falling!"

Riley glanced up and spotted the plummeting Todd, whose yells were just starting to reach them. "Erica!" Riley yelled.

Erica was caught between two situations. Shade had reached her and was swinging wildly with his dark fists. It was taking all her concentration to draw vines up to protect herself and strike out at him, just to keep up with the assault. She had heard Riley's call, and she knew that Todd was falling. She was the only one who could save him, but there was no way to do so with Shade fighting her so close.

Shade's fists swung and grabbed the vines, tearing them away. He hadn't managed to land a hit on Erica yet. Suddenly, a shield appeared around her body. As she noticed it, she was filled with anger. "Protect Todd!" she yelled, having some idea that Aegis was able to focus all her power on a single individual to amplify the effect.

Todd got ever closer to the ground, still falling from a great height.

Shade tore away Erica's vines and swung one of his large dark fists.

Before it could land, a figure smacked into Shade from the side.

"Get Todd!" Riley yelled, as he slammed into Shade and shoved his hand against the PKer's chest. He unloaded all ten charges of the glove into Shade's chest, causing bright flashes of light, even as he drove Shade to the ground.

Seeing her opportunity, Erica turned and looked to the sky, trying to find the yelling and falling Todd. He was still a hundred or so feet in the air, but he'd be on the ground in seconds. She reached out and drew vines from the ground. The vines stretched up at an angle, since she wasn't close to where he was going to hit the ground.

Then, her vision went black, and the world's sounds and sights faded from her.

"No!" she screamed, but the sound was trapped beneath the shadows that had encompassed her.

Riley was grabbed and thrown from Shade, only after all ten charges from his glove were expelled. He landed a dozen feet away, but quickly got to his feet. He risked a single glance to Erica, only to realize that she was encompassed in shadows. His eyes widened. He heard Todd's shouting, and then—

Thump.

Riley turned and saw Todd's body on the ground. The field around him shattered, as the damage of his fall was applied to the shield and then to him.

A moment after the shield broke, Todd's body burst into glittering dust.

A second later, he was gone.

CHAPTER 18: DEFEND

Riley stared in disbelief. Todd was gone. For a moment, the world seemed to stop around him, only to come crashing back down as dark fingers wrapped around him and squeezed. His moment's respite was gone, as Shade took advantage of Todd's death and went right back on the offensive.

Riley couldn't free his arms. The hand gripped him tighter. He glanced over, and saw Ice Block firing at Shade, but Shade's other hand was blocking the barrage of ice fragments coming at him.

The grip on his body didn't lessen, but it wasn't increasing either. Ice Block was buying him time to act.

Riley wasn't going to stand by and get killed.

Not when he had to avenge Todd.

All throughout the battle, Riley's spike had been sunk in the Lobster. The hellion didn't seem to be aware of the spike, or perhaps with his size and appendages, he wasn't able to remove it. So Riley pulled more essence through his right hand, and then turned his left one and powered up the glove.

With a fully loaded glove, he released blast after blast into the dark energy hand.

When Riley had fired at the hand before, he wasn't being grappled by it, it was merely protecting and shielding Shade. But now, he could actually see how much his beams were weakening the hand itself. The grip lessened and lessened, as if it was losing its strength with each blast.

Riley pushed and squirmed, and pried himself from Shade's grip. He continued to fire his glove, even as he was making his escape. The moment his glove ran out of power, he stole more essence and recharged it to continue his onslaught.

Shade was forced to defend on two sides, as he was now attacked by Riley, with his hand's stability no longer certain. The light-based beams were strong against his dark powers, even if they didn't disperse them like they had with Shadow Witch's abilities.

His hands became tight fists, blocking line of sight from the heroes he was assailing. But with their counter-attack, he wasn't able to go on the offensive, without making himself vulnerable.

With his attention so concentrated on

defending himself, he didn't see the gargoyle descending from the sky.

A jet of fire streaked down and buffeted Shade in full. He hadn't been aware enough to dodge, and the gargoyle was perfectly lined up to release the full potential of the attack down upon him.

The area around Shade erupted in flames. Panic set in instantly as his arms flew up to block the scorching flames. But the second he did this, he made himself vulnerable to the oncoming attacks of Riley and Ice Block. The ice only melted after impacting and causing the full force of its damage.

Riley's beams had no issue pelting Shade.

Regardless of Shade's items, there was nothing he could be wearing that could fully protect him from the beating he was getting.

Riley was also keenly aware of the Cloak of Concealments' stats. It was actually a severe detriment to a player's stamina, which prevented them from being able to fight at length in an engagement. It was an item meant for quick and sneaky fights, but not prolonged engagements, which this one had quickly become.

Shadows streaked across the ground and

quickly covered Shade. The nearby flames were causing the shadows to warble inconsistently, but despite this, the shadows moved with purpose, drawing Shade across the ground and toward the treeline.

Riley and Ice continued to attack, but Shade left their line of sight as he was drawn behind the surrounding trees.

"Dammit!" Riley yelled, still taking aim and firing at the trees, only managing to scorch the trunks of the dark wood.

"Forget him!" Ice Block called over.

"Where's Todd?" Erica asked as she rushed over.

"We couldn't save him," said Riley. "He's gone."

Erica already had a worried look on her face when she asked, but now that Riley had gone out and said it, she grit her teeth. "We… we have to get out of here!" she said, her voice shaky.

Riley remembered how hard his guildmate Chase's first in-game death had hit him, before he realized that Chase had no problem dying in-game because his finances weren't tied to it like Riley's were. But now, Riley felt a strange urgency behind Erica's words. She knew Todd intimately.

"Shade and Witch will flee," said Riley. "They won't stick around now, they have no healer. We have to—"

"Woo!" came a female voice from a short distance away. "Ain't so tough! Give me your loot!"

Riley and Erica looked over to where the blue lobster… had been. Dancing triumphantly was Ava.

"She killed it?" Riley muttered.

"We still have the aerial and ground one!" Ice called.

Riley looked into the sky and saw the gargoyle flapping away. He looked around for the tendrils, but realized that none of them were still visible. They were gone.

"Did we win?" Aegis asked, looking around as Ava came back to join them, after her victory over the lobster.

"We didn't win," said Ice Block, as the five of them slowly gathered around. "We lost Kevin and Roger." He then looked to Riley and Erica. "And they lost one of theirs. Todd?"

"Yeah," Riley murmured, looking back to Erica, who had a faraway expression.

"What were you all doing down here?" Riley asked. "What's going on?"

Aegis was the first to speak up in response. "A little while ago, the hellions in this lair started stealing our NPCs in the city. Several groups quickly formed up and came down here. I think a bunch of players were scared, and actually signed off with the threat of pain, and now abduction. We were a group of five, but we lost two members during one of the skirmishes in the forest. There's a group a bit…" She looked around, then pointed. "That way. They're leading the NPC evacuation. We were sent to go out and get NPCs out of pods and lead them back in groups. But we kept getting engaged with the hellions."

"What can we do to help?" asked Riley.

"We need to leave," said Erica. "I need to sign off."

Riley looked back to Erica, who was practically glaring at him now.

"Alright," said Riley. "But the quickest way to do that is join the evacuation that's… that way, you said?" Riley asked, as he pointed in the direction that Aegis had.

"Yeah, that's right," said Aegis. "We can lead you back there. Maybe some more heroes have come by to bolster our numbers. We've taken out some hellions, but there's more out there, along with the two that got away from us just now."

Riley nodded. "Let's go." He wasn't sure why Erica was so concerned with getting offline now. He figured it had something to do with Todd, but he could only speculate after that.

Aegis and her two friends led them through the forest. Riley couldn't stop thinking about the loss of Todd, and knew it was the only thing on Erica's mind as well. His absence would be sorely missed until he could find some new powers, or buy some. But luckily, with how the game had been updated, there would be plenty of avenues to pursue to get powers quickly. Even if they weren't entirely cheap.

The group went uncontended as they made their way through the dark trees and the unusual colors of their surroundings.

Before long, they saw a break in the treeline. It was then that Riley spotted small glimmering gems sporadically placed around the forest. Some were behind trees, others were laying in the grass, and a few were up in the branches. He had no idea what they were for, but he kept his distance nonetheless. They broke past the treeline and found themselves near a tall natural stone wall, much like the one that Todd had tunneled through to get them there originally.

Standing near the wall was a gathering of other players. Against the mountain wall was a blue glowing portal, which Riley recognized immediately. His eyes darted from figure to figure, and that was when he noticed a strange mirage… or a field, or something. As he got closer to the group of players, he recognized Parviz, Brenda, and Laura. Or at least 'one' of the Lauras, as there were several on the outskirts of the group, watching the treeline.

Laura was the first to notice them, as she was on guard duty. "Riley? Erica? How'd you get down here? Aegis, where are the others that were in your group?"

"We ran into some serious trouble while looking for NPCs," said Aegis. "We lost two of our friends, and then we met up with these guys."

"Hey Laura," said Riley. "We had no idea what was going on. I found Todd and Erica back at the bunker, and we knew something was wrong, so we started searching around."

"You must've left before I was able to

get a clone there," said Laura. "I've sent clones to some of the hotter grouping spots, but everything happened so quickly." Her gaze darted to each of the new arrivals, before she asked, "Where's Todd, then?"

Riley glanced to Erica, who still had a faraway expression. He sighed and looked back to Laura and explained as quickly as he could what had happened with Todd, Shadow, and Shade.

After learning of Todd's death, Laura's hands clenched into fists.

Almost immediately after Riley's explanation, Erica was quick to speak. "You're evacuating NPCs through the portal?" she asked urgently. "Does it go up to the city? Can I get back to Bunker 7 this way?"

Parviz pointed to the blue portal he had created against the stone wall. "Yeah, right over there, takes you to the middle of the city, it shouldn't be a far—"

Before Parviz could finish explaining, Erica was already darting off, running in a mad dash toward the portal.

"Where's she going?" asked a man who was standing nearby. "We need everyone for—"

"Don't worry about it," said Laura, who shot a glance over to the man that had spoken. "She has to leave. We'll be fine without her."

Riley was much closer to the strange mirage effect that he'd noticed earlier. As he looked over to it, he realized that it wasn't actually a mirage, but some sort of window effect on the ground. It was almost like a mirror made of vapor and glass, but none of it was physical. It was a few inches over the grass, and occasionally there would be glimpses of the cityscape above. Riley's brows lifted. "What's this?" he asked, pointing to the wispy glass mirror a short distance away.

"That's my 'be everywhere at once' trick," said Parviz. "You like it?"

Riley blinked a few times, looking over to Parviz. "I don't get it. You made it?"

Parviz nodded. "One of the hellions we beat dropped it." Parviz held up his hand and displayed a ring that looked strangely like an eye.

"What the hell is that?" Riley asked.

"It's an oculus ring," said Parviz. "We killed this monster with a third eye… and… well, I think I got its extra eye. But it lets me cast a far-sight effect, that lets me view things far away."

"Anywhere?" Riley asked.

"Anywhere I've been, and can already visualize," said Parviz. "So I can use it to set up way better portal systems, as long as I've already been there. My powers just got even better."

Riley looked to the portal, and then to the far-sight effect. "Is this how you got down here? Originally we had Todd with us, but how did you find the lair?"

"That was me," said the man nearby that had spoken up earlier about Erica leaving. He had platinum blonde hair as well as a white suit jacket and various pieces of jewelry. The jewelry was probably special items, and he also had a brooch on his jacket that looked like a cloud. "The name's Wisper."

Parviz gestured with his thumb. "This guy turns into mist and can go through porous stuff, like dirt, walls, and other things. But some surfaces slow him down. We were down in the tunnels, just as you said you were. But we encountered a few hellions, and beat them. That's when I got the eye. So then Wisper here has the idea to take me through the ground, cause he can encapsulate someone else in his mist and bring them with him. So we found this forest cave and ended up portaling the rest of the group down here. That's when I had the idea to use the oculus ring to get people out of here."

Riley looked to the forest, and then back to their group, noticing a few other people he didn't recognize. "How many have you saved? How many are there? There were tons of pods still back there."

"Not enough," said Laura. "Wisper scouted around and got a loose layout of the cave. It's just a giant circle, maybe a mile from center to edge, give or take. It's huge. Much bigger than the lair we found the other day. This place is a full-fledged nest, for what appears to be a decently sized hellion clan. We've had a number of heroes join up to help. I've got Carla, Chase, and Seth in a group. And a couple other groups of people I'm not too familiar with. But with Aegis's team having taken losses… and then Todd, well, I'm wondering if I shouldn't have bolstered the teams even more. These hellions are pretty strong."

"They're fighting for their home and guild," said Riley, crossing his arms. It was then that he noticed Brenda walking up from nearby, with her crossbow over her shoulder. She'd been on the far right perimeter when he and the others had approached. When their gazes met, she spoke up. "What sort of hellions did you fight out there?" she asked.

Riley thought for a minute. "Some subterranean thing with tentacles, a flying gargoyle, and we managed to kill a blue lobster. But we lost Todd."

"I managed to kill a blue lobster," said Ava from nearby, with crossed arms and a narrowed gaze at Riley.

Despite having just mentioned Todd, Riley couldn't help but smile a little at Ava's comment. "Right, the lobster was your kill. Have you met our friend Carla?" he asked, thinking they'd definitely get along… or clash terribly.

"Who?" Ava asked.

"Nevermind," said Riley, who then looked over to Laura again. "What's with the colored gems out there? The ones in the grass and on the trees. Not like, the people pods, but I noticed a bunch of coin-sized gems out there."

Laura pointed over to a guy who was lying against a three-foot high rock. He had his arms back with his hands on his head, seemingly content in the middle of enemy territory. "That's Gem. He makes gemstones that are different colors. Some explode, some are frost based, some are paralysis. None of them heal though. So he's placed all sorts of trap-gems out there. He can trigger them based on proximity or remotely, or timed. So… he's kind of slacking while we wait to be attacked."

"I heard that," the man named Gem called over.

Laura turned her head suddenly to the side. "Movement, left side," she called out loud enough for everyone in the vicinity to hear. Each of them turned their heads and looked in the direction she'd indicated.

Gem turned his head sluggishly. He had on a blue jacket that had a glittering liner inside of it. Around his neck was a necklace of all sorts of gems. On his wrists were multiple bangles with even more gems hanging off of them as well. Even his black hair seemed to strangely sparkle. "Hmm, probably shouldn't kill them," he murmured, when he noticed the cause of the commotion.

A multitude of differently clothed figures were running out from the treeline.

Laura had placed four separate clones of herself all spread out around them, between where they'd gathered their group of heroes, and the treeline. The nearest clone headed closer to the oncoming NPCs. "Get to the blue portal!" she instructed and pointed to the glowing portal on the stone wall. "Hurry! Hurry!" she called urgently, trying to get the easily hundred-strong group of NPCs to move quicker.

As the NPCs all dashed for the portal, four differently clothed players all congregated around Laura's clone.

Riley didn't recognize anyone from the group of four. He kept back as the NPCs all ran for safety. For all he knew, there were thousands of NPCs down in this place, all trapped for some nefarious purpose. Surely they could rescue some of them, but what about the ones they couldn't? What would happen to them? How would it harm the city economically, and how would it benefit the hellions?

"How many hellions have we killed so far?" asked Riley, looking to Parviz, as Laura seemed mostly distracted with speaking to the group that had just returned.

"Hmm… three in the tunnels," Parviz murmured. "Plus the one Ava killed."

"These guys killed four," said one of Laura's nearby clones.

"So, that's eight," said Parviz. "We fought three others earlier, but they ran. Then we had two try and mess with us a little after that, and we killed them both. So I guess we're at ten, unless the groups out there have taken care of any."

"Do we know how many there are?" Riley asked.

Parviz shook his head. "No idea. We had no clue this nest was even down here. I'm sure there's a bunch of nests we don't know about. There could be fifty hellions out there."

A few seconds later, Riley watched as Laura's clone stepped away from the group of four, who then turned right back around and headed into the forest.

"They're going after more?" asked Riley.

"Yeah, we have a lot of ground to cover," said Laura. "We have to protect a central portal location, and save groups of NPCs, without putting too many of them at risk. I have a feeling the hellions need whatever they're doing to complete, or complete as much as it can, since they're not just burning us out of their nest." Laura pulled a communication device from her pocket and queued up a number. She held it to her ear. "Beth? How're things going on your end? Lang just returned with his group."

Laura nodded and glanced over to the forest. "Alright, do your best. Keep an eye out, there could be some PKers in the area with shadow-based powers. It's unlikely they'll attack, just be aware." A few silent seconds passed. "Alright, see you then." Laura lowered the cell and glanced over to watch as Lang's group disappeared back into the forest. She promptly dialed another number and spoke again, "Seth, how's the search?" There was a pause, before Laura rolled her eyes. "That's too many for a group of your size, you're putting too many at risk, I said to keep things at twenty-five NPCs a person." Laura shook her head and placed her other hand on her hip. "Well tell Carla that it doesn't matter how many hellions she kills, if we don't save NPCs! Head back here immediately, stop searching, get those NPCs back here."

She then hung up and slid the device back into her pocket. "Ugh," she groaned, and glanced between Parviz and Riley. "Chase is able to send out those bots and quickly free NPCs from those pods, and Seth can lay energy net traps. And when you toss in Carla's ego for thinking she's a total badass, well… they've got about two hundred NPCs with them. Which is too many for three people to protect."

"Sounds like Carla," Riley murmured.

"Yeah," Laura groaned. "She was probably pushing Chase and Seth to free more so she could outdo the other groups, which all have more members."

"Should some of us go out and intercept them, to boost them up?" asked Riley, looking back out to the surrounding heroes.

"Hmm, maybe. How's your stamina looking?" Laura asked, looking over at Aegis.

Aegis had been speaking quietly with Ava and Ice Block, but when Laura spoke to her, she looked over. "Huh? Stamina? Um… let me check. It doesn't feel too low right now." She pulled up her status screen. "Yeah, it looks like I'm at about fifty percent stam, what about you two?" she asked Ice and Ava.

"I'm closing in on thirty-five," said Ice.

"I'm down at twenty," said Ava. "I had to put out a lot of power with that lobster. But I can eat something and recover some of it, if need be."

Aegis nodded and looked to Laura. "Should we eat?"

Laura rested her hands on her hips as she took account of all the surrounding heroes once more. "We need to hold this position, and we took some losses the last time you went out. I'm worried about those two hellions you fought. If they team up with some others, that could be pretty bad for us if we're not careful. We're spread a bit thin, and I feel like I'd only be compounding the risk by sending out a smaller group to intercept them. So let's stick here for now. The longer this goes on, the higher the chance of more hellions coming online. I'll switch out some group members when they get back, and we can send a stronger team out."

"Alright, we'll take a snack break then," said Aegis.

"Sounds good," said Laura, who then looked to Riley. "How're you doing? How's your health?"

Riley managed a half smile. "Uh… it could be better. I took some serious damage from that fight earlier, and only rejuvenated a small portion of my own health before Ava killed the lobster. So I guess I should eat something too."

"Do it," said Laura. "There's no telling what can happen down here. I don't want to lose anyone else."

"Wish I could pre-emptively boost everyone," said Riley, as he opened his inventory and took out a snack bar that would replenish his health a little.

Consumable items weren't exactly 'cheap' but the small financial burden was worth the risk, when it was making sure that he was preventing a possible death in case they were attacked.

"Yeah, none of our powers are perfect," Laura sighed. "I'm never able to output the damage Carla can. I can't heal either. I'm constantly losing clones, which hurts my total stam until I rest and eat. Each clone I lose lowers my stats. My biggest asset is being able to be in several places at once."

"Which is incredibly useful," said Riley. "How else would we be able to tell people about what's going on? Or keep a watch on things."

"Well, Chase can do the same thing, to an extent," said Laura. "But he has a bit more utility with those bots of his."

"Yeah, I suppose," said Riley. He took a few bites of his snack bar and chewed them in thought, before saying, "Have you thought about changing up the items your clones have? They make healing equipment, as well as other utility items, if you wanted to try something different."

Laura's lips quirked from side to side, seemingly thinking about that very notion. "Yeah… but if I do too many things, I'm not sure I'd be good at the roles I'm trying to do. A healing item will only be as strong as the stats going into it. And if we already have a healer, then it's a wasted clone. If I have a clone with a rope, or a net, or whatever, then if it never gets used, it's less damage I'm putting out."

Riley nodded. "I guess you're right. None of us are going to be amazing at every circumstance."

"Like real heroes from comic books and TV shows," said Parviz from nearby.

"Yeah, very true," said Riley in agreement. "We just have to do what we can, with what we have."

Parviz slowly smiled. "Well, with this new far-sight ring, I'm feeling pretty good about being able to—"

A terrible roar reverberated across the small clearing where all of them were gathered. Riley's eyes widened as he suddenly felt… less than himself. There was a strange new icon at the bottom of his vision. Everyone turned to the forest, but Riley was quick to check his status effects. "Our resistances are lower!" he shouted.

"Which ones?" Brenda yelled back, still having kept a short distance away as she readied her crossbow and aimed at the forest.

"All of them!" said Riley. "Mine are only at fifty percent! Everyone might've been affected differently though."

No one else was given a chance to check before a tall, multi-legged creature pushed past the tall trees and came through the canopy. At first, it resembled some sort of spider. Its legs were thin and a dark black, the ends of those feet sharp like spikes. Its body was a dark blue oval abdomen covered in tiny bristles. Its face was more like the beak of a squid than an actual spider. It was almost like some sort of squid-arachnid hybrid, with no apparent eyes.

"Why's it gotta be so tall!" Ava called out.

Its legs moved like pistons, smashing and stabbing into the dark dirt. If anyone was going to get into melee with it, it was likely that they might get impaled.

Riley caught a bit of movement in the trees, just to the left of the spider-squid.

"Something's in the trees!" Riley called.

But he was just a moment too late, as a jet of fire shot out from the treetops and scoured a line across the clearing they were in against the wall. It separated their ranks in half, leaving Laura, Riley, Gem, and Parviz on one side, while Aegis, Ava, Ice, Brenda, and Wisper were on the other.

At this point, Gem realized they were in some trouble, and stood up. He was a foot away from the burning flames that had streaked across the grass, but he seemed unfazed. "Screw you, buddy," he murmured and held up his hand. With a twitch of his fingers, he detonated a frost gem in the tree tops, close to where the hidden gargoyle was.

The gargoyle had been perched close to the small blue gem, which it hadn't noticed lodged in the other side of the tree. A burst of frost erupted around it, and flash froze the tree and branches, along with the gargoyle's left leg and wing, temporarily immobilizing it. But the gargoyle was quick to direct some localized flames to melt itself free.

The spider lumbered forward on quick-jabbing feet. It let out a screech and subsequent gunshot sound, similar to the roar earlier. A distortion of sound and air emanated from its beak, which was as small as a coffee cup, but as quick as a gunshot. It tore through the air and smacked right into Wisper, knocking him back a dozen feet.

Wisper lay on the ground unmoving for two whole seconds, before he got up. "That thing stuns!" he managed to say. "And hurts like hell!"

Ice Block quickly formed new spears of ice and hurled them at the spider, only to have a new burst of flames leave the gargoyle's mouth and melt the spears mid-air, as the flames were hitting them from the front.

Gem was quick to trigger several nearby gems, all on the ground around the spider's legs.

Multiple explosions buffeted the spider's thin legs, causing it to stumble to the side, almost falling over but managing to catch itself at the last second and fire off another sound blast.

The blast zoomed past them and decimated the rock he'd been resting against earlier.

Three red bolts smacked into the spider a moment later, and caused it to fall back against the trees, its legs a tangled mess.

"Time to kill something!" Brenda shouted as she took aim again.

She was about to pull the trigger when something dark suddenly obscured her vision.

She looked up from the crossbow and found herself staring into the red eyes of an entity that had deep blue-gray skin and a humanoid appearance. There was a series of short horns protruding from its hairless skull, creating a 'crown.' Its feet ended in talons, and its fingers looked just as sharp.

For a moment, she didn't act. She wasn't paralyzed by any sort of effect, but instead, she found herself too surprised by its sudden presence. In that split second of hesitation, the hellion struck with its fist, hitting her across the face and sending her reeling back. The force wasn't incredibly powerful, but it had been fast.

But it wasn't enough to put Brenda on the ground. She swung with her weighty crossbow and bashed the hellion across the face, reciprocating its attack.

The sharp-featured hellion started swinging and kicking, but Brenda matched it with deflections and attacks from her crossbow, using it as if it was a melee weapon. She was about to connect another heavy blow when the hellion suddenly disappeared.

The crossbow swung wide, leaving her wide-eyed as all she hit was air.

A moment later, she found herself no longer engaged with the monster. She turned her head from side to side, trying to find it. It was nowhere to be seen. She saw the battle with the gargoyle and spider continue to rage on, as the gargoyle kept up a rapid defense of the spider. She couldn't stand around idly forever, waiting for the weird humanoid hellion to reappear. She lifted the crossbow and took aim at the slowly recovering spider-like creature.

Just as she was pulling the trigger, something hit her from behind. She swung her weapon around, but as she did, all she managed to hit was more air. There was nothing behind her, despite the damage she'd taken. She reached back and swiped at her back to see if there was anything on her, but there was nothing.

"What the hell?" she yelled as the impacts on her back came to a stop.

She looked around quickly, but couldn't find her assailant. "Come out!" she shouted.

"Who are you yelling at?" Wisper grunted, as he was stumbling forward, still recovering from the hard hit the spider had dealt him.

"There's a hellion, it can teleport, or go invisible or something!" she growled.

"Somehow it's hitting me. I don't know!"

"Well, call out if you see it again," said Wisper as he brought his hands up and narrowed his sights on the gargoyle up in the tree. "A couple hellions shouldn't be giving us this much trouble."

His vision suddenly became obscured. He glanced up, trying to figure out what the dark form in front of him was.

"Not so fast," came a hiss from in front of him.

Before he could react, his outstretched arms were grabbed, and he was flung onto his back. He landed hard, wincing from the impact. "Ugh," he groaned.

As he looked up to see his assailant, it was nowhere to be seen and the ground seemed to be shaking beneath him.

He pulled himself up, only for two tall tendrils to burst from the ground on either side of him. His face and body were pelted with bits of dirt and debris. Then, the tentacles came smashing down around him, smacking him to the ground. They constricted tightly and kept him from moving.

But everyone was having the same problem.

Tendrils were striking up through the ground and flailing about at all the nearby hero players. There were several on each side of the flames, not counting the two that seized Wisper.

Wisper was a little sluggish from all the hits he'd taken, but he finally managed to act. In an instant, his body turned entirely into vapor. The tendrils sunk through the no-longer physical form of Wisper. His wisp-body turned, and he sunk into the ground.

Across the area, Riley had already sunk his spike into the soft and furred central body of the spider, since it was the most vulnerable. He wasn't sure how strong it was in comparison to the gargoyle, but he just needed an easy target to work with, so he could start helping those around him. He couldn't get a proper angle on his hero companions, so it took him two helpings of essence in order to get them all, and then another to power up his glove. He wasted no time in attacking the gargoyle as quickly as he could.

But the tendril hellion had other things in mind.

The subterranean hellion's appendages appeared all around them, but there didn't seem to be enough for 'everyone' as Laura's clones, and herself, were left alone.

Riley found himself firing at the tendrils of the hellion, trying to mount as much damage as he could in order to drive it back underground. It seemed as though the hellions they'd fought earlier had regrouped with a few friends. Brenda was yelling about some sort of disappearing hellion, and the spider was definitely new.

For a moment, Riley froze mid-shot. He turned his head, looking to Brenda. Wisper was gone at this point, but Riley remembered that singular attribute about the hellion in that nest they'd found the other day. He watched and waited to see if it would show up again, but it wasn't forthcoming and he didn't want to spend too much time waiting for it. Could it really teleport around at will? Was it displaying any other powers? What if it was really fast and could move with incredible speed for short amounts of time when it wanted to?

Laura's copies closed in on the nearest tendrils, hacking and slicing at them with their respective swords and axes.

Gem was throwing his premade rocks at the tendril next to him, causing it to freeze, but a blast of flame from the gargoyle in the treetops quickly melted it free, probably causing very little damage to the hellion itself. "Dammit, forgot about that one," he growled. "Someone take out that gargoyle!"

"Guys, I'm useless while my portals are active! Do I keep them open?" asked Parviz.

"Seth's group will be back really soon. Let's keep it open for now!" Laura called back, as she aimed down the iron sights of her revolver, and let loose individual shots into the treetop that the gargoyle was hiding out in.

Apparently, the revolver fire was the last straw, as the gargoyle leapt from its partially-hidden spot in the canopy to fly up into the "sky."

Riley already knew that he couldn't easily hit the gargoyle, even if his attacks would probably cause it the most damage.

The spider had righted itself, given a reprieve in the commotion of the subterranean hellion's arrival. It fired off a jet of sound at Parviz.

Parviz saw it coming, but there wasn't much he could do. He was about to dodge when he saw a green glow appear around him. The sound-shot smacked into the shield, and shattered it in an instant, but no damage came through to harm him directly. Luckily, the shield had absorbed it all. "Thanks!" he called out, as he then took the time to run for whatever cover he could behind some large stones.

Ice went back on aerial duty, launching bursts of ice into the sky.

Brenda set her focus on the spider, launching bolts at it when she could, while keeping a close eye on her surroundings.

Riley wished he'd been given more time to eat. The duration of his 'meal' was ten minutes to fully heal himself. When they'd been assailed by the roar, it counted as being attacked, and the effect was broken. He was only brought up to seventy-two percent health.

"I've got a lot of movement on the far right!" Laura yelled.

Most of the gathered players were too busy with the current hellions to worry about any new arrivals. Aegis was doing her best to keep shields up. Wisper was nowhere to be found. Ava was trying to find a way around the flames to get to the spider.

From where Riley was facing the forest, he could see the movement Laura had mentioned. He looked over and spotted numerous dark figures moving through the trees.

"I think they're our NPCs!" Riley called back.

Several seconds later, the first figures broke from the treeline, dashing towards the gathered heroes.

Riley had seen how the NPCs from Lang's group had moved. This group… was entirely different.

Their fingers were gnarled and swiping forward as they ran, as if they were trying to climb through the very air and space they were propelling themselves toward. Their jaws hung low, their mouths agape. They ran faster than the NPCs Riley had seen earlier.

"There's something wrong with the NPCs!" Riley yelled, taking aim at the horde.

The mass of NPCs continued to pour from the treeline.

Laura's nearest clone turned and pointed to the portal. "Get to the portal!" she said, but she only then heard Riley's comment, realizing he was right.

The NPCs weren't moving toward the portal. They were moving towards all of them.

It didn't take long for Laura's closest

copy to get mauled, even as she swung her sword, trying to cut down the nearest ones.

Riley started firing, aiming for their heads for maximum damage.

Parviz stared with wide eyes as the NPCs flooded towards them. "Are those… zombies?"

CHAPTER 19: SURROUNDED

Riley's beams tore and burned into the torsos of the encroaching horde. As they neared, it was becoming easier to discern the pock-marked skin and the gray-blue areas of their flesh. These NPCs were somehow diseased.

But Riley had an idea. It was probably a waste of time, but he had to try. He'd tried this before, on the first occasion that they'd dealt with player-made zombies, but maybe this was a different circumstance. He drained a new charge of essence from the spider, which still seemed concerned on hunting Parviz down.

With that essence, he fired a flash at the oncoming zombies, just like he would if he was trying to heal nearby friends.

The flash of energy suddenly buffed each of the zombies, giving them a damage boost, since they were currently classified as damage dealers.

Unfortunately, despite being 'healed' and affected by the attribute-cleansing effect of his belt, the zombies were undisturbed, and continued to run for them.

Only now, they were buffed for increased damage output.

"Crap, I didn't just…" Riley murmured.

"Did you just buff all of them?" Laura yelled. "What the hell?"

"I'm sorry! I thought I could reverse the zombie effect!" Riley defended himself.

"You're barely a healer!" Laura replied. "You're a support class, not a healer! You can't eliminate effects that strong!"

"Well now I know!" Riley shot back, frustrated that he was getting chewed out by Laura, despite already knowing that he'd screwed up.

Parviz dashed around the area, as the spider kept up its relentless assault on him. It seemed as though the hellions had some idea that he was their way out, or at least, the way out for the NPCs.

"Parviz," said Riley. "Do your portal thing on these zombies! I think they're from Seth's group, so we won't need the portal right now!"

"Sounds good to me," said Parviz, mostly to himself. "Someone deal with that spider!" he called out more loudly. He lifted his hands and reformed the red portal at the ground, making it as large as he possibly could—which was around a hundred feet in diameter. Then, he threw a blue portal into the sky. Or at least, the ceiling of the cave they were in, since there wasn't actually a sky.

He'd positioned the portal so that it appeared directly in front of the zombies at the front of the group. The zombie-NPCs weren't very intelligent. Regular NPCs had base-level artificial intelligence. Without that, when they were only in zombie attack mode, even basic instincts and logic were removed from their minds.

The zombies plummeted into the portal by the dozens. Some of the ones on the outer edges managed to get around it, but they were easily picked off by Riley's beams.

Gem was able to trigger several explosions to help corral the zombies into a narrower column, driving them into the red portal.

There was roughly one hundred or so feet between where the zombies were coming from, and where the spider continued to lumber about.

From that area, three figures emerged.

"Guys! There's… oh, you found out!" Seth called, as he led Carla and the cyberized Chase from the treeline, only to have dozens of zombies on their left, and a giant spider on their right.

Seth quickly surveyed the situation. "Carla, focus on—"

"Don't tell me what to do!" Carla huffed, and headed right past him, towards the main group. But she didn't get far before she started flinging her famous lotuses to explode against the tendrils that had poked up from the ground.

Seth looked to Chase. "Chase, go ahead and—"

"I'm on it," Chase said, not nearly as short with Seth as Carla was, but also not waiting to hear him out. There were four basketball sized spider-bots around him. They rushed forward, each one having a quick-firing assault turret configuration, which let them unload on the nearby giant spider.

"Alright, alright, everyone's busy," said Seth, who looked around for something to attack. He noticed that the zombies were all flowing down into a portal.

"Don't get too close to the spider!" Parviz yelled.

Seth looked to Parviz, then to the spider. He could see the spider's legs were very deadly in appearance. But a few moments later, he realized why he was told not to get closer.

Body after body fell from the sky. They smacked and splatted against the ground. Some of them hit the large spider, sending it down to the ground from the repeated impacts.

With each landing, the zombies caused falling damage to whatever they hit and then promptly dispersed into particles and gore.

Seth backed up and veered off to the side to take a slightly longer angle around, to get to the main group. He spotted Brenda on the other side of the flames. She seemed to be swinging at something, but then, in the blink of an eye, whatever she was attacking disappeared.

The gargoyle dove and blasted the area with flames, as if it was trying to disrupt the gathered player's cohesion.

From Riley's vantage, the damage on the spider-hellion seemed to be mounting. How much health could it possibly have? It was large and had a strong attack and appendages that looked as if they could cause serious damage. It wasn't armored like the lobster. Surely it was ready to fall?

"I need healing!" Parviz called.

Riley directed his attention to Parviz, trying to keep his distance from the tendrils. He drew out more essence, and shot a replenishing helping of it toward the portal maker, causing several others in his line of sight to heal as well. But the healing was still minimal. Laura was right, he wasn't a healer, and everyone was taking a lot of damage from the hellions.

"Brenda, can you get any heals out? Carla? What about you?" Riley called.

"Busy blowing stuff the hell up!" Carla shouted back, as if it was an absurd question.

Riley had trouble seeing Brenda through the various flames that separated them.

"There's a hellion that keeps disappearing and attacking me!" she replied. "I need help over here!"

A sharp cracking of wood sounded from nearby.

Riley turned his head and looked to the dark wooded trees with their thick canopies.

A creature emerged from the forest. A hanging, drooling maw, with teeth the size of Riley's fingers, and rows of them stretching several feet wide. Its features were angular, and its skin was made up of the same blue-gray that everything else seemed to be made up of. Its carapace was made of what looked to be a thick leather hide with tiny blue bristles. It was so large that it had trouble working its way through the trees and had to push them over or aside, in order to get into the clearing.

The strength it would've taken to have simply toppled a tree as easily as it was doing must've been immense.

Its bulky torso strode into the

clearing on two thick arms and legs. It moved like some sort of feline, or wolf. But it had a strange appearance that made it seem like it could walk on its hind legs alone.

In Riley's mind, it looked like a combination between some sort of abomination of a rhinoceros, and the agile features of a big cat.

"I got this one!" Ava shouted, as she diverted toward the new hellion. It took her only a short time to cross the distance toward it. Its two beady eyes found her as she neared.

Ava's boots arced with electricity as she rushed toward it.

The rhino-like hellion didn't give her a chance to close the distance entirely before it leapt into the air.

It moved quicker than Riley could've anticipated, but he managed to yell, "Ava needs help!" just as the hellion assailed her with its massive, boulder-sized claws.

Ava was quick to act, jumping into a sharp upward kick, but the hellion's head smacked her aside as its claws ripped into the ground.

Ava was knocked back, stumbling from

the sudden impact.

The hellion's maw opened, showing off those glistening teeth as it went to chomp her.

A beam cut through the air and hit inside the monster's mouth, giving it a sudden pause, just long enough for Ava to dodge and run around the hellion.

Another beam ripped out of Riley's glove, and another and another.

The hellion's maw closed shut and the beams singed its hide, but the monster seemed unfazed by the attacks.

Riley didn't like what he was seeing. He had a feeling that this creature was going to give Ava a lot of trouble, and they were going to need more help against it.

A quick glance across the battlefield showed him that each of the paragons around him was having trouble.

Wisper finally revealed himself again, flying out of the dirt only to become physical again and stumble, clutching his arm. "I couldn't take the underground one! It's got this weird energy… It's tough!"

"This disappearing hellion is screwing us up something bad!" Aegis called, as she was on the same side of the aerial hellion’s flames, along with Brenda and Ice. Riley and Ava were out towards the edge of the flames, mostly engaging the new arrival.

Carla and Chase were engaged with both the spider and the subterranean hellion.

Seth was repositioning, dealing with the zombie stragglers that weren't going into the portal.

Laura's clones were stretched thin. She'd lost several and had very few around, along with whichever ones she'd sent through the portal to warn other hero-players about what was going on.

Parviz was constantly assailed by shots from the gargoyle and the spider, while Gem did what he could to freeze and explode his rocks, in any direction that he could throw them.

"More movement, hard right!" Laura shouted.

Riley was one of the few people around to notice.

It didn't take more than a few seconds of looking at the treeline to realize what was coming.

"More zombies!" Riley yelled.

A soft beeping sounded, almost entirely muted by the sound of battle all around them. Laura pulled her cell up to her ear and quickly answered it.

"What's going on?" she asked.

She was silent as she listened.

"Alright," she said, "do what you can, but if you have to—"

Her words were cut short as something slammed into the ground nearby with a resounding *thump*. A gust of air blew across everyone, and even slightly abated some of the nearby flames.

She turned, her eyes wide. A several-foot wide and deep crater had extinguished the flames around it. A light gust of air brushed across her body a moment later. She was maybe thirty or forty feet from the impact, staring at the monstrosity standing in the crater's center.

Unlike the hellions they'd encountered thus far in the cavern, this one seemed entirely comprised of pale white bones. Two glimmering purple eyes rested in a sharp and slanted bovine skull, with two horns jutting from the sides. The skull was similar to an actual bovine's, but its body was anything but. As if connected by some sort of unseen force, a dozen spines undulated beneath it, as if it was some sort of weird cow-skull octopus made of bone spines.

It pulled itself up and hovered just a foot into the air. With minimal movement of its skull, it took in the scene around it. Then, without warning, one of the spines whipped up, displaying the pointed fang-like end of its bone-tendril. The almost spike-like bone shot across the air and lodged into the spider hellion that had been taking so much damage.

The spider screamed, but didn't unleash any sort of detrimental effect. Instead of affecting those around it, its body suddenly changed and shifted. Its furred central body became plated with white bone, jutting out all around it, armoring itself. Its narrow legs followed suit, becoming thicker, more durable.

Carla's red lotuses were still exploding against it, but now, the armored spider didn't seem to be backing away. Instead, it leapt through the air and assaulted Chase and Carla directly, smashing its sharp feet down and stabbing rapidly.

"This thing has to die! It's going to buff them!" Laura shouted.

Riley was already all too aware of the new hellion’s arrival. Its ability to buff the spider hadn't been lost on him. He pulled his glove up and was about to fire, but he found himself out of charge. He attempted to draw more essence, but none was forthcoming. He looked over and saw his spike lying uselessly on the ground. He quickly drew it back to his palm, so he could find a new target.

In that time, the bovine-skulled hellion threw another spike. This one caught one of the tentacles jutting from the ground.

In seconds, each of the subterranean tendrils evolved, gaining bone-armor and increased sharpness and toughness. They moved more slowly, but were stronger as they smacked around the area.

The next bone-spike pierced the air like a bullet.

The previously vulnerable gargoyle increased to two times its normal size. Its body was now more easily assailed by Ice Block's attacks, but the small pellets weren't having nearly the damaging effect that they once were.

"This is bad!" Ice Block yelled.

One by one, each of the gathered hellions gained the properties of the skulled hellion, before anyone could mount an attack against it.

"We have to get out of here!" Riley yelled. "We can't deal with this without help!"

"Help's not coming!" Laura yelled. "The other groups are making their own way out, and all the freed NPCs are zombies now! It's just us!"

There was nothing but chaos all around, as each of the surrounding hero-players was engaged with hellions that were now armored.

Riley looked to Parviz. He was their only escape. "Parviz, portal us out of here! Get us back to the city!"

Parviz had taken a small amount of cover near some rocks. He glanced to Riley and immediately followed the instruction. The portals he'd created disappeared. Instead, a new red one appeared a short distance away from him, while he set up a blue one in Gargantuan City, using the far-sight item he had. "Portal's up! Everyone retreat!"

"I'll try to cover us!" Laura said as she drew in her few remaining copies, having them engage the all-too powerful hellions.

Without delay, the gathered paragons all disengaged from the hellions they'd been fighting. Brenda, Ice, and Aegis all risked running through the flames to get to the portal. Chase ran for the portal, but used his two remaining bots to distract the armored spider. Ava was still exchanging blows with the rhino-feline hellion, but when two of Laura's copies came in close, she immediately turned and ran.

Parviz was the first to get through the portal, because if he went down, their escape would be lost. Seth threw his electrified nets out to slow any advance from the larger hellions, before rushing into the portal along with Gem and Wisper.

One by one, the rest of the heroes fled into the portal, even as they were assailed by the ranged attacks from the spider and aerial hellion.

It wasn't long before Laura, Carla, and Riley were the last ones around.

Everything was happening in the span of seconds. It just so happened that Carla and Riley were the farthest from the portal. For Carla, she was still tossing lotuses, while Riley was doing his best to dodge the tendrils and fire-breathing gargoyle.

"Hurry it up!" Laura called, as she jumped into the portal a moment later.

Carla was about ten feet ahead of

Riley. They both closed in on the portal, only for Carla to throw some more lotuses out to help cover Riley, just as she herself went through the portal.

Riley rushed to the circular red-glowing area. He leapt into the air, knowing he was about to have that terrible sick feeling from going through a portal, but he'd take it if it meant getting away from the hellions.

His vision flashed red as pain streaked through his body, coming from his back. He was caught mid-air by something. He found himself dangling just a foot above the portal.

His body turned, but not of his own volition.

He found himself face-to-face with the bovine-skulled hellion.

A terrible raking voice sounded from the hellion player's skull, even though no mouth moved. "You've disrupted our plans, but we'll settle the score by ending a few of you. I hope you weren't too attached to this character."

A strange sensation flowed over Riley's form. He was able to lift his hands, and saw that his skin was shifting and hardening, like bone.

The hellion's voice sounded again. "Don't worry, the armor-buff my limbs provide won't keep us from killing you. You'll be able to make a new character soon, but first… we're going to have a little fun with the pain feature, just because you messed with our—"

In the lower peripherals of Riley's vision, he noticed the sudden absence of red, as Parviz's portal diminished behind him.

Then, there was a strange mirage flicker around him. The red glow returned, and he felt himself falling along with the bovine-skulled hellion.

The cave vanished from his vision, along with everything else, as he blacked out.

CHAPTER 20:
UNEXPECTED CONSEQUENCE

Riley's eyes opened. But it wasn't the game world that welcomed him. Instead, he found himself staring into his visor. He pulled it off and turned his head, looking around his apartment. His head was spinning, and it was difficult to focus. Everything slowly began to clear up and for a brief moment, he didn't understand what was going on. Shouldn't he be in the game? What happened?

It was that strange feeling, much like if you'd just watched a TV show, but it broke to commercial and you couldn't remember what you were watching. But then he did. He'd been seized by that bovine-skulled hellion, but then he'd fallen through… one of Parviz's portals?

If that was true, then he was still vulnerable in the game. He wasn't sure what had caused the disconnect, but he had to log back in and make sure he wasn't dead.

He quickly restarted the visor and laid back down. He had a mild desire to use the bathroom, but he hadn't drank *too* much earlier, so he could surely hold it for a bit longer. He had to find out if his character was in danger. Or worse, dead.

The countdown in the visor reached zero, and an instant later, the world around him went dark again as his mind was pulled into the game.

Sounds assaulted his ears before his eyes could even open. The drone of nearby vehicles, glass shattering in the distance, along with dull thumps, which could've been explosions, or even buildings crumbling.

When his eyes opened, he found himself looking up at the blue sky of Sigil Online. He leaned up slowly.

"You're back!" came Laura's familiar voice.

Riley turned his head, spotting her standing nearby. She was accompanied by Parviz, Carla, and Chase.

"What happened?" Riley asked.

"Uh…" Laura murmured. "What do you remember?"

"That tentacle bone-skull thing. It impaled me in the back, and kept me from getting into the portal," he replied. "But then… I fell." He looked to Parviz. "You recreated the portal beneath me, didn't you? You used your far-sight to see back into the cave?"

Parviz nodded. "Yeah. Carla said you were right behind her. Seconds were ticking by and Laura thought something might've stopped you."

"Where's the cow-skull hellion?" Riley asked. "Didn't it fall through with me? Did you kill it?"

"You were the only thing that came through Parviz's portal," Carla said, her arms crossed against her chest. "And that was a solid hour ago. We've been watching your damn body ever since."

"An hour?" Riley asked, looking to each of their faces, as if it was some sort of joke.

"Yeah," said Chase. "That hellion must've kept itself out of the portal somehow. Of course, once you were through, Parviz immediately closed it. We were a bit confused and worried when we saw you all… well, your body had gotten a little bit of that bone-armor, just like what it was buffing the other hellions with. You looked kinda hellion-like at the time. But it wore off and disintegrated about ten or so minutes after you came through the portal. Do you have any debilitating effects?"

Riley brought his hand up and gestured to create his status screen. "I must've gotten disconnected or something, and then blacked out… I don't know," he murmured, trying to explain the weird hour difference. "But…" he trailed off as he looked at his status screen. "Yeah, everything looks normal. No debuffs or anything," he said. But then he noticed his hand. He could see it. Where was his glove? He turned his hand and checked himself over. He was missing his left-handed glove as well. But not only that, the slits at the center of his hands were now gone. The sigil tattoo on his palm was still there, but the slit was nowhere to be seen.

"What happened to my gloves?"

"Did you take them off? We can't remove your gear," said Laura.

"I didn't," Riley said, "and I know… I just… they aren't here. What the heck is going on with my character?"

As he studied his palms, something registered in the back of his mind. He quickly motioned to bring his status screen back up. He'd only checked to see if there was something weird with his status effects, such as a debilitating effect. He hadn't checked anything else. He quickly perused every detail of the status screen.

-

Relinquisher

Level: 72

Tier: Three

Status: Healthy

Hit points: 38%

Buffs: / Debuffs:

Stats: (+15)

Power: 15

Constitution: 25

Toughness: 25

Mind: 10

Stamina: 22

Dexterity: 26

Luck: 5

-

"No way," Riley muttered. His eyes stared at the line of text that read 'Tier: Three.' His eyebrows lifted. He was in disbelief. Shouldn't something cool have happened? Like when he glowed and became tier-two? Or had something happened, but he'd blacked out and missed it?

"What? What's wrong?" Laura asked.

Riley's mind was in overdrive. Some of his items were gone and now he was tier-three? But how? He didn't answer Laura right away. He quickly switched the holographic tab to his inventory. Most of his consumable items were still there. But the item he was most curious about was gone. The sphere that Aaron had given him was missing. He looked at his gear slots and saw that it was only the two gloves that were missing as well. So somehow, he'd gained tier-three and lost the tier-three sphere, along with the two gloves he'd been equipped with.

"Riley!" Laura spoke up louder. "What are you staring at? What's going on?"

Riley finally looked up from his status screen. "I'm… I… I hit tier-three!"

"What!" Carla gasped. "You're kidding me? How the hell did you do that?"

Riley shook his head. "I have no idea, but it says it right here."

"I didn't know tier-three was in the game," said Chase. "Are you sure you're reading it right?"

Riley nodded. "It says it right here, I swear. I'm missing some items, but… somehow I hit tier-three."

"Well, you didn't glow or anything cool when you came out of the portal," Laura murmured, tapping her chin.

"I don't know. Maybe…maybe there isn't anything that happens when you get to tier-three?" he said, unsure of just about everything at this point. "I imagine the game might've done something or showed me something when I hit tier-three, but I blacked out and must've missed it. I haven't heard about anything like this before."

Of course, that wasn't entirely the truth. He knew about tier-three because Aaron had told him about it, and had also given him that tier-three sphere to use in an emergency. A little secret that he'd failed to divulge to the rest of them, despite the fact that he considered them his friends. Perhaps he shouldn't have given Aaron so much crap over his secret, when he was harboring his own now.

Now that no one was pestering him with questions he didn't have answers to, he finally took account of his surroundings. They were on the roof of some building. It wasn't too high up, since there were much taller buildings around them. It was roughly four or five stories, at most.

"How far are we from the bunker?" Riley asked, as he gradually moved to stand.

"Just a block away," said Parviz, who was still watching Riley as if he might spontaneously combust, or something.

"So like, do you have any new powers?" Carla asked.

Riley blinked, then looked back down at his hands. "Uh…" he murmured, as he remembered that his hands no longer had the slits in them, which was how his powers had worked before. He turned away from his friends and held his right arm out. He tried to think about his powers, about activating them or triggering them in some way. But nothing happened. He also didn't have that strange in-game sense that he *could* do anything. When he threw his spikes around before, he'd had a notion in the back of his mind that he was able to do it. But now, he had no inclinations whatsoever.

He turned and looked at Parviz. "Let me touch you," he said, as he reached out with his right hand.

"Huh?" Parviz asked as he noticeably tensed up when Riley placed his hand on his shoulder.

The moment Riley's hand rested on Parviz's shoulder, the tattoo on Riley's hand glowed a dull white.

Parviz's eyes followed what Riley had done. "What… what does that mean? Why is your hand glowing? What did you do?"

"I'm not sure," said Riley. "Does it hurt?"

"I didn't feel anything happen," said Parviz.

"Hmm, let me check my stats," said

Riley, as he removed his hand with the softly glowing tattoo. He brought up his status screen and checked it over.

"I'll do the same." Parviz then brought up his stats as well. "Hmm," he murmured. "I don't see anything unusual. How about you?"

Riley scanned the lines and noticed that his max stamina had been reduced by twenty percent. There was also a buff that simply had a blank portrait icon, and the name 'Parviz' above it. "Whatever it is, it's using twenty percent of my stamina," Riley murmured. "Let me check something." He reached out and touched Parviz again, but nothing happened. "Hmm, doesn't deactivate that way… so let me try thinking about it." Riley concentrated. After a brief moment of wanting the effect to stop, it did. The glow on his hand faded and his max stamina returned to normal. It was under half from the fight earlier, but losing twenty percent of the maximum wasn't actually affecting what he currently had.

Riley quirked his lips to the side. "Let me try something." He reached back out with his left hand and touched Parviz's arm, but he didn't think about attempting to activate his powers. This time, nothing happened. He then touched Parviz's arm one more time with his left hand, and thought about his powers, whatever they may be. When his hand made contact, the tattoo on his left palm glowed a soft white.

"So it's a mental trigger," Riley mused. "But what does the glow mean?"

"Maybe your character is bugged?" Chase asked.

"Maybe," Riley half-agreed. He looked over to Laura. "Touch my hand, just for a few seconds."

Laura shrugged. "Alright," she said, and reached out to set her hand on top of Riley's.

Riley didn't try to empower Laura when they made contact. But after a couple seconds of Laura's hand resting on his, he made a mental effort to empower or activate his powers on her.

This time, his right hand's tattoo lit up as well, while the other was still glowing.

Riley brought both his hands up and looked between them.

"So, what's it mean?" Laura asked, as she then brought up her stat page to see if anything had changed. "I'm not seeing anything."

"Hmm," Riley murmured. He looked around and noticed one of Chase's spider bots sitting beside him. It had a turret configuration, ready to fire on any hostiles that might come near.

Riley looked to Parviz, and then to Laura. Then, he got an idea.

In the blink of an eye, a clone of Riley separated from himself. Then, he created another.

"What the hell!" Carla yelled, as suddenly three versions of Riley were standing amongst the group.

"You… you have my powers now?" Laura asked with wide eyes.

Riley felt a rush of potential inside him. He looked at Laura, then to his two copies. He made an effort to assume direct control over one of them, and in an instant, his vision flipped to one of the copies. He lifted his arms and looked down at them as he turned his arms and hands. "Woah," he whispered.

"But if you just took Laura's powers," said Chase. "Does that mean—"

Without giving Chase a moment to even finish his sentence, Riley aimed his right hand away from them. With a mere thought, a red portal opened. Then, he lifted his left hand, and created a blue one twenty feet away from it.

"You have both of our powers?" Parviz yelled.

Despite having just done it himself, Riley could only stand there in disbelief as Chase, Carla, Parviz, and Laura all started talking at once. He couldn't keep track of what they were saying. All he could do was stare at the portals he'd just made, through the eyes of a copy of himself that he'd just created.

His mouth was hanging open. The possibilities stretched endlessly before him.

"Can you take anyone's powers?" asked Chase.

"How many can you steal at once?" Laura questioned.

"Don't even think about stealing my lotuses!" Carla quipped.

"Stop talking!" Riley yelled. "Just… give me a second here, this… this is a lot to take in." Riley brought his hands up to his head as he took a couple steps back, just staring at the things he'd created. "Let me check something," he said, as he looked at his status screen again.

Taking Parviz's powers had used twenty percent of his maximum stamina. Doing the same for Laura had taken another twenty percent. The two copies took five percent each, and the two portals also took ten percent each. He was currently at thirty percent stamina. "Do your portals normally take ten percent stam?" Riley asked. He then looked to Laura. "And do your clones take five percent?"

Laura shook her head. "My clones take one percent, but if I make too many, they don't have enough stats to last very long."

"My portals only take five percent of my stamina," said Parviz. "If I dispel one of them, four percent of the stamina is slowly rejuvenated over a minute. So I can't just keep rapid-firing portals."

"So I definitely have harder limits then," Riley said. "I can take your powers, but it's harder on my stamina."

"There's items out there that’ll boost your max stamina," said Chase. "Items, temporary food buffs, and all sorts of things."

"Yeah, you're right." Riley nodded. "This kind of changes my entire outlook on what my character can do."

"I bet you can even steal a hellion's powers," said Laura. "That'll be pretty cool."

"Yeah, I could've used that when we—" Riley stopped mid-sentence as he remembered everything that had 'just' happened in the hellion lair, despite it being over an hour ago for everyone else. He quickly looked to Laura. "We lost Todd," he said. Laura already knew it, but it was now becoming a reality all over again to him. "We're going to be down a paragon for a while, until he can get some powers. He'll probably have to do what Seth did. Did... everyone else make it out? Where's Seth, Brenda, and the others? What's going on with the city?"

His four friends all exchanged looks before looking back to him. Laura was the first one to speak up. "You know that economic report that gets released every hour, and can be found on the billboards?"

Riley nodded. He hadn't used a billboard in a while, since most of the quests were meant for solo or low-level players.

"Well, the last report had Gargantuan City at a steep decline, due to all the NPCs that were stolen, many of which were killed. We saved a bunch, but due to the loss, the NPCs that are left are now on a heightened alert status, which means that they won't go about their business like they usually do. They'll be more reserved and stay inside, or go out only sporadically and during the day."

"So, our NPC services are gonna be screwed up for a week or so?" Riley asked.

Laura nodded. "Yeah, roughly. The city won't be populating as many quests on the billboard, and the ones that are available won't pay too great. NPC workers and guards are going to be incredibly expensive to hire, as the demand will exceed the supply, depending on how many players are still trying to hire them. We took a serious hit with their abduction. We still don't even know what they were doing with our NPCs."

"They were turning them into zombies," Parviz spoke up. "I thought that much was evident?"

"They were sticking them in those pods," said Riley, remembering what he'd seen when he first arrived in the cave. "It was only when we… or you guys were saving them that the whole zombie thing started. At least, that's what it looked like. Whichever hellion turns NPCs into zombies must be a part of their clan. And when we started saving them, they must've decided that zombie NPCs were better than letting them get away."

Riley paused, thinking back to the things he'd seen down in the cave. "There was some weird-looking fruit on some of the trees. Did anyone try and grab any?"

Laura shook her head. "No, I saw it as well, but we were busy trying to save the NPCs."

"I didn't think to grab any either," Chase murmured.

"So, they stole a bunch of our NPCs and tried turning them into fruit?" Carla asked, with a bit of skepticism. "So what's the plan now? We regrouping and heading back down there? As much as I hate Riley being tier-three before me, I'm sure he's ready to go bash some skulls in with his whole… power-stealing… power," Carla said, gesturing to Riley as she spoke.

"I'd really love to test myself out, but… I think I need to pop offline for a bit," said Riley. "I need to use the bathroom and get something to eat. But I can head back online afterwards."

"I think that's a good idea," said Laura. "I was messaging the Vanguard Alliance leader. They're trying to form a group of whoever they can get together. But most of us were down there fighting and wearing ourselves out, so we should all eat and regenerate what we lost. That's what Seth and the others are already doing. Hopefully, Erica will head back online after she checks in on Todd."

Riley nodded. "I better head off then, so I can hurry back." With a mere thought, he released Laura's powers, and the two clones of himself disappeared. He didn't relinquish Parviz's powers. "Should be able to get down pretty…" He thought about it for a second. "Actually, I don't think I'm going to try and portal. I don't know why, but every time I go through them, I just feel terrible. I'm just going to climb down using my ring," he said, referring to his Ring of Expert Climbing.

"Alright, try and hurry back," said Laura, as Riley made his way to the side of the roof. "Parviz, portal us over to the bunker."

"Sure thing," said Parviz, as he created a nearby portal, as well as one as far down the street he could see. It didn't take long for them all to jump through the portal, excluding Riley.

Riley maneuvered over the edge of the roof and made his way down. He was much happier to take a few more minutes getting back to the bunker, than risk getting that strange sick and dizzy feeling again. The more he thought about it, the more he wondered if that was what had caused his blackout. Was he unable to handle portaling around for some reason? Was it something wrong with his character? Did it have anything to do with how he got tier-three? These were questions he didn't expect to find easy answers to.

When Riley reached the street, he took a quick glance around to gain his bearings. He was only down the street from Bunker 7. There were a couple NPCs walking around, which relieved him somewhat. It meant that the initial 'threat' was over, and some of the NPCs had returned to their virtual lives. Hopefully the city would recover quickly from losing a couple thousand of them. If they were lucky, the game's world AI would implement some quests that would alleviate some of the stress, such as having players run taxis on their own, or construct sturdier buildings or… something. He wasn't sure. He'd never delved too deep into the city-building aspect of the game, which was still being fleshed out by the developers.

A short walk saw him back to the bunker. There were a few familiar faces inside, but Laura and the others had surely already logged off. So he headed down to his apartment to do the same.

His mind was still reeling from the whole blackout scenario, and having reached tier-three. It was just so unreal. Reaching tier-three when he hadn't heard of anyone else doing it, other than Aaron in a limited capacity, was just such a special feeling, like he was on top of the world, like he could do anything.

A small smile crept across his lips as he began thinking about his guildmates, and what it would be like to combine some of their powers. He opened the door to his bunker apartment and stepped inside.

He must've still been in a bit of a daydream, because it took him a couple seconds to realize there was someone sitting on his bed. His eyes went wide. "Who're you?" he asked, as the finely-dressed black-suited man stood up.

"I'm Roger Dallas. I'm with the Apendia crisis team. We need to talk."

"Crisis team?" Riley asked. "Crisis team for what? What's going on? You're… a mod or something?" Riley already had a lot on his mind from hitting tier-three, along with everything else that had happened that day. "Wait, is this about me hitting tier-three?"

Mr. Dallas held up a hand to stop

Riley's many questions. "Let me explain," he said. "I'm with the crisis team for health-related issues. We monitor abnormalities in the connection between the rig that's monitoring your brain, and the signals and data that arrive in the game. We temporarily store that information and actively run an algorithm to find anything that might be amiss."

Riley had never heard of such a thing, but from the way Mr. Dallas was speaking, he was starting to get worried.

"And something's wrong with my connection?" Riley asked.

"Potentially," said Mr. Dallas. "A member of the crisis team is sent to anyone that the algorithm marks as having an unusual connection to the game. This goes beyond anything that might be considered merely lag, connectivity problems, or outages. For legal reasons, I do have to tell you that Apendia is not claiming responsibility for anything that might be discovered."

"Like what?" Riley asked, his brow furrowing.

"That'll be for a trained medical physician to decide," said Mr. Dallas. "We've sent you an email and scheduled you a free appointment at a clinic closest to your home residence that can do a thorough check up on your brain. If you can't make the appointment, you can reschedule via email, or decline it altogether. This is merely a courtesy that Apendia provides to its users, such as yourself."

"So… I'm not in any type of trouble or anything?" Riley asked, partially suspicious of the whole thing.

Mr. Dallas had kept a serious expression the entire time. "Not that I'm aware of, no," he stated. "In the email you'll be receiving, you'll be able to contact me directly for any questions relating to your appointment at the clinic. Do you have any questions for me now?"

Riley glanced away. This was all so sudden and unexpected. He really had no idea. "So, I have to go get my brain checked out, because you detected something weird going on?" Riley's eyes suddenly widened—he wasn't sure why it hadn't occurred to him minutes ago. "Wait, does this have anything to do with me blacking out earlier?"

Upon speaking of blacking out, Mr. Dallas's brows lifted. "You've been blacking out?"

Riley nodded. "Earlier, I blacked out

when I went through a portal. I'd been fighting a hellion at the time. But usually when I go through a portal, I just get a really weird feeling, like… I'm sick or something, but it passes pretty quickly. Also, does this have anything to do with the pain update? Because I've been having the weird sick feeling for a while now."

For a moment, Mr. Dallas didn't say anything, as if he was trying to think carefully on his words. "I would highly recommend taking that appointment to see a physician, and as soon as you are able."

After a few moments of silence, Riley asked again. "And what about the pain update? Wasn't that a fluke? Is it getting rolled back? Is it causing any problems?"

Mr. Dallas held a hand up again, as if to quiet Riley. "I cannot speak on anything other than what I've told you already. You don't have to log out now, but I would advise doing so, and getting checked out as soon as you're able. If you have no other questions pertaining to your appointment, then I wish you well."

Riley wasn't sure what else to ask. It seemed as though Mr. Dallas wasn't going to answer anything he actually wanted answered.

"Yeah, um… that's fine, I guess, thanks

for the notification," said Riley. "That's all."

"Have a pleasant day." Mr. Dallas bid him farewell, and a moment later, disappeared. Usually when someone teleported or died, there was a cool particle effect or flash of light. But Mr. Dallas was simply there one moment, and gone the next, as if he'd never been there in the first place.

Riley stood there for several long seconds, trying to process this new information. Eventually he shook his head and walked over to lay down on his virtual bed. "What a messed up day," he murmured. He brought up the in-game menu system and navigated to logout. Seconds later, the game world faded and the real world welcomed him back.

CHAPTER 21: ON THE MIND

Two days later.

Riley sat in a tucked-away booth at Paragon Cafe.

A cup of coffee sat in front of him, but it was no longer steaming and hadn't been touched since the waiter placed it in front of him.

His back had remained against the booth since he sat down. His eyes hadn't left the coffee mug in five minutes. He didn't even notice Aaron until the other boy was slipping down into the seat across from him.

"What's up?" Aaron asked in a soft and sincere tone. He'd been friends with Riley too long not to notice that something was bothering him.

Riley's gaze went to his best friend. "A lot," he murmured.

"Like?" Aaron pressured.

Riley breathed in slowly, and exhaled. "I had a weird visit from a member of Apendia's crisis team. They detected something weird from the connection on my headset, so they set me up with an appointment at a clinic nearby. So, yesterday, I went." Riley paused and licked his lips, chewing on the lower one before speaking again. "They discovered a benign tumor in my head. It's against my brain."

Aaron's eyes widened. His lips parted, but before he could say anything, Riley continued.

"They said that surgery wasn't recommended, but that they want me to come in from time to time to monitor it and make sure it doesn't become a larger issue. They think it will remain benign and… not be a problem."

Aaron's brow furrowed. "That sounds… not great, but not awful either. Luckily you were able to catch it, but from what you said, it… isn't a problem?"

Riley looked away, then slowly back to Aaron. "As far as my health is concerned, they deemed it 'not a problem.' But I mentioned I play Sigil Online, and I've been having a weird sick feeling in the game when I go through portals. I figured there may be some sort of connection. Well, apparently there is. According to the doctor I spoke with, the tumor is in an area that might be affected if my brain is under an unusual 'workload' as they put it. They said a lot of stuff I didn't entirely understand, but the gist of what I understood is that when I go through a portal, more data is running through the headset at that moment, and it's causing some… undesirable effects, due to where the tumor is on my brain. So their recommendation was to not play Sigil Online.

Ever again."

"You're quitting Sigil?" Aaron asked.

Riley narrowed his eyes. "Of course I'm not quitting!" he said abruptly. "I'd be out on the street in months if I did that. So, the way I figure it, is if I'm really careful about what I'm doing in Sigil, I can… prevent the weird effects."

"Was the doctor worried that the game might make the tumor worse, or anything?"

Riley shrugged. "He didn't seem to make that accusation. Just that doing high-intensity stuff, like going through a portal suddenly, would put an abnormal amount of stress on my brain, which agitates that area and gives me the nausea and vertigo in-game. Which, admittedly, is something I don't want to deal with. I knew going through portals was causing it, but now I know why. So… no portals for me."

"That's rough," Aaron murmured. "But it could be a lot worse. I'm glad it isn't."

Riley nodded, and finally managed a half smile. "Yeah, it sucks, but you're right."

"Did he imply anything had caused the tumor?" Aaron asked. "Like, playing with the headset on isn't the cause, is it?"

Riley shook his head. "I asked him about that, and he said that the headset rigs, no matter which manufacturer they're from, are fully tested and put through a lot of high standards to make sure they don't cause any harm like that. But apparently they all work the same way, which is safe."

"Yeah, but something's going on, don't you think?" Aaron asked. "At least, maybe as far as Sigil is concerned. Remember how there was that player who died when they implemented the pain patch?"

"Yeah, I remember. I brought up the whole pain in-game thing, but the doctor was under the impression that it would only work the brain harder, and not actually cause any physical harm… to a healthy person."

"To a healthy person?" Aaron asked.

Riley sighed. "Yeah, apparently there's this weird gray area right now, as far as VR is concerned. If you're healthy, with no problems, like degenerative diseases or problems with your nerves, or… you know, problems with your brain, then the headsets are harmless. But there's apparently some ongoing testing where they're trying to find out if VR is speeding up certain health issues, or working in unison with them, to result in the possibility that it may lead to death."

"So doesn't that worry you?" Aaron asked, leaning forward. "It sounds like the doctor doesn't know if the headset might be more of a problem, given your situation. Doesn't having a tumor make you 'not healthy'?"

Riley shook his head. "I don't know. We spoke for about half an hour, and I was starting to lose my mind with all the stuff we talked about. I guess I could give them a call and try and speak with the doctor again. Or maybe discuss some finer points with him on my next visit in three months."

"Well, he did tell you to stop playing Sigil, right?"

Riley nodded. "He told me to 'not use VR hardware, to be on the safe side,' but as I was saying before, they didn't have any concrete evidence that continuing to play would for certain harm me."

"But it sounds like there's still a bit of a risk, don't you think?" Aaron asked.

"Sure, I imagine there's some," said Riley. "The pain update might even make the portal thing worse, if more information such as sensory data like touch and feel are being transmitted as well. But I feel fine when I play normally. I'll just… be careful, and keep away from anything that works like a portal or a teleportation."

"Didn't you tell me that there was a player who used to teleport you around, back when you were Radiance?"

"Yeah, his name was Teller. He ended up siding with those guys that were trying to PK us when we fought you. But I never felt sick after he teleported me around. But then again, there was a brief delay between where I was and where I ended up. So maybe the problem is that a portal makes it all too quick, and there's just too much data from where I was and where I'm ending up. But when it's a teleport, maybe it's… different somehow? I don't know, I haven't teleported in a while." Riley sighed. He reached up and rubbed at his temples. "I kinda don't want to think about it right now."

"Sorry," Aaron murmured. "I'm sure it's been tough to deal with."

"Yeah, along with some other things that have happened."

"Other things?" Aaron asked.

"I made a bad call the other day," Riley spoke, his eyes once again staring at the table. "You remember Todd, our earth mover? Could pull up barricades and—"

"Yeah, I remember him," said Aaron.

"Yeah, well… he's dead." Riley's brow furrowed as he spoke, then looked up to Aaron. "And it's my fault."

Aaron shook his head. "Come on now, you can't blame yourself for someone losing their character. Sigil is a lot easier to get back into than it used to be. Sure, it sucks when your character is wiped. You know that as well as anyone, but you can't—"

"No, not his character, him," said Riley. His hands had moved to his lap as he began to fidget. "He died in the game because I trusted Shadow Witch not to turn on us. But she did. And we got trapped between her, Shade, and some hellions. Todd ended up getting killed. But… I found out yesterday that he also passed away. According to Seth, who spoke to Erica, Todd had some health issues. Seth couldn't remember what Erica said he had, but it had to do with his nervous system. Apparently it wasn't a major detriment to him, but it prevented him from moving around a lot, or something. I'm not sure. All I know is that it was just enough, and combined with the pain update and being killed in the game, it was too much. Now he's dead. Just like that girl we saw on the news the other day, and the several others that have popped up since then."

Aaron's gaze lowered to the table.

"So I can't help but wonder if maybe the same thing might not happen to me, if I end up dying in Sigil. Will the experience be too much for my brain to take? The sick feeling has only gotten worse, and now with pain and all the extra information from that… What's going to happen if I die in Sigil again? But like I said, I can't quit. I don't think I'd ever be able to do anything else. So I figure… I might as well keep playing, despite the risk. Maybe this tumor isn't that bad, and maybe it's not enough to really harm me, you know? Surely the doctors would've said something if it had a higher chance of happening, right?"

Aaron looked across the table at his friend. "I don't want you to die, Riley. Sigil or not. I don't want to lose my best friend, just to play some game."

"I'm going to be careful," said Riley. "I'll be as careful as I can, I promise. Which… kind of leads me to the next thing I wanted to talk to you about."

"There's more?" Aaron asked, with raised brows. "I'm not sure I can take much more news from you at this point."

"Well, the only other bad news is that our guild is slowly falling into shambles from people who haven't been online, to people who deserted us, like Shell. And then

Erica is apparently taking a break from the game, because of Todd. I can only imagine that she doesn't want to see me ever again. But I don't blame her."

"You can't think like that," Aaron spoke up.

"I know… but it's easier said than done," Riley countered. "But that's all the bad stuff. So, let's move on to the one good thing I can tell you."

"That sounds good," said Aaron.

Riley then recounted the events of the fight from the other day in the hellion's subterranean lair. He told his friend everything from the moment he'd left Neon Nest, to the moments leading up to him crossing the threshold through the portal and passing out.

"I thought you said there was good news?" Aaron finally interrupted, after listening for several minutes.

"There is," said Riley, a bit more anxiously as he was nearing the end of his drawn-out story. "When I got back into the game and checked my character, I found out that… well, for one, an hour had passed. My two gloves were gone, including the one you'd just made for me, which was really upsetting at the time. But more importantly," Riley then lowered his voice. "The tier-three sphere was gone."

"Gone? What happened?" Aaron sat up a bit more in his seat.

"I don't really know, but now I'm tier-three," he said as his lips curled into a big grin.

"What?" Aaron gasped, but he kept his voice low as well. "Really? You can't be serious!"

Riley nodded with a big grin on his face. "And instead of shooting those spikes out of my hands, I can actually steal other people's powers, but only up to two, and in a more limited capacity, but still… I can essentially steal powers for real now."

"Man, I bet that's going to be so much fun. Probably a bit hectic, but fun. So…" Aaron trailed off, glancing away, seemingly thinking on something. "My crafter friends and I thought that the sphere might help us permanently hit tier-three… but wow, I had no idea that something like that could happen. That's amazing!" he said in an excited but hushed tone. "Wow, I'm going to have to tell the others."

"You're not going to tell them that it happened to me specifically, right?" Riley asked. "This is still something I want to keep secret… well, as much as I can. Everyone in my guild is going to know, since my powers are going to be all different now."

"Oh no, of course not," said Aaron. "I'll keep your identity a secret. I'll just… hmm, I'll have to think of a way of letting them know about the possibility, without revealing that I gave you a sphere and let you into our secret tier-three club. Even though you already went and exceeded what we were doing." Aaron laughed.

Riley was definitely feeling a bit better after their bleaker talk earlier, but he got to thinking back to the attack on their city. "So yeah, that's pretty much all the news I wanted to let you in on, but I did want to ask, how is your city doing? We had that huge attack I was telling you about, but I was wondering if other cities were having the same problem as us. I've heard about attacks on the news, but nothing as big as what happened in Gargantuan."

"Things have been pretty good, all things considered," said Aaron. "We still have hellion roamers, but most of what I hear happening is actually over in your city and a couple of the others. We don't have nearly the trouble in my city that you guys seem to have in yours. But then again, we have a lot more active clans, which patrol the city and head down into the underground pretty often. There's not much hellion clan activity at all. Unfortunately, I think you're getting the worst of it."

"Sure feels that way lately," Riley mused with a sigh. "Maybe the heroes from your city will pop over and help us out a little. What do you think?" he asked with a half smile.

Aaron laughed and shook his head. "I don't think so, not unless there's a solid benefit to them, but who knows? Only takes one attack on our city from some big hellion clan. Then, they'd all rally against that clan and try to destroy them if they could find them."

"Wish our city's guilds had that sort of cohesion." Riley scratched at the side of his head. "But yeah, that's about it. Tier-three… who'da thought, right?"

"That's so crazy," Aaron admitted, shaking his head. "I don't know of anyone who has a permanent tier-three status. It was permanent, right? There wasn't some sort of timed effect?"

Riley nodded. "I checked. There wasn't any sort of timer on any of it. I'm permanently tier-three powered. I gotta say, between the whole tumor thing, and then the whole ability to steal two people's powers, I've had a lot on my mind. I haven't been able to sleep too well. Been a stressful couple of days."

"I imagine so," said Aaron.

A brief silence fell between the two, and Aaron pulled out his cellphone. He checked the time and slid it back into his pocket. "Well, I was planning on doing some stuff, but I'm in no rush to leave. Did you want to talk some more? Even if you just wanna vent about… whatever?"

Riley shook his head. "No, it's alright. I think I should head back and just think about things for a bit, then I'll probably head online and go see Warcry. Haven't spoke to her in a while. Figure I could let her know what's going on and I guess see what she's been up to."

Aaron smiled, and slowly stood up. "Well, thanks for letting me know, and seriously… be careful. Listen to the doctors if they really think you shouldn't be playing Sigil. I'm sure you can find something, I dunno. Or, hell, why not be more of a crafter and less of a fighter?" Aaron said, letting his lips curl at the obvious joke.

Riley smiled at Aaron's humor. "I'll

see you later," was his only response.

"See you later," Aaron said before turning and heading off.

CHAPTER 22: ROOKBANE

'Building' in Sigil Online was a relatively simple matter. Players could go into the rooms they owned and bring up a building tab, letting them move furniture around or place items that were in their inventory. If they had the materials and the schematics to make a piece of furniture, they could even craft certain things inside the room. Some pieces of furniture would require a workshop. Others did not.

Riley had moved the few pieces of furniture in his room from time to time. But there wasn't a huge reason to do so. A piece of furniture like a bed, or a lamp or cabinet, would either serve an aesthetic purpose or a practical one. A shelf could display a trophy. A bed, when used to log out, would give a 'well rested' buff to the player when they returned to the game after so many hours.

For Riley, there wasn't a whole lot for him to do with his room. He had the simple items, but never attempted to delve further into crafting, workbenches, or anything of that sort.

Riley found himself thinking about the building feature in the game as he sat on his virtual bed. The hellions seemed to be able to build wherever they wanted, and generally chose underground areas, which had been expanded upon by the developers. From what he'd read, hellions could technically build anywhere, as long as they had the materials. Hero players could only 'build' inside buildings they owned, unless their powers allowed for makeshift construction, like Todd's.

A tinge of sadness ran through him as he remembered Todd.

Todd was one of the players that had been in Seth's party when he'd returned to the game. One of the first few people to give him a chance. Now Todd was gone, and Erica had fled the game.

And if he wasn't careful, maybe he too would end up like Todd.

Riley shook his head, trying to pull his thoughts away from such depressing matters.

He was about to head over to see Warcry today. He'd already queued up a taxi from the lounge terminal. Due to the lower populace of NPCs, and the turmoil their city was in, the wait time was a lot longer than usual. Taxis from other cities wouldn't enter Gargantuan due to its threat status.

With a quick gesture, he checked the time on his user interface. The taxi would be available in just a couple minutes. So it was best to go ahead and head out to wait for it.

It didn't take long to leave his room, head up the stairs, and go through the lounge. There were familiar faces standing around, conversing, but none of them were guildmates, or even close to being considered a friend.

He pushed open the door to Bunker 7 and walked out. He looked across the street, then up into the sky. There weren't any explosions as far as he could hear. No flying fortresses. No giant monsters. The buildings looked… well, they looked a little banged up, since their NPC population had taken a hit, and couldn't easily go out to repair all of them from the normal wear-and-tear of heroes and hellions.

"Where you off to?" came an all too familiar female voice.

Riley whipped around and found himself face to face with Glint. She'd been standing against the wall, just behind the opening door.

"What are you doing here?" Riley countered, startled by her presence.

"Just waiting on a taxi. You?" Glint asked, lifting a brow at him. She tilted her head, allowing her almost glimmering hair to fall from her shoulder.

"Same," Riley replied. "Long wait?"

Glint nodded. "Yeah, it should be here any minute though."

"Yeah, mine too," Riley replied. "Wait, are you going to Colossal City?"

"Sure am," Glint confirmed. "You?"

"Yeah, actually. I guess the taxi is gonna take both of us?"

"If it gets here," Glint said with a sigh. "This is the spot it queued me up to arrive at. Been standing around for about ten minutes already."

Riley nodded. "What're your plans?" he asked curiously.

Glint shrugged, and finally took the opportunity to step forward "I was gonna hit the market district. See if there's anything worth getting. You?"

"Was going to visit a friend," Riley answered, feeling that divulging such a fact wouldn't put him in any danger. Not that he felt Glint would turn on him… but after Shadow Witch the other day, and everything that ensued from that, he wasn't sure if he should really trust anyone outside of the guild at this point.

"I heard there was a big fight down in one of the hellion lairs a few days ago," said Glint. "Were you down there? The news said that some paragons got taken out, but so did a bunch hellions. But they caused some serious NPC damage?"

Riley's lips parted. He thought about what he was going to say, and took a moment before speaking. "Yeah, I was." He looked away, then back to Glint. "Ran into Shadow. And Shade."

Glint instantaneously grimaced at the mention of Shadow Witch. "Eugh. Really? I bet that wasn't fun. Let me guess, they popped out of nowhere when you were fighting some hellions?"

Riley rolled his shoulders. "Worse," he murmured. "She was by herself, and seemed to run into us on accident. I kinda figured it might be best if we let her tag along with us. We had no idea what was going on with the NPCs or anything. I thought it was the best solution, at the time, but all I ended up doing was getting a friend killed… for real."

Glint's brow furrowed. "What? What are you talking about?"

Riley explained what happened to Todd, and the fight that had killed him. He left out the majority of what had happened afterward, other than that they managed to get away.

"Damn, that's… that's terrible." Glint shook her head. "Wish I could've been there. I can see invisible players, you know."

Riley had been looking away, but looked back to Glint when she mentioned that. "You can see people who are cloaked? Like, with that cloak of concealment item?"

Glint nodded. "Sure can. I can see just about any sort of cloak effect. I can spot camouflage as well. Just a part of my paragon status, I guess."

Riley pondered what Glint said. He never remembered her being able to do that. Was it actually an item she had that let her see invisibility, but she didn't want to admit it?

It was then that something clicked in the back of his head. "Huh…" he murmured. "Shadow actually asked if you were around when we ran into her. I remember now."

"Yeah, she's aware that I've been trying to find people to group with," said Glint. "I think someone told her I approached you guys to join up with you."

"So she knows that you can see

invisibility?"

Glint nodded. "Yeah, she's aware. I'm a huge threat to her and Shade's guilds. I can see invisibility, and I know where they like to hide and how they prefer to attack."

Riley wondered if Glint really was telling the truth about actually being fully out of Shadow's guild. Why would Shadow have asked about her otherwise? If that was the case, then maybe Glint really was trying to make things right. But could he really vouch for Glint, given what had happened with Shadow?

Glint glanced to the side. "I hope that's our ride," she said, and took another step forward.

Riley turned and saw a lone blue car heading down the street. It wasn't moving very fast, and only had one occupant, the driver.

Unlike previous taxis that Riley had taken in the past, this one didn't have any sign on top that said anything about the destination or who had ordered it.

Glint and Riley stood side by side as the blue car pulled up. The driver, a man with a buzz cut and weathered features, turned his head to look at them. He reached up and touched something on the inside door.

The window descended slowly, and once it had lowered all the way, he spoke.

"You two heading to Colossal?" he asked, looking between them. His voice sounded older than he looked.

"Yes," said Glint and Riley, almost in unison.

"Well, get on in," the man said, and with another press of a button from within the car, the two side doors opened.

Riley let Glint approach the nearest one, while he walked around the vehicle and got in on the other side, just to save the driver a couple extra seconds and quicken their travel. Once in, he pulled the door shut and looked to the driver. "You're… a player, aren't you?" he asked.

"Kinda impolite to ask that, isn't it?" the man chuckled and shook his head. Within moments, the car started moving again, heading down the street. "But yeah, I am. Figured I could make some quick and easy money running a taxi around."

"It was a bit more expensive to queue you up," Glint commented. "So does that mean there's no NPCs running taxis?"

"I dunno about that," said the driver. "Just that I've been busy nonstop since the other day, when we had that incident. I get into the car, I start up the taxi service program, and 'boom,' automatically given directions and everything," he said, as he gestured to a GPS interface built into the dash of the car. "Easy money. Well, as long as something doesn't happen."

"At least you should be able to get away if something goes wrong," Riley commented.

"Yeah, yeah, I imagine I'm a little faster than most people. Some of them hellions move pretty quick though," the driver said, nodding a little while he spoke. He was wearing very plain clothes. A black shirt, a pair of denim pants. Nothing about his attire would've given away that he was a player. But the vehicle and his demeanor had caused Riley to think he might've been.

"So, Colossal City," the driver murmured. "You both getting out of the city permanently? Wouldn't blame you, I guess. Some folks are saying that we're going to be the next Uber City. But at least Uber has all those PKer hero players running amok. I think they keep the hellions in check, don't they?"

"I don't really know," Riley commented.

"I believe you're right," Glint spoke up. "At least, that's what I've heard as well."

"Yep." The driver nodded some more. "Bet that's a tough place. I'm sure the hellions want a whole city to call their own. But the way I hear it, they can live and colonize the underground areas just fine. Heck, they can even go out there into the areas outside the city, right? Not sure why they want their own city."

Riley sat there, looking between the driver and out the front window. He hadn't expected so much conversation from him, but it was getting him thinking. Were the hellions trying to seize Gargantuan City?

"The city gives them a prime location to farm the NPCs," said Glint. She turned her head and looked out the window, watching the buildings pass by. The city around them was particularly quiet and mostly devoid of pedestrians. "But they must know that if the city is put into too much turmoil, that the NPCs will mostly stop spawning. So yes, they must have some other intent."

"Mhmm," said the driver. "But better minds than mine need to figure it out. All I can do is drive around." He chuckled again. "Been saving up for some powers, but maybe at the end of this week, I can finally get something from the pact system. I hate to say it, especially if you two have been in the thick of things with these hellions, but I've made a lot more money because of it. As far as taxiing people around is concerned."

"Pact powers can be pretty expensive, that's for sure," said Glint. "I don't blame you," she reassured him. "You've got to make whatever you can, when you can. And there's nothing wrong with running a taxi. It's a service most people need."

"Why do they call it the pact system, anyway?" the driver asked. "I've been meaning to ask someone."

"Oh, generally because it involves being bestowed powers from an item that players are able to craft," said Glint. "Most of the powers are things that other people can have. So you're not going to get anything truly original, for one. Also, using a pact item will lower your stats. So if it's a superpower that requires mind, it'll generally lower another stat, like power or toughness, making you weaker than you'd be if you would've just found anything else on your own."

"Ah, well that makes a lot of sense then," said the driver.

Riley was silent as the driver

continued to speak. Occasionally Glint would reply, but mostly they both allowed the man to ramble. Conversation was probably part of the fun for the man.

Riley stared out the window. They were nearing the outskirts of Gargantuan City. You could barely tell that the city was under such a plight. The hellions had focused their attention mostly on the NPCs and not so much the structures. But that could change. There was no telling what the hellion clans were truly after. Laura had spoken to him about the alliance they were trying to get their guild into. According to her, the Vanguard was incredibly busy, trying to mobilize its player base into patrol and attack teams, but the hellions were numerous and hard to find. Since the pain update, and since the news of people actually dying in real life, a good number of people were 'waiting it out,' to see if the developers would do anything. Which meant less paragons willing to get into PVP conflicts.

But so far, nothing had changed. It was up to the heroes to deal with the hellions that were slowly taking over parts of the city. The developers weren't going to magically come to their aid.

Riley thought of Warcry. He hoped that maybe after speaking to her he might gain some special insight on a way to fight the hellions. Or maybe Colossal City was so well-off that she and her Rooks of War could come to their aid, as they had before. But then again, his problems weren't Warcry's problems. Warcry had come to his aid when he needed her. There was no longer any debt between them. They were even.

He glanced out the front window of the car. They were passing the threshold between the two cities, marked only by some meager signs, one of which said 'Welcome to Colossal City.' Another said 'Now leaving Garg,' but the rest of the sign was bent and broken.

Riley continued to stare out the window, watching as they neared the shorter structures on the outskirts of Colossal City. It was then that something caught his attention. There was an unusually dark formation of clouds slowly swirling above the cityscape. It was like some sort of localized storm, all focused on a part of the city beyond their view.

"Do you see those clouds?" Riley asked, dipping down a little and pointing out the front windshield of the car.

The driver lowered his head. "Hmm, yeah, that's weird."

Glint had tilted down to get a better look. "Never seen anything like it. Could be a player's powers? Hellion or paragon. Or even an event of some sort. You think they might be getting hit with an invasion event or something?"

"No idea, but that's around the same area that I was heading," said Riley.

"Yeah, the market district is back in that direction as well," said Glint.

The driver sighed. "Well, at the first sign of hellions, I'm dropping you guys off on the closest curb. The system will refund you for the percentage of the trip I didn't get you, but I'm not risking the car, or my life, on getting you under a cloud that might have been made by hellions."

The driver continued to navigate his way through the city. There were other cars on the street, and the sidewalks were more populated with NPCs than in Gargantuan.

The further they went, the harder it was to see the dark clouds, as more buildings began to obstruct their view.

Riley was craning his head and ducking in his seat, just trying to see out the car. Then, he realized he could just lower the window.

With the windshield down, he stuck his head and part of his torso out of the car, and twisted about as the car turned down another street.

"What are you doing?" the driver called back, aggravated, since one of his passengers was halfway out of the vehicle.

"Trying to see if anything's going on with that cloud!" Riley replied, as he gripped the roof of the car for support.

"If you fall out, I'm not responsible!"

"I've got him, I've got him," Glint sighed, as she reached over and grabbed his pant leg. She rolled her eyes. "We're going to be there soon enough, Radi—uh, Relinquish—eh, let's just go with Riley. It's Riley, right?"

"Yeah, that's fine," Riley groaned. No one ever called him Relinquisher.

"We're almost there. Just a couple more streets," said the driver.

Several seconds later, a loud *thump* sounded in the distance, coming from the same direction that Riley had seen the cloud, if his suspicions were correct.

A moment later came a loud crunch, followed by a distant sound of shattering glass.

"Something's going on!" Riley said, but couldn't see anything.

"I can hear it!" the driver yelled. "That's it, I can't risk it. You both are getting out."

"What? But we're almost there!" Riley said, and quickly slunk back into the car. "Just get us to the end of the street!"

"Fine, fine, the end of the street, but no further!" the man said as he drove faster. Several cars were heading past them, but they were the only vehicle on their side of the street.

The car came to an abrupt halt, forcing Riley and Glint to rock forward in their seats. "This is it," said the driver. He pressed a button on his dashboard, and the two side doors opened simultaneously. "Out you go. And don't think I'm sticking around to taxi you back."

"Thanks," Riley murmured as he quickly got out of the vehicle. He didn't waste a moment as he ran around the corner of the street. He looked into the sky and saw the edges of the circular billowing clouds. They were almost coal-black and swirling more rapidly now. Riley wondered if there might be a tornado forming, but the clouds were only up in the sky, with nothing coming down from them. Despite the lack of cyclone, there was a distinct rushing wind sound drowning out most of the other nearby sounds. Usually you could hear vehicles driving down the street, or people shouting, or fighting on the rare occasion. But all he could hear was the rushing wind.

"Wait up!" Glint had to yell to be heard over the wind as she chased after him.

Riley turned his head. "The market district is up the street, just keep going! I'm going to check out this storm."

"I'm coming with you!" Glint replied. "What if there's hellions? You can't solo anything!"

Riley darted down the street with Glint right on his heels. He knew she was sort of right. If Glint knew what his old powers were, then she knew that he didn't have any decent solo capability. But now that he was tier-three, he had a lot more potential. But that potential was only as good as the players around him. With her nearby, he could seize her powers at the very least.

The structures around them stretched into the sky. Office buildings, and who knew what else. Riley wasn't too concerned. He was heading toward another intersection at the end of the block. If he took a right, it'd get him on a collision course for whatever was beneath the storm. He kept pumping his arms as he ran. He had no idea what he was going to find, but as he neared the end of the block and was just about to turn, he realized that despite approaching from a different angle, Warcry's Rook Den should be right over—

Riley turned the corner and stopped. Glint almost ran into him as she turned to see what he was looking at.

But it wasn't *what* he was seeing. It was the distinct lack of what he was seeing.

The Rook Den, the nearby shorter structures, and a larger section of the block were all smashed into rubble.

Figures darted around. Streams, bolts, and rays of different colors were firing off in different directions. Some of them impacted the nearby high rises.

Riley couldn't make out anything from the distance, but the complete destruction of the Rook Den, along with everything else in the area, struck him with dread. What the hell could've caused such destruction? Was it some kind of explosion, or powerful weapon? Was there an enormous monster in the vicinity? Was this an invasion event?

He tried to focus on what the distant players were fighting. He saw various insect-like figures. Each of them was pale white in carapace and had distinct features, such as looking like a mantis, a roach, and even something that resembled an assassin insect. But most curious of all was the fact that all their bodies seemed unnaturally armored, as if they had somehow been imbued to be stronger. In that instant, Riley thought of the bovine-skulled hellion which had buffed the hellions down in the cave.

There weren't many of them, and for each one he saw, there seemed to be a dozen players fighting them.

The droning sound of wind above their heads was slowly alleviating. Riley looked up and watched as the dark clouds rapidly dispersed, as if the energy keeping them swirling and aloft was now gone. Second by second, the clouds lessened, and soon the clear sky above was revealed, along with beaming sunlight.

He looked out to the street before him.

Now that the winds were dying down, the sounds of fighting began to assault his ears. Without giving it further thought, he ran down the street, heading towards the mass of distant figures.

"Wait!" Glint called, as she raced to catch up to him. "You don't know what you're getting into!"

"We've gotta help them!" Riley replied, without even turning his head. The closer he got, the easier he was able to make out the details of the players and the monsters they were fighting. The players were mostly dressed in a similar dark, plain-clothed fashion, which was the loose signature clothing style for Warcry's Rooks of War.

There were plenty of alarms going off in Riley's head. This was the first bit of action he'd seen since discovering the tumor in his head. He knew he probably shouldn't be in the game at all, and if anything, he probably shouldn't be rushing into a fight like this.

But if it wasn't for Warcry and her guild, he'd have died when Shadow Witch and Shade's guild had come for him in Death's Chasm. He knew Warcry wasn't keeping score, but he couldn't help himself. If she was in danger, and he could help, he was going to do everything in his power to do so.

As he raced ahead and ran past large chunks of debris and fallen buildings, he noticed that there weren't many monsters left. Bursts of particles exploded from the monsters, or hellions, whichever they happened to be. One by one, Warcry's Rooks were taking them down. By the time he reached the closest player, there was no longer any fighting going on. Everyone was looking for their next target, but none remained.

"What happened here?" Riley asked, coming up to the closest player.

The figure turned around quickly and spotted Riley. The player had short red hair and a pair of green-tinted spectacles. Huh?" the guy asked, as if he didn't understand the question. He looked Riley over for just a second, then spotted Glint running up behind him. "Just get here?"

"Yeah, we saw the storm, figured you might need some help, but it looks like everything's over?" Riley asked.

The man nodded and pointed with his thumb over his shoulder. "Yeah man, we took care of them, but they messed us up pretty bad. Big ol' hellion popped outta nowhere, then it armored up and got real tough. It leveled the whole block it looks like. Then a bunch of all kinds of hellions came from the sky. It was crazy. They had a bunch of servant monsters with them too."

"Servant monsters?" Riley asked. "The hellions brought NPCs with them?"

The man nodded. "That's right. They matched their armor color and everything. The whole lot of them were pale, like bone."

"That must be The Pale Ones," said Glint. "But I didn't think their lair was over here?"

Riley looked to Glint, as she stepped up beside him. "You know where their lair is?"

"I thought it was over in Gargantuan," said Glint. "Shadow Witch spoke about them a couple times, when I was listening in on meetings. They have a couple quick entrances to the surface, but they're well hidden."

"Group leaders! Form up! I want head counts! Kill counts!" a woman's voice shouted. "Hurry up!"

"Welp, gotta go," the man said, before he turned and darted off to where a woman was yelling orders. She had deep red hair, shaved on one side. There was a prominent set of red coiling tribal tattoos on her arms. She was dressed in a red shirt and black cargo pants, the same sort of clothing she always had, since Riley had first met her.

"Is that Warcry?" Glint asked.

"Yeah, this is where her hideout was,"

said Riley. "I imagine there were a few other venues in the area, but man, everything's gone."

"I can see that," Glint murmured.

The two of them watched as almost a dozen individuals went over to where Warcry was standing. They spoke for about ten minutes before they started to disperse. Almost immediately, the various people who'd been talking to Warcry all started calling out to different members of their guild.

"She sure seems to know what she's doing," said Glint. "You rolled with her when you were still on good terms with Shadow and Glasser, right?"

Riley sighed. "Yeah, feels like it was forever ago. But I was with Warcry since the beginning."

"Well, here she comes," said Glint, gesturing with a nod.

Riley glanced back over to where Warcry was, but she was already halfway to them. He smiled as she closed the distance. "Hellion problems?" he asked.

Before answering, Warcry extended her arms and gave him a big hug, lifting him off his feet in the process. "I've missed you!" she said, in that intense voice of hers.

"Where've you been? You don't stop by enough!"

Riley was promptly set back down and all he could do at first was smile. Despite having her entire guild hall crushed, along with most of the block, Warcry was still able to smile and greet him.

"Sorry," Riley sighed. "Been really busy in Gargantuan."

Warcry nodded. "Well, it's not a good enough excuse, but I guess it'll do. Were you in the fight?" she asked, before looking over to Glint. Her brows furrowed. "Who're you? You look familiar."

"This is Glint," Riley spoke up. "She's…uh—"

"I'm one of the people you fought when you came to Riley's rescue in Death's Chasm. Unfortunately, I was a bit too blind to see my mistake at the time but I've come around. Albeit a little late. Hope there's no hard feelings?"

Warcry looked between the two of them. "If Riley's vouching for you, then I guess I have no problem with you now. We won that fight after all."

Glint half smiled. "You sure did."

Warcry returned her attention to Riley. "So what're you doing here? I'd invite you in…" She turned and gestured to the expansive pile of rubble nearby. "But we're currently remodeling."

Riley's lips curled from ear to ear. "I just kinda wanted to chat, actually. But yeah, it seems like you're gonna have your hands full for a bit." Riley then realized that with Glint at his side, he couldn't really have a private conversation with Warcry.

"Hey, uh… Glint? Would you mind giving us a minute in private?" he asked. "Not to be rude or anything, of course."

Glint shrugged. "Sure thing," she said, and without further issue, she walked over to where the Rook Den once stood.

Once Glint was out of earshot, Riley sighed. "So, I don't mean to put anything more on your plate right now, but I just felt like I should tell you what's going on with me."

Warcry's brow furrowed. "What do you mean? Is something wrong?"

Riley then told her about everything that had happened over the past week. The tumor. The hellions in their city. The death of Todd. And finally, his achievement of hitting tier-three.

"Tier-three?" Warcry asked. "I heard rumors about people hitting tier-three for limited durations with the help of items. But I didn't know anyone was able to hit it permanently."

"It certainly feels permanent," said Riley. "I guess I really lucked out this time. I think my new powers are going to allow me to achieve some really interesting things, but I haven't told a whole lot of people yet. I'm worried that if word gets out, that I might be targeted, either by PKers, or hellions." Riley then went into a little detail about what his powers entailed, and how he was able to steal powers in a limited capacity.

"Huh," Warcry murmured. "Definitely sounds like you're going to have your work cut out for you, with learning how to play with these new powers. You're going to have to change things up, depending on what you're fighting and who's around you. I'm sure you'll figure it out, though. I'm really proud of you. I guess you didn't have much choice in the matter, but… if anyone was going to hit tier-three, I'm glad it was you. But that whole tumor business, you're sure it's not a problem? It really sounded like it's more than, you know, the flu."

Riley shook his head. "I'm sure it *is* a problem, but one I can manage. It's definitely something I'm going to have to worry about, especially since I don't want to portal around. But I think I'm going to be able to deal with it. I just need to be careful."

"Well, see that you do," said Warcry. "I know we don't group anymore, but I'm still glad that you're around. I'd be torn up if something happened to you. You know it's true."

Riley scratched at the side of his head. He was never all that great at emotional stuff. "I appreciate it," was all he said at first. He looked away, then back to Warcry. "So, enough about me. What exactly happened here?"

Warcry turned her head and glanced around their surroundings, then back to him. She looked into the sky as if she was trying to think of where to start. "Well, there was this enormous white hellion. Taller than the buildings, certainly taller than the Rook Den. It looked like some big beetle, and then it grew this weird bone-like armor. It was really tough, and I'm not sure how much damage we even managed to do to it. It came in and started smashing the block. We did our best to engage it, and I'm pretty sure we caused it a helluva lot of damage. It had a bunch of its clan friends with it."

"Yeah, I think they're called The Pale Ones," said Riley. "At least, that's what Glint said."

Warcry nodded. "That's what I've heard on the forums. They had some serious firepower in their ranks. The big one was a bit slow, but man… it sure smashed us. We were able to fight off the smaller ones well enough, but I think some of them might've even been minions. Unfortunately for us, we lost all our own minions when the big one came smashing in."

"You had minions?" Riley asked.

"Yeah, we decided that if we spent some money on NPC guards, we could keep more of our number out on the streets, or leveling. But it looks like that money was kinda wasted. I'm really not sure what our losses are totaling. We've got a lot of rebuilding to do. We'll have to contract some NPC gatherers for resource gathering, or I guess I could task some more of my people to it. I sent one group to the market district for basic supplies, but maybe I'll send another group out for actual resource gathering. I have a feeling we're going to need the majority of our money… which can't be accessed until the den is rebuilt. It's all still there, but we won't have access until then." Warcry took another look around. "So, sounds like you got hit by… what? The Royals? We got hit by The Pale Ones today. I wonder if they're coordinating their efforts. If that's the case, then things are a bit worse than just one group of hellions acting up."

"The Royals? So that's what the blue ones are called, huh?" he asked, before thinking for a moment, remembering how he saw one hellion that was paler than The Royals. It was the hellion that had buffed the nearby royal clan members and then stabbed him… which consequently gave him his powers. "I think you're right," he said. "But we're having difficulty coordinating with the other paragon guilds in Gargantuan. We haven't been able to really join this alliance that Laura is trying to get us into. I think she has some contact person she speaks with, and we kinda get assigned things to do. Apparently the alliance is being really cautious with new members, because it doesn't want spies that would sell out their plans to either PK guilds or all the hellion ones."

"Speaking of sellouts," Warcry murmured, before gesturing with her thumb over to Glint, who was just standing and looking around aimlessly. "Isn't that what Shadow Witch's guild has been up to?"

Riley's brows lifted. "What do you mean?"

Warcry tilted her head and rested her hands on her hips. "Shadow's guild has been working with hellions. At least, that's what I hear. She uses her people to scout potential targets, and finds out if players are frequenting certain areas, and ends up selling that info to hellion guilds on private forums and stuff. Kind of like how people would sell info on the locations of rare spawns. They're doing the same thing, but with paragon hunting grounds and locations."

Riley stared at the ground, as he thought back to when Shadow had been with him in the cave the other day. "If Shadow is helping them, then I don't think she has good relations with The Royals, because I think they attacked Shade as well as us."

Warcry shrugged. "All I know is that she's been playing things safe, selling out paragons for profit. Maybe that's something you should talk to Glint over there about."

Riley sighed. "I'm not sure if she has any recent knowledge of what Shadow has been up to, but I'll talk to her. Maybe if we…" He trailed off as he began to think. He crossed his arms and stared at the ground. "Maybe we could try and cause some hostility between the hellion clans. Or at least get a better idea of which ones specifically are aligned, and try and cast some bad blood between them."

"How do you expect to do that?" asked Warcry. "Not like hellions are going to just believe anything some random guy has to say to them. If they'd even be willing to hear you out in the first place."

"Hmm," Riley murmured. He looked back over to Glint. "Not me, but maybe Glint. I'll have to talk it over with her, and see what she knows and what she's willing to do. But if things work out, we might be able to at least cast some doubt between the hellion clans."

"Whatever works," said Warcry. "All I know is that if we don't start hitting their lairs and really lowering their numbers, we're going to see harder and harder losses. They don't have NPCs that they have to take care of like we do. They can just rebuild their lairs if they get broken down and destroyed. I imagine it's still expensive, but I feel like they currently have a huge advantage over us."

Riley stood there for a few silent moments. He stared at the destruction around him, but soon enough found his gaze going to Glint. "Well, maybe we need to do something more than just simply attacking their lairs outright."

Warcry tilted her head. "You look like you've got some sort of plan brewing in your head."

The corner of Riley's lips curled. "I think I have an idea."

CHAPTER 23:
THE PLAN

Two days later, Riley was back in Paragon Cafe, sitting alone in a booth. It was evening, but he still had a cup of coffee in front of him. It was about half full as he cradled it between his hands. His attention was on the televisions in the cafe. There were three in his direct view. His eyes flit between them, following the stories on each.

One was talking about a game currently being developed. They had the lead developer answering questions about it. It was some sort of space game, but Riley wasn't paying a whole lot of attention to the details. Starting in a new game wasn't really on his list of priorities. Even if he were to die in Sigil Online, he still had a better chance of working back up from nothing with the help of his friends. Sure, a new game would have more opportunity to 'hit it big,' but so did Sigil Online.

On one of the other televisions, a news

report about another in-game death was brought to light. The death wasn't in Sigil Online, but a whole different game that had also implemented pain at the exact same time. The news report then segued into a health alert. One of the news agencies had a purported medical expert talking about the potential hazards of the life-like immersion headsets and virtual reality, and the strain it could put on a person's brain and body.

Well, Riley wasn't too sure that the immersion headset he owned was the culprit for the tumor he had, but it certainly did seem to be causing some sort of health issue for him.

But it was a third monitor that mostly had his attention. He could just barely make out the audio over the din of sound around him, but there were subtitles. The show in question was a prominent one that spent most of its time covering different story and social aspects of various immersion video games. The show had just discussed the death of two paragons that were ambushed out in one of the PVE zones, in an area that Riley hadn't been to. The paragons had been assailed by a group of five hellions that were able to burrow under the ground and lie in wait.

Movement near the door to the cafe caught Riley's attention. He glanced over and spotted Aaron coming in. His arrival brought a smile to Riley's lips, and Aaron quickly made his way over.

Aaron sat across from him and sighed. "Sorry it took me so long, I've been busy with my buddies."

"Your buddies?" Riley asked.

"Yeah, you know, the group of people who I created the…" He trailed off and lowered his voice. "The tier-three spheres with?"

Riley's brows lifted. "Oh, right, them."

Aaron nodded. "We've been trying to up production of the spheres."

"Did you tell them about me?"

Aaron gave Riley a sheepish look. "I didn't tell them about you specifically, but I told them I had it on good authority that there might be the potential of permanent tier-three, and we should all try to figure out if we can make it happen. Which means more spheres."

"Well, I wouldn't have even had that sphere in my pocket if you guys hadn't made them," admitted Riley. "So I guess there's no harm in it."

"I kinda figured the same thing." Aaron smirked. "So, what's on the conversational agenda for today?"

Riley's gaze kept diverting to the nearest television, as if he was splitting his attention between it and Aaron.

Aaron was quick to notice, and looked over as well. "Something interesting on the TV?"

"Uh, well…" Riley murmured. "Hopefully there's going to be. I thought they might've run the story by now, but I haven't seen it. I'm starting to worry that it's not going to be released at all."

"What story?" Aaron asked.

Riley shot Aaron a smirk. "A little plan I'm cooking up."

"Are you going to tell me what it is?" Aaron asked. "Am I going to be somehow involved in this plan?"

"Hopefully," said Riley. "We could really use everyone that we can get. Laura's contact in the alliance isn't willing to dedicate any members towards my plan, which, to be fair, we couldn't give them precise details about."

"Am I going to get precise details

about it?" Aaron asked, teasingly.

Before Riley could say another word, the words "And today in Gargantuan City—" reached his ears.

Riley and Aaron both turned their heads at the same time. There was no commentator on screen, and the TV had shifted to what appeared to be a recording from inside Sigil Online, from a player's viewpoint.

The player was behind a ten-foot tall stone pillar. They seemed to be in some sort of structure, like a parking garage, or a sub-basement within the city. It was large and very open, with wooden pallets and crates, and various run-down machinery. It could've easily been some sort of abandoned factory.

The player's view was focused on a wide hole in the ground, across the room. The player wasn't speaking and there was no real way to determine if they were a hellion, or paragon.

A figure crawled out of the hole, but it was hard to make out their exact details, other than their short blue hair and dark clothing. The figure reached down and helped another person, who had an orange-reddish halo, out of the hole. The halo glowed bright, as if it was superheated or something. The player looked to be a woman, with neck-length orange hair and a red jacket. A third humanoid figure with bat-like wings also climbed out. He, or she, was wearing a cloak of concealment, but wasn't invisible.

The three figures ran off, away from the player who was recording. The player's viewpoint followed them as they ran past several other pillars and crates, and saw them head through an opening in one of the nearby stone walls. Once they vanished from sight, the player's attention went back to the hole they'd left.

"I wonder what they were doing down there?" came a younger male voice. It was either the player who was recording the video, or someone behind them. "They seemed to be in a hurry." It was likely that the player who was recording had been streaming their 'investigation' and was talking to their viewers.

Five seconds passed.

Then ten.

"Should we go over and check it out?" the male voice asked.

Then twenty.

Then, the player's view shook, and a

bright light emanated from the hole in the ground.

A burst of fire jetted from the hole and buffeted the ceiling of the room they were in. The flames caught nearby crates on fire, and just as quickly as it had appeared, it subsided.

"What the hell was that? What was down there?" the male voice asked, before the video went dark.

The television flipped the scene back to one of the news commentators, Susan Graff. "This incident happened yesterday afternoon in Gargantuan City. Apparently, a few paragon saboteurs decided to hit a hellion lair with a powerful explosion. We've tried to discover which hellion clan was hit, but we haven't been able to determine the target. What *is* evident is that one of the players involved, Burning Halo, is seen in the video as being one of the attackers. We've tried reaching out to Burning Halo for word on what went down, as it seems pretty exciting, but we've received no reply. In related news, Gargantuan City's NPC populace is still recovering from a devastating hellion-masterminded attack from last week. We're still—"

"That's it," said Riley with a big grin on his face as he looked over to Aaron.

"They actually played it."

Aaron gave Riley a suspicious look. "What's the big deal about that video? Paragons fight hellions all the time."

"True," said Riley. "And the news loves to report on any little incidents that seem interesting, especially when footage is sent to them for free. Like that footage was."

"Alright, enough mystery, just tell me what it all means," said Aaron, seemingly getting tired of the charade.

Riley looked back to the television, then back to Aaron. He lowered his voice, but could still be heard clearly. "So, you remember Glint?"

"Not really?" said Aaron.

"Doesn't matter," Riley said dismissively. "She used to be part of Shadow Witch's group."

"I remember Shadow Witch," said Aaron.

"Well, Glint still has friends in Shadow Witch's guild, which is a PKer guild, and also a guild that happens to be helping one of the big hellion clans in the area. Namely, The Pale Ones. There was some speculation that Shadow and Shade were helping The Royals, the blue-armored hellions in our area, but after the fight in the caves, it seems as though that relationship might've gone bad. But anyway, Glint had her friends attack The Pale Ones' secondary lair. It's not their main one, it was mostly a resource-generation location that was supposed to be kept secret. She also had that streamer friend of hers go to that location, just on a fake whim, to be able to record their getaway. And now with some footage capturing Burning Halo leaving the scene with two others, The Pale Ones are going to hopefully think that Shadow Witch's guild is backstabbing them."

Aaron stared off in the distance as he listened, but when Riley finished, he looked back to him. "And how does that help anybody exactly?"

Riley sighed. "So, Shadow's guild has been selling player location info to this hellion clan. We're going to turn them against her, so that she and her guild, and maybe even Shade's guild, are now actively fighting the hellions as well. So instead of this crazy paragon vs. PKer vs. hellion conflict we have in Gargantuan, it'll be a bit more even."

"Sounds like a good plan," said Aaron. "I guess?"

"Well, that's not all of it," said

Riley. "The second phase is where we push the advantage. We're going to head out with Glint and go to one of the entrances to The Pale Ones' main lair. Apparently it's well defended, so we'd have a poor chance of fighting our way in with just our guild, but the idea is that the hellions on guard duty might be willing to hear Glint out if she offers to sell them info about Shadow's guild and hideout locations, and also their whereabouts and tactics."

"You think the hellions would be willing to hear her out?" asked Aaron. "Seems a bit hopeful to me."

"Well, the idea is that she's going to go there alone, with us waiting nearby in case things go south. She walks up to their front door alone, and apparently they may recognize her from being in Shadow's guild, because Shadow had a lot of in-person dealings with The Pale Ones, and Glint was usually around at the time. So… the plan at that point is to lure as many of The Pale Ones out as we can, on a time-sensitive attack, to hit Shadow Witch's group. Which is all a bluff. We just want to lure them out so that we can then attack their lair, when it's least defended… which is going to be hard no matter how we look at it."

"And you're inviting me to this party?" Aaron asked with a smirk.

"If you wanna come, absolutely. We'd love to have you, and, well, we could use every paragon, or greater, that we can get," said Riley.

"Hmm," Aaron murmured. "Well, I think it's a step in the right direction for turning the tide in Gargantuan, if things are as bad as they're saying on the news, and also what you've described. So yeah, I can definitely be there."

"Great. The plan is to lure as many of The Pale Ones away as we can, then sneak in. So, on site it'll just be The Bunker Brawlers, though unfortunately, we're not as many as we were when we made the guild, but with you, it helps. With the element of surprise, and with them hopefully away from their lair, along with the fact that two of us are tier-three, it should be enough."

"I like it," said Aaron. "It'll be nice to help you guys out, *and* I'll get to see how cool your power-stealing powers are. Have you thought about any interesting combos?"

Riley couldn't keep from grinning. "It'll all depend on what happens at the lair, but yeah, I've given it some thought."

CHAPTER 24: THE PALE ONES

One day later, Riley stood in an alleyway between two neighboring warehouses on the outskirts of Gargantuan City. It was a part of the city he hadn't frequented before. Gargantuan was a big place, and there were plenty of areas he'd never stepped foot in. With the advent of hellions, most of the players in Gargantuan pushed more towards the center for defensive purposes. This left the outskirts as a key haven and lair-building area for hellions.

Riley looked at each of the faces around him. Their numbers had definitely fallen as of late, but hopefully it would be enough.

Among the gathered players was Laura, the duplicator, who still had yet to achieve paragon, despite her high stats.

Carla, the Chromatic Lotus.

Chase, their spider-bot maker.

Amber Impaler, who had to be coaxed

into even showing up, as he wasn't a big fan of pain being part of the game.

Brenda, also known as Crossbolt, who would be able to lay down just as much damage as Carla, at least on single targets.

There was Parviz, who was apprehensive about the endeavor, but realized how vital he was to making sure things worked out well, especially since he was their main form of escape.

Red Shotgun and her partner Green Melter made a very powerful close combat team. Red and Green had higher stats than most of them, and were nearly on par with Aaron's stats in his bug form, but Aaron, or Arbiter, was still the single most powerful paragon in their group. Currently, Aaron was still in his human form, as he hadn't secretly used his tier-three sphere yet.

With Glint on her way and Riley, that made eleven.

Unfortunately, the death of Todd had seen Erica absent from the game. Shell's abandonment had mostly gone unnoticed, but Snow, along with Constructor and Blue Mist, had also been absent from guild activities as of late. They'd ignored Laura's messages for several days, and had just yesterday removed themselves from the guild.

There was also Seth and Marcella. They were still in the guild, but as fate would have it, they had set that night as a date night a week in advance and had made reservations at some nice restaurant, and weren't going to renege on their night out together, which nobody blamed them for.

The only member of their group who wasn't in the alley was Glint. They didn't have direct line of sight on her, but thanks to a little minion-crafting on Chase's part, he had one of his spider-bots set up as an observer in the warehouse that The Pale Ones used as the entrance to their main lair. Chase had configured one of his other bots to act as a sort of projector, so that they could all see what was going on in the warehouse. It looked a lot like the building that had been in the video he'd seen the other day, where Glint's friends assaulted the secondary lair of The Pale Ones. Glint didn't know if the clan had any more lairs than two, and she also didn't know how extensive the lair was beneath the surface. If it was anything like The Royals’ cave lair that they'd been in with all the trees, then it was likely that it could be huge. An eleven-strong group was going to have a lot of ground to cover.

The Bunker Brawlers were all huddled in a group, a safe distance from the warehouse itself. They watched the bot-based projection on the wall with anticipation, but also boredom.

"So, where is she?" asked Amber Impaler, his arms crossed. "We've been here for half an hour."

"We had to get into position before she started heading over," said Riley. "We may have the element of surprise, but we don't know what all those pale hellions can do. They may have something that works like a proximity alert. Luckily, we were able to use this projector setup to safely scout a spot to lay low."

"Spider-bots are a lot stealthier than my shimmering far sight effect," said Parviz. "Especially since I've never been in this area before. I can only use the far sight ability by thinking of a place I've already been and can visually remember."

Chase's bot was discreetly located near a cracked window on an upper story of the warehouse. It was able to see inside and outside, and had a good vantage on the street leading up to the warehouse.

"So, once the hellions follow Glint, we're going to sneak in?" asked Parviz.

"Yeah, that's right," Riley confirmed. "We lure the pale hellions out, and then Chase will see how far he can get into their tunnels with the spider-bot." He then looked to Chase. "You can't stealth them, can you?"

Chase shook his head. "Not yet. Maybe when I hit tier-two? But right now, no stealth. They're pretty quiet when they move slowly, but if they have to run, their metal legs will click a lot."

"We're all going to run over and sneak into the warehouse from a side entrance that Chase scouted," Riley continued, just so the plan was fresh in everyone's mind.

"Do we know where their tunnel entrance is?" asked Red.

"Let me pan over to it," said Chase, as he controlled his spider-bot to orient its camera towards the inside of the warehouse. "See that stack of crates against the wall? You can't tell from this angle, but there's a large gap between them and the wall, and there's a decently large hole in the floor over there. Hopefully it's the right entrance, and not some trap-entrance."

"That's why we'll send the bot in first," said Riley. "Then we'll follow behind it, once we know it leads to the main lair. We'll go in, do as much damage as we can, and kill any hellions we see. If we're lucky, this raid will give them a serious setback, until we can rally other guilds or paragons to help us. Or, to give more time to the Vanguard Alliance to make whatever moves they're working towards."

"Yeah, the alliance," Amber Impaler sneered. "The one that's been ordering our guild around, and dangling entry to their exclusive little club over our head as a reward. Bunch of arrogant—"

He was quickly cut off as Chase held his hand up to silence everyone. "I've got someone on the street," he said, as the spider-bot was now looking outside the warehouse. A single figure could be seen in the distance, making their way to the large rundown building.

"Looks like Glint, that's her silvery hair and attire," said Riley.

"Kinda reminds me of Seth," Amber murmured.

Walking down the street towards the warehouse was Glint. She appeared just as she had the other day when Riley had met her on their little ordeal in Colossal City. She walked casually, seemingly in no hurry. There wasn't any wind in the streets. Everything around her was still and silent, save for her footfalls. There were street lights interspersed around, illuminating the street, but not the alleys. The moon was eerily absent from the night sky.

"And they're not just going to attack her?" asked Carla. "She's out there all alone… Don't hellions usually kill on sight?"

"Well, the plan is hinging on the fact that they won't attack on sight," said Riley. "Glint said she's been around some of the pale hellions before when she was with Shadow Witch. So hopefully they'll at least give her a chance to talk, since she's just walking right up to their main lair's entrance."

"And what happens if they attack her?" asked Red.

"I'll just drop a portal under her," said Parviz. "We evac her, and then we all get the hell out of here."

"Sounds simple enough," said Red, who leaned against Green Melter's shoulder.

The gathered players all watched as Glint went down the street. For about a minute, nobody said anything. But then, the shadows shifted and contorted near the entrance to the warehouse. The warehouse's semi-open two-sided doors weren't illuminated by the street lights, and the shadows seemed oddly thicker in the direct vicinity around it.

"What's that?" asked Carla, pointing at the spot in the projection. "It's like the shadows are moving."

"I see it," said Chase, who leaned in to try and get a better look. As he did, the shadows took the form and shape of a robed figure. Unlike the typical cloaked humanoid player, this figure was unusually tall, with a long robe that went down to its feet. The sleeves hung down and it almost looked like an apparition as it left the shadows.

"I hope it's not some NPC guard," said Laura. "It won't even try to talk to her if it is."

"Shh, shh, let me set it for audio too," said Chase, as he reached his hand out toward the spider-bot. The robot shifted subtly and a small speaker appeared behind a slide-away panel.

Glint neared the robed figure. The group of paragons couldn't make out any details other than the long black robe of the entity.

"Hey," said Glint casually. She came to a stop and rested her hands on her hips. "I got info on the whereabouts of Shadow Witch and her crew. I know where they're gonna be later. I hear you guys might be interested."

The partially distorted audio from what

Glint was saying came over the small speaker on the spider-bot, allowing everyone to hear it.

The robed figure stood silent for a short time, as if sizing Glint up. Or perhaps waiting for something else.

A low raspy voice came slowly from it, even though none of its true features could be seen. "Glimmer… wasn't it?"

Glint sighed. "It's Glint," she corrected. "I used to run with Shadow Witch's crew, but I ditched them. I heard they attacked one of your bases. So, do you wanna get some revenge, or not? You know how it is, you send some currency my way if the intel checks out. And of course, you don't kill me."

Again, the figure was silent for an ominous amount of time. Then, the raspy voice came again. "Now… is not the best time."

Hearing this, Riley couldn't help but be reminded that hellions were just players like everyone else. Sure, they were more akin to player-killers, who progressed in the game through killing others, but they were still people, with their own ambitions, strengths, and weaknesses.

Glint waited to see if he was going to

say anything else. She glanced around, wanting to make sure that there wasn't anyone getting in position to ambush her. She had the ability to see through stealth, but even she couldn't see anything amiss in the area beyond the hooded entity. "I can't guarantee I'm going to have info this good ever again. This is your chance. If you don't want it, that's fine. I'm just saying, this is your opportunity if you want to take it."

"What's this paragon talking about?" came a deeper growling voice from further behind the robed figure.

An imposing creature slid from the mass of shadows that seemed to encompass the street directly outside the warehouse's main door.

The form that exited the shadows looked like some sort of humanoid white goliath beetle. Its armored exoskeleton gleamed in the dull light of the nearest street lamps. It stood on two segmented back legs that ended in small claws that clicked heavily against the stone street. It boasted an almost circular thorax and a sharply angled head with two sharp pincers jutting from the sides. Its two sets of arms were much like its feet, but longer. It lumbered into position beside the hooded figure. If the robed entity was roughly seven feet tall, this hellion was easily ten.

"She has information on the whereabouts of Shadow Witch and her clan," came the voice from the hooded figure.

Glint watched the tall beetle. Its eyes were purely black, and it was impossible for her to tell where it was looking, unless its head turned. It seemed to be placing all of its attention on her.

"We don't need it," came the deep voice from the beetle.

"But," said the hooded figure, "The Witch and her clan attacked—"

"It doesn't matter!" the beetle hellion roared. "We're moving out! Somebody, go ahead and kill her!"

Glint's arms fell to her sides as she heard the order to have her killed.

A moment later, something else moved from the shadows that the hellions had walked out of. It was as if the shadows outside the warehouse were linked to something else, like some sort of shadow-passage that only they could utilize.

The shape that burst from the shadows had the same white exoskeleton as the beetle. Its body continued to pour from the shadows, coming to unimaginable lengths. At first, it looked as if it was flying or gliding, but countless tiny 'feeler' legs were propelling it forward along the ground. It seemed to be an incredibly long centipede-like hellion, roughly five feet wide, two feet tall, and… well, there didn't seem to be an end to its length yet.

The centipede shot toward Glint, causing her to immediately turn and run. Her arm went out and from her palm came an intense light that radiated all around her, bathing the street in luminescence, as if the sun itself had come from her palm.

"Portal her out of there!" said Riley, just as the brilliant light flashed. Even from where they were in the other street, they could see the light from over the buildings.

"She's moving!" said Parviz. "I can't even see her!" At that point, they were all squinting from whatever Glint had done.

Parviz kept watching as best he could. His hand was already out, ready to aim his near-instantaneous portal ability, using the projected image of the street as his way of seeing the location.

"Do you see her?" asked Laura.

"Do you?" Parviz snapped back. The

radiant light was only now beginning to dissipate. Parviz could make out the writhing body of the centipede moving around the street. Then, he spotted a figure, but instead of Glint being on the ground, she was suspended in the air between the buildings. It took Parviz a few more seconds to realize what he was seeing. She appeared to be caught in some sort of webbing.

"I have her trapped!" came a feminine hiss through the audio of the spider-bot.

"I can't see anything! Where is she?" came a chittering growl that emanated from a swift-moving source in the street, surely belonging to the centipede.

Some off-screen hellion seemed to be speaking to the centipede that was diving around with his pincers at the ready to cut into Glint, once it was able to find her. The ability she used must've blinded the centipede, and surely several other hellions, except for whichever one had caught her.

"I can't portal her out of there if she's up in the air like that! I can't move the portal, and she won't be able to drop into it!" said Parviz frantically. "What are we going to do?"

"There's not that many of 'em, let's

get in there and kick their asses," said Red Shotgun. "That's what we came to do anyway, right?"

Riley watched the projection and shook his head. "It's not a great idea, but I guess it's all we can do. Let's do it! Parviz, portal us over there, but stay back here with Chase. That'll give us the safest escape possible, and Chase can still monitor the situation and use any spare bots to help out."

Chase nodded in agreement, as Parviz created a red portal on the side of the building on Glint's right. The portal was in an area that the centipede wasn't diving around. The light from Glint's hand had subsided completely by now, and the robed hellion was nowhere to be seen, but the goliath beetle was shielding its head with two of its arms.

With his other hand, Parviz opened a blue portal against the wall beside the projection from the spider-bot.

"Everybody go!" said Laura, who was the first to dive into the portal. Red and Green rushed in, and Laura's clones followed, one after another.

"Dammit," Riley mumbled to himself as he took a few steps back. "I… I think I'll just run over, I don't want to risk passing out."

"You better hurry!" said Carla, who then went through the portal, followed quickly by Amber Impaler and Brenda.

Riley turned to run, but a firm hand took hold of his shoulder. He looked over and saw Aaron. Or, more appropriately, Arbiter, as Aaron must've used the sphere in the last minute to discreetly become his Arbiter form. "I got an idea," said Aaron.

"Get going, we'll hold down this street," said Chase, urging them on.

"Don't fall," said Aaron, as he swiftly and effortlessly hoisted Riley over his shoulder.

"Uh, ok!" said Riley, trying to balance as well as he could, while being carried like a sack of potatoes. He'd barely finished his comment before Aaron leapt from the ground and onto the nearby building. The moment he landed, he leapt again, heading over to the next rooftop. The world rushed by for Riley as Aaron leapt around, closing the distance swiftly on their destination.

When they landed on the same building that had the exit portal that Parviz had created, Riley could already hear the shotgun blasts from Red, and the sharp hiss from Green's acid. A thick, acrid stench filled the air, as things started to melt and burn.

Riley was able to turn his head and partly survey the area, as Aaron was about to leap down to the street level.

A terrible roar emanated from the street below. Everything shook around him. It was like some sort of tremendous earthquake. It quickly set Aaron off balance. He fell over and dropped Riley on the roof. Then came the sound of an explosion… but without any heat, just a gust of wind that buffeted the rooftop of the three-story warehouse they were on.

Riley scrambled to his feet. A great smoky cloud had formed, engulfing the entire street below. It stretched far into the sky.

Riley craned his neck and found himself staring up at a gradually forming storm that grew bigger and bigger as the smoke from the street quickly coalesced into the strange dark cloud.

That was when he caught movement in the smoke itself. His gaze lowered and watched as a gleaming white exoskeletal arm rose into the sky. All of the nearby warehouses and buildings were only about three stories high. The monstrosity stood somewhere between seventy and a hundred feet tall. It was impossible for Riley to discern accurately with nothing close to its height nearby. It towered above everything. It was truly enormous, larger than most world bosses he'd seen. What sort of hellion could take such a form of this magnitude? As the smoke cleared and increased the size of the storm cloud above, the enormous goliath beetle's form was revealed.

It was then that he remembered Warcry's Rook Den and how it had been smashed into the ground, as if something had come along and pulverized the whole block into rubble.

This was the hellion responsible. Whereas Warcry had her whole guild to try and fight such a thing, unsuccessfully, they had less than a dozen.

Despair filled Riley's mind. For several seconds, he didn't even move as he tried to come to terms with the sheer size and scope of the hellion before him, despite how there were still other hellions around as well.

But there was one thing they had that Warcry, her guild, and all the players in that area didn't. Or more specifically, one thing *Riley* had.

Riley's lips curled. He turned to

Aaron, who was standing a few feet away. "Try and keep that thing distracted. It's huge, but… maybe you can fight it? Just buy me some time!"

"I don't care what stats I have, that thing's enormous! It's going to have some insane power behind anything it does, based on size alone! The hell are you going to do?" Aaron called, as Riley was already rushing to the side of the roof.

"Don't worry about me!" Riley called back.

Using his Ring of Expert Climbing, he was able to grab onto the side of the roof and descend it as if he was going down a ladder. He looked below, as he quickly made his way down the three-story brick building. The sound of Red Shotgun was easily discernable, as her powers were the loudest. There was still some measure of smoke in the area, along with debris and dust from the nearby structures that the enormous hellion had smashed into when it took its larger size.

With a meager glance around, he could see the ever-moving insanely long centipede. He spotted Amber Impaler's glowing orange tendrils stabbing repeatedly into the centipede-hellion's body. Just because these creatures were large didn't mean that they were immune to damage. They had stats like everything else, which meant that they could die, just like everything else.

As Riley reached the street level, he saw several of Laura's clones running by. "Use your mortars on that big one!" one of them shouted.

Riley knew immediately that Laura was calling out to Chase, and that Chase would surely hear the comment from the safety of the other street. With a large monstrosity like the goliath hellion, the mortars would be perfect, as it couldn't move out of the way fast enough. It was entirely unlikely that the hellion clan would be able to discern Chase and Parviz's location. Parviz had dispersed the portals after everyone had gone through, so there was no way for one of the hellions to sneak back through it.

Just as one of Laura's clones was running by, Riley reached out with his left hand and activated his left tattoo, effectively stealing Laura's powers. One down, he thought to himself as he ran toward the enormous hellion.

"Someone get me down from here!" Glint called, as she struggled in the confines of the webbing.

Riley glanced over. He had no way to

help her, so he kept running. In the corner of his eye, he spotted Green Melter heading in Glint's direction.

"I got you!" Green called. "Red, cover me!"

More shotgun blasts echoed around the street.

Riley's eyes narrowed, as he was having trouble seeing through some of the dust in the air. Part of the lengthy centipede's body was in his way, preventing him from getting closer to the enormous hellion. He veered to the right of the street to stick close to the building beside him. There was just a little room between the centipede and the wall, and if he was careful, he'd be able to sneak by.

The ground trembled beneath Riley's feet. He almost lost his footing but managed to clutch the wall of the nearby building.

The asphalt in the middle of the street began to tear and crack. A purple light glowed from the fractures, and from them, long, skeletal fingers reached out.

Riley was mesmerized. All throughout the street, these dark purple fissures formed and spawned humanoid skeletal minions that pulled their way from the ground.

"The hell are these?" Red shouted.

"We need to clear them out!" Laura replied, as her twenty copies were starting to quickly get outnumbered by the numerous skeletons. She'd been quick in ordering her duplicates to attack the skeletons that were still pulling themselves from the ground, while they were vulnerable.

"What about the big one?" Carla yelled, as her lotuses peppered the goliath hellion with high-damage explosions.

From further down the street, away from the goliath hellion itself, Brenda fired a series of red bolts from a safe distance away, taking shots at both the centipede and the enormous hellion that had seemingly came from nowhere. She kept firing, but kept a careful eye on the battle, in case anyone might need healing.

The street quickly descended into further chaos. The hero players quickly found themselves outnumbered and outmatched.

The goliath hellion was starting to move. Its lower set of arms reached out to stabilize itself further by crunching into the nearby rooftops, as one of its upper arms plummeted to the ground below, right towards Carla. Despite its huge size, the street was wide enough that nobody was clumped together.

Carla easily noticed the trouble she was in. She turned to run, but saw that she was being swarmed by a half dozen skeletons, closing in all around her. She threw her micro-lotuses to dispatch the nearby minions. The destruction was just far enough away to avoid harming her as well. With a quick glance, she looked back to the goliath's hand, which had clenched into a clawed fist. It was coming fast.

Light glinted off Aaron's exoskeleton as he leapt through the air. He shot like a dart toward the large hellion's head and smashed his own fist into its left eye.

The hellion bellowed a terrible groan. The immediate impact caused it to flinch and momentarily lose its grip on the nearby buildings. Its head teetered away as it roared. Its arms came up, seeking to protect itself as Aaron landed on its armored torso and began leaping around on its shoulders, kicking and punching its head and face. Despite looking incredibly armored and invincible, it appeared to be in obvious pain from Aaron's attacks, if its roaring was any indication.

Aaron's attack had bought Carla some freedom, as she redirected her attention to tossing lotuses to clear out more of the skeletons that were pestering the other heroes.

With everything going on, and since he hadn't made a grand entrance himself, Riley was going relatively unnoticed as he skirted around the right side of the street, avoiding the centipede. He did his best not to get too close to any of the skeletons, even though a few were clacking his way. Their bodies were noisy when they moved around.

Two skeletons were up ahead, coming right for him as he closed in on the giant hellion. He wouldn't easily be able to get past them and he had no offensive capabilities. He wasn't sure how he was going—

From behind him, two red bolts smacked into the two skeletons and detonated against their torsos, sending bones flying about, which then dissolved into particles.

Riley was thankful that Brenda was so observant. Now, he had his opening. Time seemed to slow as he closed those last few feet on the hellion's clawed foot. He was almost there!

Then, his right hand pressed against the foot of the enormous hellion. His palm glowed, and in an instant, he'd stolen its power.

His lips curled.

CHAPTER 25: CRIMSON

With a mere thought, Riley's form grew exponentially. His vision rushed higher and higher. He couldn't explain the feeling overtaking him. He was simply growing larger, his body heavier. Thankfully, his clothes grew with him.

He could see over the rooftops of the nearby buildings, but then, the growing stopped. Almost as if he was in a daze, he stared at the goliath hellion, who still stood twice his current height.

Why did he stop growing? Wasn't he

supposed to be as tall as the goliath hellion?

The hellion had managed to shield its face from Aaron.

Aaron had been forced to land on one of the nearby rooftops to assess the situation. That was when he caught sight of Riley's transformation.

Riley began to move, but his body was sluggish, as if every movement was taking extra long to achieve.

"Ha ha!" bellowed the beetle before him. "You thought you could take my power?" the hellion asked, its words slow. "It seems you could only take what I was capable of when I was only tier-two."

With that, the hellion grabbed one of the nearby buildings, once again steadying itself as it swung one of its upper arms at Riley.

Riley, being more nimble, was able to slowly swoop beneath the oncoming clawed fist, but before he could take a step towards the hellion, he looked to the street to make sure that he wasn't about to step on any of his friends. In that moment of uncertainty, the hellion grabbed him by his hair and lifted him up into the air.

There was an immense pressure on his scalp as his hair was pulled in this enlarged form. His feet left the ground. He could hear the commotion below, but had returned his gaze to the large hellion before him.

The hellion was tier-three, just like him. He wasn't able to take the hellion's full size. But… perhaps he didn't need to.

Instead of attacking, Riley reached out with his left hand and opened it wide.

A bright light formed as particles appeared out of nowhere and coalesced. A new pair of shoes smashed into the ground below, taking out several skeletons.

Using Laura's power of duplication, Riley created a copy of himself. He willed his clone to aid him, hoping the rudimentary AI would be smart enough to help him out, without him needing to take it over completely.

Riley Two—as Riley figured the clone's name to be—reached up, grabbed the hellion's arm, and pulled it down, so that Riley was now standing of his own accord. Then, Riley moved his arm further to the right side of the street and repeated the duplication process.

Just as before, particles shimmered and

the ground shook as a third Riley appeared. The street was becoming packed as Riley Three moved into position and grappled with the hellion's upper left arm.

"What?" the hellion roared, seemingly in disbelief at what was going on. "How?"

The hellion released its grip on Riley's hair, allowing him to pull back just a bit, while his two clones seized and grappled with the hellion's upper arms. The hellion was forced to release its hold on the nearby buildings that it was using to stabilize itself, as its legs didn't seem capable of supporting its sheer size alone.

Once those lower arms released the rooftops and grabbed at his clones, Riley seized the opportunity to step forward as quick as he could, which, admittedly, was a little slow.

But at that size, his speed was still faster than the much larger hellion.

Riley turned with his shoulder to the hellion and as he reached it, he pushed into it with his arm and elbow, and all the strength he could muster.

"No!" the hellion roared as its massive body was driven back. One of its legs lifted as it tried to steady itself, but it would be impossible for it to regain its footing as it was forced back.

The rest seemed to flow in slow motion as Riley shoved into the hellion, which fell back and smashed into the warehouse that housed the entrance tunnel to its clan's lair.

Riley and his clones were also brought down with the much larger hellion. He directed them with his mind to keep the hellion on the ground.

"Arbiter!" Riley called. "Damage!"

Compared to Riley's slow movements, Aaron practically zipped around, leaping from one of the rooftops and landing on the fallen hellion's chest, just above Riley's head. Aaron ran up and went right for the goliath hellion's vulnerable face, where he started to punch. Aaron's long, chitinous fingers seemed almost fragile, but were actually powerful.

Riley's lips curled into a grin, but before he could fully form it, a sharp pain pierced his lower back, as if someone was pinching him with sharp metal fingers. It didn't hurt any less just because he was large.

He turned his head slowly and managed to see over his shoulder. The long centipede had climbed up his leg and back, completely unbeknownst to him. He hadn't even felt it. Its sharp pincers were lodged in his back. Then, a second later, his vision flashed red again as the centipede pulled its pincers out, only to bite again.

With slow, strained movements due to the throbbing pain in his back, Riley pulled a knee forward and used his hands to push himself up to a kneeling position. Something brushed against his leg, but any sort of sensation dealing with touch was… unusual, to say the least. But still, it felt like something was there. He glanced down and saw another centipede scurrying quickly around his legs. Riley's eyes widened. The centipede was able to break into two? Were there more?

"Defend Riley!" came Laura's voice from far behind him.

A few seconds later, three mortars came raining down upon the large hellion's body as Riley's clones kept it well-restrained. There was no telling how much health a hellion like that had, but it was surely the best use of Aaron's abilities to eliminate the goliath hellion as quickly as possible and apparently, with the aid of Chase's mortars.

But now, Riley had troubles of his own. When he was regular-sized, he'd gone mostly unnoticed, but now, he was the second most noticeable player in the street.

He went to grab the centipede, hoping to pry it off his leg.

The centipede moved far too fast for him and as he went to grab it, it bit his hand. He winced as another sharp pain streaked through him. The pincers in his back tightened, causing him more pain.

He was starting to think that increasing his size wasn't the best plan, now that he realized how vulnerable he was. He hadn't taken the time to check his health to find out if it got a boost from having increased size. It was likely that he somehow got a defensive boost for being larger, but he wasn't positive. The centipede was hitting pretty hard with its two sets of pincers. He was cresting below seventy percent health.

He wasn't sure what would happen if he lost his main body. Would his consciousness go to one of the other two? Did his 'core' body matter? Laura tended to protect her core body, but did she do it from an efficiency standpoint? He'd never seen her use a copy to create another copy, as far as he could remember.

So for all he knew, he *really* needed to

keep his core body alive. Which meant he had to take another risk.

He willed his body to shrink to its normal size. He had hoped it would happen in an instant, but instead, it happened slowly. The goliath hellion had released a bunch of smoke when it transformed, and it had also seemed quicker. But then again, Riley was only stealing the hellion's tier-two capabilities, and not his tier-three.

The centipede chomped repeatedly into his back, even as he shrunk in size. The centipede by his feet was plunging its pincers towards him, but a burst of green acid splashed in its face and seared it for several seconds, before it burst into particles. A quick series of shotgun sounds came from behind him, and a few moments later, the aching pain in his back subsided. Bit by bit, he shrunk in size, until he was back to normal. He stumbled forward, disoriented from being small again. Or at least, regular sized. He turned around and watched as the centipede that had been biting him dove toward Red Shotgun and Green Melter, who were both blasting it heavily. The centipede broke off into another segment, only for the two women to damage it hard enough to kill it within seconds.

Riley quickly glanced around and saw the end of the centipede, which looked noticeably smaller. Whatever Red and Green were doing was working.

In the corner of his eye, he caught a bright flash. He turned just in time to see one of Laura's duplicates get stabbed through the heart by a skeleton with a sharp dagger made of bone.

Riley's first instinct was to reach out and blast it with his glove, but he no longer had any sort of weapon. It was just him and the powers he'd taken from Laura and the goliath.

There were still dozens of skeletons, and more were still rising from the ground. "Anyone got eyes on the robed hellion?" Riley called out. "Must be some kind of lich!"

Amber ran by, stabbing his orange tentacles through the ribcages of skeletons, shattering them in seconds. "Forget that, they're easy to kill! Find the damn spider that's skittering around and making those damn webs!"

"I second that!" Glint yelled from nearby, but Riley couldn't find her. There were still a lot of skeletons, and segments of the centipede blocking his view.

Brenda's bolts and Carla's lotuses were doing a good job of skeleton removal, but there seemed to be no end to them.

"Up there!" Brenda shouted, as she let loose several explosive bolts up at one of the nearby buildings.

Riley turned just in time to see the bolts smash into the buildings and blow up chunks of it, but he didn't see what she was shooting at.

He figured that they had it under control, and it wasn't as if he had any available stamina to do much else. He was almost tapped out with the two clones being super-sized. He kept an eye on them, making sure that they were doing their job of keeping the goliath down. It had been taking all of their strength just to keep the goliath's arms restrained.

Suddenly, a bright burst of light filled the street.

Riley squinted, almost about to shield his eyes as he thought Glint might've used her blinding light again, but the light wasn’t coming from where Glint was.

The goliath hellion's body had become glimmering particles that shimmered and shined. Then, they faded.

The enormous hellion was dead.

"Goliath is down!" came the chittering hiss from the centipede.

There were no other hellion voices that responded. It appeared as though the robed lich figure had taken a hidden position nearby, or had triggered his powers and ran. The white spider several of Riley's guildies had claimed to see was nowhere in sight either.

Feeling that his clones were at too much of a disadvantage against the remaining enemies, Riley willed the two of them to shrink to normal size and run to him. Once they did, he absorbed them and regained some of the stamina he'd been using to create them and keep them in their enlarged forms.

In the corner of his eye, he'd been keeping watch on the centipede hellion, but with only it and the skeletons, it was quickly getting whittled down to smaller and smaller segments, even as it split off. Riley noticed that some smaller segments of its long body tried to run at different times, but Brenda was usually able to damage it, while Red and Green dealt with most of it.

Now that Riley had no use for Laura's or the enormous hellion's power, seeing it as more of a disadvantage than advantage, he ran over to Red, who was faced away from him. "Red, let me borrow your power," he said as he placed his left hand on her shoulder for just a moment, to exchange Laura's powers with Red's.

"Sure thing," Red replied, barely paying him any mind as he gained her shotgun pellet ability.

Riley found himself side by side with Red on the right and Green on the left. He tested out Red's power and destroyed a few skeletons, using just a couple volleys that he was able to create by punching and concentrating on using Red's powers.

"I think they're thinning out," said Riley hopefully.

"Doesn't look like it to me!" said Red, who kept up her attacks.

Brenda, who had been separated from Carla, was starting to get enclosed by some of the skeletons. She was just barely managing to destroy them before they reached her.

Riley glanced over to where Aaron should've been, since he'd made quick work of the large hellion. He didn't see him anywhere. He kept glancing around, while trying to keep up with new skeletons that were clawing their way out of the ground. How many more skeletons could the lich make?

Surely there was some kind of limit!

A familiar voice groaned, and Riley caught movement in the corner of his eye. "Help me!" the robed lich yelled, as he fell in the street.

It was then that Riley caught Aaron walking out from a nearby alley, where the lich must've been lurking.

A short centipede segment practically leapt over to intercept Aaron, but a quick triple shot from Brenda took care of it.

Aaron started wailing on the fallen lich. Riley had no doubt that the lich would be dead in seconds.

In the same moment, Red Shotgun and Green Melter fell to the ground on either side of him.

Riley glanced over to Red, then to Green. What the hell? Had they been hit?

"Red?" he called, about to step over to her when one of the skeletons closed in on him. He had to shoot it with the red pellet energy blast that he'd stolen from Red Shotgun, but a single volley decimated the skeleton. He quickly knelt beside her, punching the air and destroying any skeletons that continued to near them. "Red? Are you alright?" he asked. "Someone! Get over here!" he called as he shook Red's arm, then looked over to Green. Neither of them were moving, but their bodies weren't breaking into particles, which meant that they weren't dead. Were they just asleep? Or Paralyzed?

Two of Laura's clones rushed over to help. Both of them were wielding swords which cleaved through the skeletons that got close. "What's wrong with them?" came Laura's voice from further away.

"I don't know! They're not moving!" Riley called back.

A burst of light glimmered in the corner of his eye. He looked over and saw that Aaron had dealt with the lich. His friend quickly dashed over to him, slaying any skeletons in his path. The glowing fissures in the ground began to fade and close, as the lich had been defeated.

Riley took a quick glance around, noticing that there was no sign of the centipede. Had it been destroyed? Or had part of it escaped?

"Did anyone kill that spider?" Carla yelled as they mopped up the remaining skeletons, which weren't much of a problem when they weren't being reinforced by an endless supply.

"I don't see it!" Amber Impaler replied, as he ducked into the nearby alleyways, trying to find it.

Riley returned his attention to Red, shaking her arm. "Red, wake up!" he urged, but there was no response from her.

Aaron arrived at his side. "What happened? Did they get hit with something?"

"I don't know!" Riley exclaimed. "They just dropped. I didn't see anything happen."

Laura was the next to arrive in their little group, just as one of her remaining clones slayed the last skeleton in the street. She was down to six, plus her core body.

"Brenda! Carla! Try and heal them!" Laura yelled, looking over to where the other two young women were.

Carla was running over, but Brenda took careful aim and shot a green glowing bolt at Green Melter.

Once Carla was close enough, she quickly created a green lotus and threw it to Red. It burst into green particles against her, but there was no noticeable change in either of them.

"Damn, what the hell happened to them,"

Laura murmured. "It's almost like…" She trailed off, then looked to Riley.

Riley looked up to her. "Like what?"

"Like when you blacked out after coming through the portal after that fight in the cave," she responded. "You just went unconscious and crumpled. Maybe something similar happened to them?"

"Maybe they got disconnected from the game," said Carla, who was still glancing over her shoulder, as if looking for more enemies. "You know, maybe their Internet provider went down, or they had a power outage."

"I guess it's possible," said Riley, who slowly stood back up. "But… what do we do?"

"All we can do is just watch them until they come back," said Laura. "I guess we can bring them back to Bunker 7. That spider is still nearby, but it's not going to attack us if we—" Laura's eyes were drawn up to the sky.

Riley had noticed a glint of light in the sky as well, and had looked up just as she did.

Amber Impaler, Glint, and Brenda all started to gather around them, but now everyone was looking into the sky.

"The hell is that?" Amber was the first to speak.

Far above in the night sky, a dozen orange-glowing circles slowly expanded.

"What are they?" Aaron asked.

The glowing circles were easily several hundred feet above them, but none were on the outskirts of the city. They didn't seem to be above anything in particular. They appeared random.

The strange discs stopped expanding. It was difficult to see how large they'd gotten. A moment later, amber meteor-like objects descended upon Gargantuan City.

"Is it an invasion?" Riley asked, as the portals in the sky spit orange-glowing meteors down upon the city.

"This might be something else," said Glint, who stared into the sky. "Did you all hear what that hellion said?" She looked down to Riley. "It sounded like they were all heading out somewhere. Like, maybe they knew this was about to happen?"

"So this is some sort of hellion attack?" Laura asked.

"Most likely," said Glint. "They didn't want anything to do with the ruse. They had something more important going on, and this has to be it."

"But their warehouse is smashed," said Amber, pointing over to where the goliath hellion had fallen back on the building and leveled it. "Shouldn't we dig the entrance out and try and destroy their lair?"

Riley glanced over to the smashed building. "That's what we came here for," he said. "But it's not going to be a quick run-in, now."

"Just super-size yourself again, and dig the entrance out," said Amber. "Easy."

Riley gestured down to Red and Green. "What about them? We can't just leave them here. We need them to take the lair. It could still have a ton of NPC defenses. The hellions we killed might be able to rally their friends to sign on and attack us while we're down there. We don't have the element of surprise anymore, and we're down two of our higher levels."

A blue portal opened nearby. First came Parviz, then Chase.

"Guys! The portals in the sky!" Parviz exclaimed.

"We know," said Riley. "We're trying to work out what to do about—"

"No no no!" Parviz shook his head and pointed up at them. "Look!"

"Yeah, we saw them!" said Laura, even as she looked up into the sky.

The orange portals were shrinking. But one by one, new ones grew and opened from small pinpoints. The locations of the portals had changed, and once the portals reached full-size, new meteors rained down upon the city.

"They're dropping in troops! It's the Crimsons, I read about them on the forums. They're all reddish, like The Pale Ones were white, and The Royals were blue. They're doing some sort of mass invasion," said Parviz.

"What? How do you know?" asked Glint.

"I used my far sight to get a closer look at the portals," said Parviz. "And I can see where they're coming from. It's like, this massive cavern, with a bunch of those dark amber pods. There's a whole army of red demon-like things getting into them."

"You can see through the portals?" asked Riley.

Parviz nodded. "Yeah, they're unloading this army on Gargantuan through the portals. We're about to get wrecked, hard."

"What happened to Red and Green?" Chase asked, waiting for a moment of silence in the conversation. "Are they ok?"

"We don't know," said Riley. "They just collapsed. They might've gotten disconnected. But unless they come back, we're down two players, and we need to protect them."

"So what's the plan?" asked Glint, still new to being with the group of players around her. "Attack The Pale Ones' lair? Defend the city? Protect Red and Green? We can't do all of them."

Riley glanced back into the sky. "Parviz, you said you could see into the area that the hellions were forming up from. How many troops were left?"

"Um, I didn't get the best look before the portal ended up closing," said Parviz. "But from what I saw, maybe thirty percent? Or twenty?"

"What are you thinking?" Laura asked, her sights on Riley.

"I'm thinking we need to hit the Crimson clan when they least expect it. We might've dealt a serious blow to The Pale Ones by eliminating some of their players. We can always try hitting their lair another time, but this attack is huge. We have to put a stop to it, else we might lose the entire city." Riley glanced back to Parviz. "Can you use your ring again, right when one of the portals starts to open, and cast a portal in the room these things are in?"

"Yeah, sure," said Parviz. "You wanna attack the whole army?"

"Not the army, just whoever is in charge," said Riley. "I say we put a stop to them, and maybe have a chance at destabilizing the attack. The players in the city will start forming up and defend it… but this might be the final nail in the coffin for Gargantuan unless we can stop whoever's up there. We should wait just a little longer until they've launched more of their troops. We have no idea how strong they are."

"And what about Red and Green?" asked Laura. "We can't just leave them here."

Riley looked down between them, then glanced around at his guildmates. Then, his gaze fell to Aaron. He knew that Aaron didn't have an unlimited amount of time in his Arbiter form, and he didn't want to tell the others about it, nor did he want to risk

Aaron losing his true fighting capabilities in the thick of the next fight. "Aaron, can you carry them both back to Bunker 7? There should be other players there, at least. It's one of the more durable buildings, if this hellion attack gets bad."

Aaron nodded. "I can," he said, not offering up any disagreement. It seemed that Riley might've been right about Aaron not having much longer in his tier-three form.

"Then go do that now," said Riley. "I don't want that spider taking advantage if it's just you, after we've left."

"Alright, good luck," said Aaron. He quickly hoisted Red Shotgun over one arm, and Green Melter over the other. For Aaron, it seemed almost effortless. Then, he leapt to one of the nearby buildings. The moment he landed, he leapt again, heading off in the direction of Bunker 7, towards where many of the hellion-filled meteors were falling.

"How are we all on health and stamina?" asked Laura.

"I'm alright," said Carla.

"Same," said Brenda.

"Fine here," said Amber.

"Me too," said Parviz.

"I'm down a couple bots, but I can still manage to build some stuff," said Chase.

"I'm good," said Glint, "if you still want me along for the ride."

"We'll need all the help we can get," said Riley. "Are we good to go then?"

"Those portals have opened and reformed a few more times," said Chase. "If we don't go soon, we might miss our chance."

"Then let's do it," said Riley. "Parviz, do your thing."

"Here we go," said Parviz, as he used the ability of his ring to cast the far sight effect up in the sky, near one of the newly created portals. As he did, a small circular mirage appeared in front of him, which he used to see the faraway spot in the sky. The portal was still opening and hadn't dropped a meteor yet. "I just see the meteor… We'll have to wait for it to move out of the way," he said as he grit his teeth, looking down at the window-like mirage before him.

Laura moved closer to Riley. "Are you going to be alright going through the portal?"

Riley had already realized that he was going to have to risk it. He nodded. "Yeah, just once shouldn't be so bad. We don't have much of a choice, do we?"

"You don't have to go," said Laura. "You can just go back with Aaron and defend the bunker. We can manage without you."

"Just one time won't make a difference," said Riley. "It's fine, I'm coming with you."

Laura relented with a nod. She stepped away and drew her other clones nearby in a line, ready to go through the portal once Parviz had made it.

"Meteor's down!" Parviz called as he quickly drew his arms up, one to the far sight effect in front of him, the other to the ground nearby. A blue portal opened on the wall of a nearby building just in front of them. Unlike the portals the hellions were using, there was no way to see where it led until they'd walked through.

"Let's go!" said Parviz. Now that he'd created the portals, he let his far sight ability dissipate, since he didn't need to see into the structure that the army was being launched from.

"Me first!" said Amber, who ran through the portal.

Glint was next, followed by Chase and Carla.

Laura with her six clones rushed through the portal, Brenda right behind her.

Finally, Riley steeled himself mentally for what he imagined might be a tough portal exit. With Parviz on his heels, he walked quickly into the blue portal.

CHAPTER 26: THE DEAL

Riley's eyes opened. Sounds he couldn't make out assaulted him from every side. He was on the ground, somewhere. He must've passed out. But… for how long? What was going on? He pulled himself up and looked around.

Laura was standing a couple dozen feet away; her back was to him, a revolver in her hand.

A blue portal opened beneath her, and a moment later, she fell through it, just as dozens of crimson blasts pelted the area around the portal. Some of the blasts made it through, but a second later, the portal disappeared.

Riley's eyes widened. Before he could even move, something wrapped around his torso and trapped his arms against his sides. Several feet of orange-glowing tendril appeared in his vision. What was going on? His vision flashed red, and he felt a searing pain all along his body where the tendril grabbed him, as acid ate into his body and his hitpoints. Had Amber Impaler betrayed them? What was going on?

His body was lifted up and smacked down into the ground. He winced from the impact, taking some extra damage. A sudden weight appeared at the small of his back, as if someone was pressing their fist against it. Then, he felt something press against the back of his skull. It was cool against his skin and felt like metal.

"Stop!" Brenda's voice yelled from behind him. "Else Riley dies! We all know what that might mean!"

The sounds around him started to fade. The acid damage cut into his hitpoints every few seconds, but wasn't enough to kill him. But if that was her crossbow against his head, a triple explosive shot, or hell, even a single shot, would critical hit him for more hitpoints than he had left. He wouldn't survive it. Somehow, he'd taken damage after coming through the portal and passing out again. How much time had gone by?

"What's going on?" he growled from his position on the ground.

"Just doing what I have to," said Brenda from above him.

Riley turned his head, trying to take in the scenery around him.

"I don't understand," Riley said, as he saw Glint and Parviz hiding behind a red portal, while the blue one was placed on the ceiling, away from them. It looked as though he was using it as some sort of shield, but Laura was nowhere in sight. Where had she gone? Was she alright?

With a little more glancing around, he spotted Chase and Carla half-crouched behind a mechanical-looking barricade. In fact, it looked as if Chase had morphed one or more of his spider-bots into some sort of makeshift fortification.

Then he saw Amber Impaler's mass of tendrils, which had created a similar barricade in front of him in the direction of the figure about a hundred feet away. It was in that moment that Riley remembered an item Brenda had gotten a long time ago, which allowed her to spawn a single orange tendril. He'd never seen her use it. He'd utterly forgotten she'd had it.

But those thoughts were washed away as he looked across the room at the only other figure he could see.

It was a humanoid form. A reddish skull was almost hidden between a pair of dark black horns, and a black cyberized mask seemed to be a part of its torso. Its arms and lower legs were all the same reddish-orange hue as its face, while the cyberized portion made up its upper legs, torso, and smaller sections of its arms.

If anything, it looked like some sort of cyberized demon. But as Riley looked at the hellion, he realized that there were all sorts of strange half-mechanical, half-organic contraptions around him, and above him. On the ceiling was a series of ten turrets with their muzzles in his direction.

He had no idea what the other contraptions could possibly be. Some were spherical, some looked like chairs or benches. Others were pod-like. Another looked like some sort of vat, or stasis cell. There was another that looked to be some sort of viewing monitor, and behind it was some strange half-orb with red light spewing out of it.

It was then that he realized the room they were in was made of brown stone, but all the red light was casting an almost sunset-like quality to everything.

"It looks as though we are at a bit of an impasse," came the words of the cyber-demon hellion. "My name is Sage. I'm the leader of The Crimsons. And, well, now it's no real secret, that out of game, I'm Brenda's brother."

"You betrayed us?" Riley growled, speaking only loud enough for Brenda to hear.

"Loyalty only goes so far," said Brenda. "I wasn't going to let you kill my brother."

"But you're willing to kill me instead?"

"Of course I am!" Brenda's voice rose.

"Stop!" Sage called and took a few steps closer, but kept his distance from everyone.

Riley could see Parviz and Amber talking, and with a glance, he noticed that Chase and Carla were doing the same. He couldn't hear anything they were saying, but he knew they were in a tough spot. Their group was separated, betrayed, and potentially outgunned. This was bad. Real bad.

"I'll share a secret with you," Sage continued. "We're very alike, you and I. I'm not sure what your condition is, but it's evident that there's something, else your guildmates wouldn't have stopped as they did. And my sister wouldn't have used you for leverage like this."

"If I'm so expendable, why not just kill me?" Riley called over, wincing from another sting from the acid. "You're stalling. We have the upper hand, we can destroy you."

"Possibly!" Sage called back. "Who can say? You're in my nest, though, and here, I easily account for five paragons. If your friends attack from behind their barricades, the skirmish will surely claim some, if not all of them, since Brenda is also on my side. She'll dispatch you in an instant, and move to help me clean up your other guildmates. But! That's not what I want. I want to come to an arrangement."

"What?" Brenda said from behind Riley. "But we have them! We can't take the risk!"

Sage held his hand up as if to quiet his sister. "They're not stupid," he said. "If they attack, they die. It's that simple.

That one over there," he gestured toward Parviz and Glint. "He has the ability to flee. He could portal away and save himself, but he would leave everyone else stranded, and they would die. If he attempts to send his portals to save his comrades instead of himself, he and that woman taking cover with him are both dead. Them aside, we have those two over there behind the wall that surely couldn't take more than a few volleys from my turrets, and this orange fellow."

"The name's Amber Impaler!" Amber yelled, his fists clenched. "Turn off those lasers, and we'll see who wins!"

"Ah, but I *am* my lasers," Sage laughed and shook his head. "But I'm sorry, I got sidetracked there. Please, let's talk."

Riley didn't say anything at first. He looked to the three separate groups of his friends. They were all over fifty feet from him. The room was much larger than the small area they currently occupied. But the launch area that Parviz had spied earlier seemed to be cleared out. All of the invasion pods had been dispensed, and while they chatted, Gargantuan City was being destroyed.

"Alright," Riley called. "Let's talk. Can… you make this acid tendril go away?"

"Let him go, but keep him in line,"

said Sage.

"Five… four…" Brenda started to count down. "Two… one." The tendril disappeared in orange particles, and the pressure alleviated. "It only lasts for a minute anyway." Brenda's knee pressed more firmly on his back, but it was a lot better than the sting of acid.

"Thanks," Riley grunted. Then, he spoke up for Sage to hear. "So what's your deal?"

"My deal," Sage said, taking a few more steps forward, "is that we all survive this. Both in-game, and out of it. I'm not sure about the rest of your friends, but you and I, we may not survive a death in this game. Which is why Brenda has turned on you. Which I'm thankful for. I wish I had known to prepare for this, but… well, I didn't see this coming."

"It all happened really fast," Brenda said. "I'm sorry. I didn't know what to do."

Sage waved his hand dismissively. "It is what it is," he said. "But now we have to deal with the situation at hand."

"You're destroying our whole city with your invasion," Amber yelled.

"Ah, yes, yes I am," Sage agreed with a nod. "I will seize your entire city, and The

Crimsons will lay claim to it. I've already incorporated The Royals into my fold. That little venture with your city's NPCs was my doing, with the help of my portal machine over here, which just so happens to be out of commission, thanks to that flower child over there."

"Say that to my face, you horned freak!" Carla yelled as she stood up, only to be pulled back down into cover by Chase.

"You're quite a group," said Sage. "You all work together very well, and Brenda has always spoken highly of The Bunker Brawlers, despite your more recent shortcomings. But I also hear that you're looking to join the Vanguard, which have admittedly been quite a pain in my side, even if they have been relatively useless at competently forming groups to achieve any meaningful goals in Gargantuan City. The Crimsons, The Royals, and The Pale Ones have all been vying for dominance in Gargantuan, but thanks to your mess up of The Royals, and my ability to seize control of what they were doing, it worked greatly to my benefit. That time-stopper hellion, Chrono, I think you've met him a couple times now. He's a piece of work. He's going to do some great things. In fact, he *was* doing great things, until you wrecked his lair. Which, I guess I have to be thankful for as well, because it led him to The Royals, and now to me."

"So you're just collecting up all the hellions we break?" asked Riley.

"More or less," said Sage. "If the strong stick together, we can do anything. That goliath hellion you just killed thought he was the biggest and the best, and took leadership of The Pale Ones. Which was commendable, but short sighted. So Taurus, who I believe you owe your new powers to, joined us in secret. I thought their attack on Colossal City was a bit… wasteful, but I wasn't in charge of that. Your fight with the remaining Pale Ones was unexpected, but helpful. You should count yourselves lucky that Taurus wasn't there, else that fight might've gone poorly for you."

"You sure do tell your brother everything about us, don't you?" Riley grumbled.

"He's all I have to talk to," said Brenda. "He's the only family I have, and I'm all he's got. Wouldn't you do the same for that friend of yours, Aaron?"

Riley lowered his gaze, as any form of rebuke faded from his mind.

"So! What do you say?" Sage asked.

Riley looked up at him. "To what?"

Sage tilted his head to the side. "To

joining the Crimson Alliance."

"Join you?" Amber and Carla yelled, almost in unison.

"But of course!" Sage said, stepping closer, but he was still a good distance away. "Your Vanguard Alliance of Paragons could do nothing to stop me. I'm obviously the stronger power, and when I crush Gargantuan outright, I will hold full control. The hellions of the city will thrive and reach new heights, while the heroes will be forced to vacate and find new homes. There is a change on the horizon. I can feel it. The developers won't be able to sit idly by while another city is claimed by chaos. First, there was Uber City, which devolved to PVP. Now Gargantuan, claimed by hellions. The developers will have to implement a system that allows for the creation of structures and infrastructure. I'd wager my new kingdom that the next expansion deals with building. Because it has to, if this game is going to survive."

Riley was still trying to catch up with everything Sage was saying. A lot of it made sense, but his mind kept returning to the fact that their home was being destroyed. "I'm not the guild leader," said Riley. "I can't accept any sort of alliance with you."

"I hate to say it, but you can," Chase

called over. "Laura made you second-in-command officer status, you're able to do that kinda thing."

"Oh crap," Riley grumbled on the ground.

"I ask again, do you accept joining the Crimson Alliance?" Sage asked. "You can keep your guild name, if you wish. Since you'd be the only heroes in my alliance."

"Keeping our name means nothing if we can't keep our home," said Riley. "And you're destroying our home."

"You call Bunker 7 home, right?" Sage asked, looking to Brenda for confirmation. She nodded.

"That's right," said Riley.

"Then I'll leave it alone," said Sage. "Your Bunker 7 will not be harmed. No hellion in my alliance will harm you, or your home. Admittedly, there might not be as many people around to frequent it, but it'll allow you to gain your buffs and everything that heroes might need. At least, until the developers do something about building. Which, as I said, has to be what they work on next, or I will continue to claim city after city until I rule the whole game. The only way to stop that is to allow players to build their own cities, towns, structures, and I don't know, implement a better minion system."

Everything Sage was saying was making more sense by the moment. "Your brother's not a developer, is he?" Riley asked.

"Nope," said Brenda. "But he's giving you a way out of this. I suggest you take it."

"And trust you, after you just betrayed the whole group?" Riley asked.

"Hey, you'd have done the same if that was Aaron over there," said Brenda. "Tell me again, after we found out that the White Weevil was your friend, we killed him, right? That's what happened, after all he'd done?"

"No, we didn't," Riley murmured.

"Oh, right. We let him live, because he was *your* friend. I completely forgot we did that, because… you know, he did some bad stuff to paragons."

Riley sighed. "So how does this work? If we accept?"

"What? Are you serious?" Amber called, turning his head back to Riley. "We can take one hellion and Brenda!"

"I'd prefer not to be dead, Amber!" Riley shot back. "We're taking the deal and joining them. You can leave if you want to. I don't care. I've had too much today. I just want to call it a day and log off, and see what Sigil is like tomorrow, after… after everything is under this guy's control, I guess."

"Then it's settled," said Sage. "Brenda, let him up, and bring him over here. It's not that I don't trust you to not pull a fast backstab on me, but… well, I don't trust you to not pull a fast backstab on me."

Sage held out his hand, just like any hero player might do when inviting someone to their group.

Brenda got off Riley's back, and even helped him up. "I'm sorry," she murmured. "I was only going to shoot if it looked like everyone was going to kill him. I… don't want you dead, Riley," she said, keeping her voice low, just for him. She then put her crossbow to his back as Riley walked forward.

"Could you have really done it?" Riley asked. "Knowing that I might actually not wake up after you did?" He kept walking towards Sage. The turrets on the ceiling were tracking him.

"I guess we'll never know," said Brenda. "And I think it's best that way."

Riley reached Sage in what felt like minutes of walking. He turned his head and spotted the rest of his guildmates, all looking out from behind their different barricades. "Well, this'll be new," Riley murmured as he looked up to Sage, who stood about a foot taller than him. He held out his hand and shook the hand of a hellion.

EPILOGUE

Months later.

Paragon Cafe was busy as usual. People were drinking coffee, eating pancakes for dinner, and watching the latest news about their favorite games. On one television, developers were talking about a futuristic space game that was gaining fan attention while it was still in development.

On another television, an interview was starting up. Seated on the left side of the screen on a red chair was a middle-aged man with short red hair. He was thin and a little pale. On the screen, it showed his name as 'Blake Grigson.'

Across from Blake sat another man in a red chair. He had tan skin and a buzzed head. He wore a black T-shirt with 'Sigil Online: Bastions' written on the front in all white letters.

"So let me just say real quick," said Blake, the interviewer. "I'm here with Jacob Nunez, the lead developer of Sigil Online at Apendia." He gestured over to Jacob, just a couple feet away from him. "It's great to have you once again on the show Jacob, but let me just cut straight to the chase here and say, your shirt!" He held out his hands, gesturing to Jacob with raised eyebrows. "Bastions? I need to know more, right this instant!"

Jacob got a big grin on his face and sat back a bit in his seat as he tugged on the hem of his shirt to straighten out the lettering. "Bastions is the name of the next big update for Sigil Online. I know we've been throwing around the word expansion since Hellions, but nobody had to buy Hellions, and expansion kind of relays the idea that it needs to be bought. So, you can think of Bastions as an expansion, or just a huge content update for Sigil Online."

"Uh huh, uh huh," said Blake. "I still need more here, buddy, give me some juicy details. Bastions are like, forts? Fortresses? Castles or something? What are we getting in this update?"

"We ran into some definite snags with the release of Hellions and some of its subsequent content patches," said Jacob.

"Like the pain fiasco?" asked Blake a little pointedly. "I gotta say, that one really hurt. Not going to lie. I was in the game when it happened. It was not fun."

Jacob slowly sighed. "Yeah, I agree. Unfortunately, things didn't go as planned. What happened was that we handed over a large portion of code, such as new functions, and a whole lotta other stuff, to the in-game AI. And well… one of those things was the pain feature. We've fine-tuned pain in the game, to be unpleasant, so that you definitely don't want to take a lot of damage, but it won't be as agonizing as it was those first couple days. If anyone wants more information on any of that, please see the statement we released several months ago about that incident."

"Yeah, yeah, sorry to derail you there, buddy," said Blake. "Back to these bastions."

"As I was saying," Jacob went on. "Due to Hellions, we discovered that we needed to implement some systems to level the playing field. With Sigil Online: Paragons, we had a really good thing that was mostly well-contained. From that spawned hellions, to really mix things up. But in that mix-up, we… mixed things up quite a bit. And now we have to, well, allow for things to be… less mixed up."

"Yeah, I get you, I get you," said Blake. "So, how about those bastions?"

"Right," said Jacob. "Bastions is going to be the long-awaited crafting and infrastructure update. All across the board, we're adding systems to crafting, research, minions, building, supply lines, overhauling what NPCs are capable of, and how they're created for the paragon, or what players have been labeling the 'hero' side of the game. A lot of these features will be in some way open to the hellions as well, but the hellions, when they were implemented, already had a lot of these features in small ways, depending on the hellion's powers and building capabilities."

"So when you say bastions," said Blake, "you're saying players can do more than just build a warehouse, or an office, or a shop?"

"I'm saying a resourceful guild of players could build their own city," said Jacob, holding his hands out as if to relay the size of something. "Bigger than any city currently in the game. Bigger than all of those cities combined. We're letting players go absolutely crazy with this next update. The entire world could be decimated and destroyed, but built back up, entirely player designed."

"Wait, are you destroying the world?" asked Blake, leaning forward in his seat. "Are you having some cataclysmic event to bring in this new update?"

Jacob suddenly waved his hands in front of himself. "No no no, not at all. Nothing like that. No. I'm just saying, no matter what destruction may occur, like what happened with Uber City, and what has in more recent events happened in Gargantuan. Those cities were utterly changed by the events that transpired, and have not recovered to what they were. This update would allow players to rebuild those cities in different ways, or merely incorporate that land into a whole different city. In fact, with the new update, whichever clan or player owns the area could technically rename it to something else."

"So, bastions," Blake repeated, as he held his hands as if he was holding some kind of box. "I can build, with my guild, a whole fortified city… but, like, what reason would someone have to come and attack us? Like, why bother, you know? What's in it for them? They can't seize resources, only territory, right? Are you changing that too?"

Jacob nodded. "What we're doing is changing the current system. In the game's current state, containers and facilities are kind of hard-coded in. If a city building is destroyed, it's rebuilt, just as it was. If a player's apartment is destroyed, it's rebuilt just as it was. If the furniture was broken, it can't be used for its effects, and inventory in a chest can't be accessed until it's repaired completely. That's how things currently work, but in Bastions, it's all different. We're allowing facilities to be raided for resources."

"Wait, so I won't be able to have some stuff stored away safely anymore?" Blake asked.

"Well, even in the current system, a lot of players lost items in both Uber City and Gargantuan. Some players ran back and rebuilt their storage containers to pull the loot out of them and move to another city. But we've found that the system doesn't create a loyalty to one's home. There's too much safety. We want people to defend what they have, but we also want to make it so that players are able to more easily rebuild if they've lost anything. A player's character and their gear are their most valuable assets. But with bastions, we may have players without any power at all waging war against tier-two, or even tier-three players. So we're going to allow players to obtain the loot from containers that they seize. We're also doing away with instanced rooms. Which is currently how most inns work. For anyone unfamiliar with what instanced rooms means, you can have a building that's only a lounge and a basement, but the basement allows players to reach hundreds or different rooms which would all be larger than what a basement could support. It's like a bunch of mini dimensions, accessible from one location. With bastions, rooms will be expanded immeasurably, so there'll be no reason to have instanced rooms. This is going to severely change how the game currently operates, and we understand that some people might not be happy about it, but we feel it creates a lot of opportunity in the game."

"Hmm, that's a lot to take in," said Blake. "I'm not sure how I feel about being able to lose all my stuff. And what's going on with my room, if you're removing the instance of it? Does my stuff disappear?"

"First of all, one thing we're doing is that if a player dies, their items will now remain right where they are. They can store their items and money safely somewhere, and if they lose their character, they can still retrieve those things if they make a new one, and if nobody knows where those items are. Furthermore, there will be a timeframe that players are going to be warned about the change, and they'll have to find a room that isn't instanced. There's quite a lot of building space in most of the cities. But right now, a lot of it is used for NPC offices that don't really do much of anything. So, staking claims to land is going to be overhauled as well. But we feel everything is going to go relatively smoothly, with how we're envisioning the transition. We're implementing a wave of new capabilities for players to both generate and gather resources from the world itself. Currently, the cities of Sigil Online are all kind of built up together, with a vast desert around them. There's some lakes and forests out there, and other dimensions they can access, but overall, the main building area is all those cities. We're allowing the game to spread out beyond those cities, and build wherever players want to actually be. They could create a bastion in Death's Chasm, or the amber caves, the crystal fields, The Twilight Catacombs, wherever! Some of those territories are hard to get to, but if players are enterprising enough, they'd find ways to make it work, either with things they can now build, or with items they find, or with the powers of other players."

"So you're saying I can have my dream home, a little cottage out by the Crystal Shore?" asked Blake with a big smile. "There are some really nice fish out there. Absolutely gorgeous scenery. I love it. So I can build a… bastion cottage and call it my home, and live out on the Crystal Shore?"

"You absolutely can, Blake," said Jacob. "Collect some resources, send out some builders, there's a ton of ways to do it, but yes. You can have that home you've always wanted. You could just fish every day. And as long as nobody wants that spot, I doubt anyone would bother you."

"Well, I hope nobody bothers me," said Blake. "Cause I'm pretty weak in Sigil. I'm not gonna lie, but! What I am is super freaking excited for this update, even with the prospect of losing some stuff. It sounds like I'll have a lot more opportunity in the game. I mean, Hellions was absolutely crazy when it came out. It was hectic, chaotic, I feel like the whole economy was turned upside down. But now we have this huge update. It sounds a lot more stable at first, but from what you're saying, it may be just as chaotic and terrible as Hellions was. Am I wrong? I mean, answer me this; from my cottage dream home, could I employ or build NPC gatherers to gather the resources necessary to build an army of NPC warriors of some sort, let's call them 'exploding crystal spider fish,' and then march my army of spider fish on someone else's territory or bastion, and claim everything for myself. Loot, materials, whatever?"

"That's right," said Jacob. "It's all up to the players, and what the players want to set their minds to, to achieve."

"Well, it definitely sounds like it's going to shake things all up again," said Blake. "People are getting vacated from their homes, but now they can live anywhere, right? Plenty of resources for everyone to gather and fight over. Hellions are working with paragons nowadays, if Gargantuan is any indication. So who knows what the future holds for Sigil Online."

"Exactly right," said Jacob. "It'll be exciting to see what happens."

Blake leaned forward and gestured to Jacob. "Well, once again, thank you so much for coming on the show and sharing some info about Sigil Online and the soon-to-arrive Bastions update. Really looking forward to it! I think I may finally end up getting killed in the game this time around. I'm thinking my time may have come, but regardless, I'm sure it'll be a blast."

"Thanks Blake," said Jacob, giving a nod.

"And that's it, everyone," said Blake, looking to the camera. "You heard it here first, Sigil Online: Bastions. We can't wait!"

ABOUT THE AUTHOR

Jeff Sproul is a writer living in a small cabin in Alabama. It's quiet, peaceful, but there's a lot of bugs. When he's not squishing bugs and spiders, he enjoys a frozen pizza on the weekends and a daily 2 cups of coffee for his sanity.

Jeff Sproul has been writing stories for over ten years. Some of his favorite scifi and fantasy works are Isaac Asimov's Foundation series, Starship Troopers, Warhammer 40k and various anime (which would be far too long to list.)

Printed in Great Britain
by Amazon